WHAT WAS PERFECT

WHAT WAS PERFECT

UNDENIABLE TRILOGY - BOOK ONE

JOLIE MOORE

This edition published by
Moore Digital Media Inc
1125 N Fairfax Ave, Unit 46071
West Hollywood, California 90046

Cover: Najla Qamber Designs
Photo: Jenn LeBlanc Studio Smexy
eISBN: 978-1-944179-49-6
ISBN: 978-1-64414-032-1

ALSO BY JOLIE MOORE

What Was Lost

What Was True

Taming the Bad Boy

CHAPTER 1

TWENTY-ONE YEARS EARLIER...

PREPARING my muscles like Coach Popescu had drilled into me over the last five years, I aligned my toes with the curb. It was nearly the exact width of a balance beam. I drew the hot air into my lungs. It exploded out as I did first one front flip, then another, followed by a front handspring. One jump split, and I came down without a bobble. Did another handspring with a half twist. I could feel my lips spread across my teeth as I stuck the landing.

Finally.

I'd been working on that for months. Couldn't count the times I'd fallen on my ass trying to get it just right. And the one time I get it right isn't in the gym.

I bit my lip against pestering my mother with one of the two questions she wouldn't answer: when could I get back in the gym?

Coach Popescu had just said that I was on the short list to go to the Elite Qualifier in Allentown when my parents had pulled the rug out from under me.

One minute I was on my way to the Junior Olympics, the next, nearly homeless.

"Don't make a scene," Mama tut-tutted. "This isn't a movie, Izzie."

I looked left and right.

No one was watching.

Mama was being totally paranoid. It was a new trait she'd developed after my dad had walked out, and it wasn't exactly my favorite. I felt sorry for her though, so I took Mama's warning to heart and tread lightly on my Keds knock-offs. The other kids at the pool this summer had that little blue rubber label that marked their canvas sneakers as genuine. My white soles were as plain as the bleached-out summer sky above us. Everything about me screamed "discount-store poor kid."

Maybe not everything. Maybe just two things: the sneakers and the dumpster I was about to dive in.

Since Dad had disappeared with my brother, Arturo, Mom had kind of fallen apart in what felt like a split second, but what had probably been more than a year. One minute I was living in the house where I was born on Pemberton Street in Philly's version of Little Italy. In the next moment, I was living between two crack houses in Camden while dodging bullets on the way to school.

Taking heed of her warning, I stopped grabbing for the sky, and dropped my arms from where they'd been nearly pressed to my ears.

I jumped off the curb and stepped carefully toward the garbage bin. As I peered over the lip of the blue-painted metal, two distinctly different smells hit me at once—rotting garbage and freezer burn. The odor of stale ice meant only one thing.

Ice cream.

I tossed a quick look in Mama's direction. She was doing the practical shopping. Still-good produce and past-its-due-date cartons of dairy bulged from her Cousin's Supermarket bags. My mom was stealthy that way. At least when we walked home it looked like we'd been legit shopping and not scavenging like the neighborhood's stray cats.

I touched the hot metal lip. Not too bad, my flesh wouldn't burn off. With a deep breath and the move I'd used to mount the uneven parallel bars more times than I could count, I hoisted myself up. As I'd done on the lower bar thousands of times, I extended both legs out in a split and rotated them over, just hovering over a sticky spill from a partially opened box of Italian ice. In less than a second, the hot metal lip of the bin was searing the skin off my bum. But the pain was a distant concern as I kept my eyes peeled for the telltale sign of steam.

Off in the right-hand corner, I found it. I took one tentative step, then another, trying to avoid the squish of something rotten. The multicolored boxes were just out of my reach. Red, white, blue, and orange Technicolor beckoned.

One more step.

Without looking, I lurched forward.

The sound of something extruding from a plastic bag was accompanied by the smell of death. My once white sneaker was covered in maggot-filled meat.

As disgusting as it was, that didn't stop me from pursuing the ultimate prize. Shaking the muck off my ruined sneaker, I grabbed up three chocolate-covered cones that promised confectionary bliss, then did a single-armed vault out of the trash bin. Coach Popescu would have been proud of that one.

Definite ten.

CHAPTER 2

NOW

I BACKED into the empty conference room, my butt hitting the high-backed leather chair precisely in the right place for me to sink into its depths. Pressing the answer button, I put the slick black phone to my ear.

"Daniel," I answered in greeting, like it was an episode of *Cheers* and he was Norm. "Why you blowing up my ho phone?" I asked.

"Bella. Bella. Bella. You know I hate it when you talk like that."

It took all my strength not to speak into that void, not to be the innocent girl he met, the good girl he still wanted. But I shut up. Worked hard not to say something I'd regret. But Daniel Kenyon van Dijk, a man used to getting everything he wanted, couldn't just let us sit in quiet.

"I miss you, Bella. I'm in Los Angeles in a few weeks' time." His voice was both seduction and command.

"I hear that Officine Brera is all the rage. Italian country-side cooking. Almost as good as my nonna would make," I deflected. "Have your assistant make a reservation." I never said "no." Daniel Kenyon van Dijk didn't take "no" for an answer.

"Should that be for two? Are you dining with me?" he asked, like he always did when he was out here on business. As the chairman of the world's largest staffing firm, Daniel had business contacts in nearly every city on Earth. Though he didn't need one, he always found a reason to travel to the same city I was in. He'd stalked me in New York and Philadelphia. Now, he found reasons to be in L.A. at least four or five times a year. At least one of those times, I didn't say no.

"I'd love to take a ride in that cute little BMW I gave you. I haven't had a chance to check out that custom Coral Red Dakota leather."

"Daniel," I said, putting the weight of the world into a sigh. "You know that's not going to happen. We decided to just be friends."

"I miss our so-called friendship. Friends have dinner when friends are in the same town. I haven't even been invited to your new penthouse."

That he'd bought me the car or paid up two years' rent on the penthouse went without saying. To anyone in the outside world, the facts of Daniel's generosity appeared questionable. But the hundreds of thousands he'd spent on me were nothing more than a drop in the bucket for a man who had an ocean of riches and not enough life left to spend it all.

Daniel was my weakness.

Daniel was my past.

Daniel and I were not in a friendship.

Of all the words, terms, and euphemisms for our relationship, friendship would be at the bottom of the list. Former boss, former employee was far more accurate, and appropriately sanitized.

"I'm sure there is no shortage of young women willing to be your *friend*, Daniel."

He may have been seventy-two, with all the wrinkly body parts that you could imagine going with seven-plus decades of life, but he was also from one of the world's richest families. Unless the earth had spun off its axis and the economic equation had changed drastically, there would always be a supply of hot-and-cold-running women for men like Daniel. For Daniel himself.

"Insipid girls," he said into the space where I'd been doing the mental math of the supply of women and the demand of men. Conclusion: there would always be an oversupply of women.

Daniel continued, "They want to talk about hair and nails and designer clothes when they're not tap, tap, tapping on their phones. They're going to go blind before they're forty, not to mention they can't speak a word longer than five letters. A girl actually crossed her fingers and said 'hashtag city life' to me in an offline conversation." His tone was aggrieved. I had to bite the inside of my cheek to hide my laugh.

"Hashtag" don't date teenagers.

"Hashtag" rich man cliché.

I could have done a thousand of them myself, though I never would have with Daniel. He didn't have that kind of sense of humor. Maybe high-end escort services were no longer recruiting from the Ivy League. I almost felt sorry for him.

Almost.

"Daniel. I'm at work. Gotta go," I said. I needed to get him off the phone before he started waxing nostalgic about how I was the only woman who could fulfill his needs.

"Some things never change," a too-familiar voice said.

Turning away from the wall, I spun around in a chair that had cocooned me, kept me perilously unaware of my surroundings. Like it could somehow go unnoticed that I'd taken a personal call during work, I jammed the slim black phone into the leather portfolio I'd found hidden in the men's section of Saks. Men always had it better in high-end department stores and in life. This one right in front of me, especially.

I recovered quickly. "If it isn't the Wimpy Panda," I blurted out in my mean-girl voice.

I couldn't believe my eyes. There before me, sitting at the other end of my department's conference table, as if he were ruler of the free world, all the way from motherfucking New Jersey, was Jake Wu.

I'd have called security in an instant if a visitor badge hadn't been clipped to his lapel.

Jake fucking Wu. He was at the bottom of the list of people I'd never wanted to see again. Maybe second to bottom, above the guy who was listed on my birth certificate as my father.

Jake fucking Wu had taken my heart, my virginity, and stomped on both. To say that we hadn't parted amicably would probably be the world's biggest understatement—ever.

All the blood between us was...bad.

I stood, height giving me a perceived advantage.

"What the fuck are you doing at CBT? Please tell me you're not pitching a show, 'cause you're totally in the wrong place. This is Program Practices. I'm about to start our weekly progress meeting," I said, hoping to wipe that knowing smile off his face. The smile that said he was king of the realm and I was garbage, a serf not good enough to shine his shoes.

"Bella," was all he said.

My name.

Nothing more.

Bella was the nickname he'd given me many years ago. Because I was beautiful, he'd said way back then, when it was very, very good. Before it had all gone very, very bad.

At least he hadn't pretended he had no idea who in the hell I was. He'd done that act to death in high school. Somewhere on a mantle in the Garden State was a gold statuette for best actor in the role of Shittiest Rich Kid. Probably more than one shiny award gleamed after my mother carefully polished them.

He changed tack when I didn't respond. "Isabella Aconi."

"Vice President, Program Practices." I spit out my very impressive credentials. Vice President well before forty, I wanted to add, but held myself back. Instead, I ran my fingers through my hair, even though the finger fluff was wholly unnecessary. I was ninety-nine percent sure I was impeccably groomed and outfitted.

Today I was in a tailored black pencil skirt, ivory blouse tucked in. Impossible-to-walk-in heels were carefully buckled around my ankles. I'd had my brows threaded. Learned my makeup on set from a professional years ago. In the fantasy where I saw an old boyfriend, I always won the "who has aged better" game. Today was no different.

I refrained from throwing up my hands like a championship boxer, though.

Because he wasn't an old boyfriend.

He'd never been that.

Anything but—that.

Everything but—that.

"Izzie. Isabella Aconi." He drawled all seven syllables. "Look at you, all grown up. All dressed up. It's like you're a bona fide adult."

"And it looks like you're still a bona fide asshole, Wu Jian." I'd done my best imitation of his mother saying his full Chinese name. It got the tiniest wince from him.

Score.

I was about to get to the bottom of why Jake Wu was here on my patch of earth when my phone trilled its three-note notification of a text message. It wasn't my work phone, which was quietly charging back at my desk. It was my *other* phone, my ho phone, *again*. Daniel must have been on his personal jet. It was the only time I knew him to play with his phone like a millennial. A carbon copy of the behavior of the young women he claimed to despise.

I pulled the BlackBerry from the leather portfolio.

"Since when do we use BlackBerrys?" Jake asked.

"We? Is that the royal 'we'?"

"The network."

"I don't know why you're asking about network policy. But if you must know, this is a private phone."

I held my face neutral as I looked at the text.

Show me your very nice bosoms.

I typed back two characters: NO.

I pressed the "screen off" button firmly before anyone could come up behind me and see that not-appropriate-for-work exchange.

Before I could stuff it back into the zippered leather pouch, the BlackBerry trilled again.

A new text glowed: *How about your rump?*

I typed a few more characters this time: *Noooooooooo, Daniel. Absolutely not.*

Instead of turning off the screen, I shut off the phone. One day I was going to chuck the damned thing in the ocean and not look back.

But I was twelve miles from the Pacific where I stood in my Louboutins. Stuffed it back into the bottom corner of the leather instead.

Jake looked at me curiously. I held my ground. I didn't flinch until he said, "You haven't asked about your mother."

Mother.

My mother was a world-class—

Nope, wasn't going to go there. Wasn't going to let her have power over my life. Saccharin smile firmly in place, I asked, "How's *my* mother?"

"When's the last time you saw her?" he asked, jabbing at me with his question. The poking, punching, and mental sparring was full on. I didn't care. A Jersey girl, by way of Philly, a bare-knuckled fighter, I brawled to win.

"Been a bit. I'm sure all is well in Toms River," I said, nudging away that little spark of guilt the mention of my mother sometimes brought. "Nothing ever changes at Casa Wu. Maybe that should be Palace Wu now."

The modest four-thousand-square-foot home he'd grown up in had given way to a fourteen-thousand-square-foot monstrosity on their six and three-quarter acres of Jersey land. All that additional square footage was all the more reason my mother said she couldn't leave.

Those extra ten thousand excuses were all lies.

"She's thinking of retiring," he said, deflecting my jabs.

Taken aback for a second, I threw back in his face, "Maria Sofia Aconi would never retire." Because she wouldn't. My mom would be handmaid and housekeeper to the Wu clan for as long as she drew breath. I'd been happy to say goodbye and thank you very much and take my leave. I hadn't been back more than a handful of times after I drove myself to Olde Haven when I was eighteen. Maria Sofia Aconi, on the other hand, wouldn't leave Toms River except in a coffin.

"My mom brought a new girl from Nanjing." Jake actually smiled, a wolfish sort of thing that bared the result of thousands of dollars of orthodontia.

I pulled my lips up over my slightly crooked bottom teeth. Braces hadn't been in Mom's budget.

"Cheap Chinese labor doesn't just affect factories, I guess," I snapped, trying to mask my conflicting emotions of hope and upset. "No one's job is safe."

"My mom has gotten nostalgic for the flavors of home. She needs soups and vegetables, not pasta and cheese."

Yeah, I'm sure that was it. Not that my mother was

getting older and took all her vacation time. Not that my mother was a threat to his. Nope, none of that. Flavors of home. Fucking liar. They were all fucking liars over there at the Old Freehold Road compound.

Whatever.

The sparring had started before I'd figured out why in the hell this blast from the past was in my office, perched like the king of fucking Siam. That was two today. Two men from my past, invading my present. Altogether, it was two too many.

I turned away from Jake as the door swung wide, the air fluttering the asymmetrical silk ruffles on my blouse.

The rest of my staff filed in, including Daisy Fletcher, a fellow alum from Owen, the Connecticut Ivy, and low woman on the totem pole, followed by her mentor, Connor Quinlan. They whispered conspiratorially to each other as everyone from my department took seats around the table.

I'd made Connor her watchdog and my spy, but I was starting to think he'd flipped sides, or was at the very worst a double agent. Ticking through the constantly changing agenda in my head, I made a note that I was going to have to remind him where he needed to keep his loyalty if he wanted to keep his job.

"Jake, I don't know where you're supposed to be, or exactly why you're here, but I'm sure my assistant, Alexandra, can help you find where you need to go." The dismissal included a casual flip of my hand. My Freywille wide gold bangle clinked against the Piaget watch. Gold on gold had a nice sound.

I pivoted on my Louboutins, leather on carpet giving me a classic spin an Olympic skater would be proud of. Or an

Olympic gymnast doing floor exercise. As quickly as that thought went through my head, I silenced it.

Success had more than one name. I'd read that somewhere once in one of those kitschy mall stores with so-called inspirational posters. That aphorism, at least, had to be true.

No chairs squeaked. No one's phone beeped or trilled. The room was unusually silent.

Too silent.

I locked eyes with my assistant. She was paralyzed by something that looked a lot like fear. I was a witchy boss, but she'd made it past the probationary period eighteen months ago, so it wasn't like I was going to fire her tomorrow. She swiveled her head between Jake and me.

Ah, the fighting. I'd forgotten how that would look to someone who didn't know us. Neither my mom nor his dad would have blinked. They'd worried more about us being horizontal. Vertical had always been okay.

"No worries, Alex," I tossed out. "I grew up with Jake in Toms River, New Jersey. We were...more or less...next-door neighbors back then. There's nothing we haven't already said to each other."

Nothing.

I'd said I love you and I hate you more times than I'd care to admit. More times than I'd ever admit to anyone even under Abu Grahib-style torture.

In spite of my glib assurances, Alexandra Hughes looked scared. More terrified than usual, in fact. I ran a tight ship, though. The poor girl looked deathly afraid half the time she was working. But someone put the fear of God into her today.

Jake had probably said something to twist her arm and let him past the reception desk.

I raised an imperious eyebrow. Trust me on this. Even though I couldn't see my dark-brown eyebrow, it was the very definition of imperious. I'd practiced it in front of the mirror enough times to be sure. The minute I'd been promoted from Director to VP, I'd worked to make sure I had imperious down to a fine art.

The girl shrank even farther into her oversized sweater and too-baggy jeans. Needless to say, she hadn't taken my not-so-subtle recommendations for a more professional wardrobe.

"Can I talk to you?" she whispered in my direction, but her eyes flickered the other way—*again*. "About Mr. Wu."

"What about Mr. Wu?" My voice was too loud. Too shrill. But as much as I could control my eyebrow, my vocal chords had a mind of their own. "There's nothing you can tell me about Mr. Wu that I don't already know. We practically grew up together. I've seen him stumble his way through all the awkward stages of life. Looks like he still may be in one."

Wasn't exactly true, with his flawless hair gelled into place and square jaw shaved clean, but I wasn't ready to put away my boxing gloves quite yet.

"Ms. Aconi," Alexandra hissed, her "Ms." tinged with extra emphasis on the "z" sound. "I have to talk to you—about why he's here."

"Is it an emergency?" My second eyebrow shot up. The message I was sending this time was that she was going to be banished to cataloguing at some videotape archive in an unair-conditioned room in the far north Valley if she didn't stop with this very public ambush.

"No, it—"

"Spit. It. Out." I had no tolerance for mealy mouthing, and less tolerance for Alexandra right now.

"The new network owners are touring today. This—"

"Ah, our new corporate overlords from China." It was like the media mergers of the nineties that I'd studied in the Ken Auletta tome, among other books. Everyone was quaking in their boots about this new buyout. "First AMC Theatres and Dick Clark Productions. Now us. Should we hazard a guess about Woo DynoMedia? You think they're in the metals business or shopping malls? Because, folks, that's who today's Chinese billionaires are. Tomorrow they're Hollywood's corporate moguls. God save us all from people looking for a little Hollywood magic."

Not one person laughed at my over-the-top humor. Usually, they made jokes along with me, or at least make polite chuckles. Now...crickets. I was bombing like a bad comedian. I glanced over at Daisy. Maybe the cooties from her trite sitcom-star boyfriend had rubbed off on me.

I averted my eyes from my staff as I tried to think of a good way to eject Jake from the room and get on with my meeting. Like an itch I couldn't reach or scratch, though, something prickled my scalp. If I hadn't been in front of a dozen people, I would have buried my fingernails in my hair, pulled my carefully tucked blouse from my skirt and patted a paper towel against my armpits, anything to make the weird feeling go away.

Jake stood. His chair rolled back silently on the industrial carpet. Instead of apologizing for being in the wrong place, he buttoned his jacket.

I looked at him for the first time. *Really* looked at him, and not my memory of who he'd been to me.

I clocked that he was wearing a suit. A very expensive three-piece suit. A bespoke suit that looked like a sheep who was way more virgin than I had tailored it, tiny little hooves clicking with needles and thread.

For a few seconds, I debated between the source of the suit. It was either high street London or Singapore. Knowing his mom, Min Li, as intimately as I did, my guess was Singapore. My scattered thoughts on wool provenance couldn't distract me from the weird vibe in the room. Everyone was moving as if they were underwater, in slow motion, while I kept trying to figure out what in the hell was going on. Normally I was in complete control of my department, my meetings, and my appearance. But now it was as if I'd been caught flat-footed for no obvious reason.

It was as though I had my ear pressed against a huge safe while a seasoned safecracker turned the dial. The spindle was whirring, looking for the notch to catch. Then the spinning stopped as one fact after another clicked into place.

Jake's last name was Wu. The company taking over my network was Woo DynoMedia. If I knew anything, it was that transliteration of Chinese characters could go more than one way. It was why cousins with the last name Zhang and Chang were written exactly the same in Chinese. But Wu and Woo?

My head swam like I'd had an entire bottle of Pinot Noir. By myself. This morning. I shook off the woozy feeling.

That Wu thing had to be a coincidence. It was probably a really popular Chinese name.

I looked at the gray faces of my staff.

Uh oh.

It wasn't a coincidence.

Oh, shit. It wasn't possible. Jake's father made cars. He was the third-biggest auto manufacturer in China. He was the Chrysler of the mainland. Cars were not television.

Of course, I'd just laid out example after example of companies that were getting in the media game.

Before I could smooth over my insults, take back my words, save face in front of my staff, Jake smoothed his hands down the wool and spoke.

"Good afternoon. I'm Jake Wu, President of Woo Dyno-Media, the new owner of the CBT Network."

Alexandra sucked in breath dramatically. Her normally immovable kinky hair seemed to tremble like a needle on a seismograph. The others had the good grace to maintain radio silence.

Everyone turned toward the hall, the move seeming choreographed.

The conference room had one set of floor-to-ceiling windows that faced outside, but a second set lined the corridor. Jake's dad and an entourage of more Chinese men came into the little room. They all did a polite bow of their heads, but otherwise remained silent.

"This is my father, Feng Wu. He's the CEO of Woo DynoAutomotive. My family sells about four million vehicles a year to customers in China and around the globe. In today's interconnected world, we're looking to diversify, bring our shareholders and customers value. And we know you here at the CBT are working hard to make the network accountable and keep the airways clean. It was nice meeting you. I'll be learning from you, so I apologize in advance for my silly questions. In the next few weeks, I'll be by to introduce myself to everyone, but if you have any questions in the meanwhile..."

Jake spelled out his CBT email address for the group. His father and the merry band of henchmen, led by Jake, nodded their goodbyes and strolled down the hallway.

Feng Wu hadn't so much as nodded in my direction or acknowledged me in any way. I wasn't a magnet for his stares, like Maria Sofia Aconi, though. I was what I'd always been, a pesky annoyance to sweep out of the way, first with overwhelming kindness, then... Well, I wasn't going to think about any of that.

The corporate drones had sucked the air from the room, leaving behind a vacuum.

The eyes cast my way ranged from accusatory to pitying.

I lifted a glass of water to my lips and drank the whole thing.

How in the hell was I supposed to come back from that? Talk about losing an audience. Instead of the silence I required, my staff started talking amongst themselves about everything but the shows on the network we were paid to supervise. The very shows I was in charge of.

I banged my faux crystal glass, empty of the water I'd gulped a second ago, against the conference table. Self-preservationists they probably were, likely thinking of how to save their own fucking necks. Because mergers always started with downsizing, rightsizing, or, in common parlance—

layoffs. I could practically see the gears turning as each and every person tried to figure out if they should update their resume at their desks or wait until they were home.

"Daisy!" My voice was Catholic-school-nun sharp. "*Grave Chase?* Can you give us an update on their production schedule?"

CHAPTER 3

TWENTY YEARS EARLIER

"GET DRESSED!" My mother's sharp command pierced that little place between sleep and wakefulness where I liked to hover. That little space was my favorite. It wasn't quite the place of nightmares, where my father and brother left me to rot in Camden, New Jersey. But it wasn't quite the place where I was fully alert and aware of rats and roaches that shared our broken-down apartment but didn't contribute one iota to the rent.

I unstuck one lid, then the other, using my sleep-sweaty hands to wipe the rocks from the corners of my eyes. I was expecting my mother's sour face, the one that would assign me bathtub- and floor-scouring duty at best, roach-stamping duty at worst.

The smile that lifted the corners of her eyes was something else entirely.

"Where are we going?" My mind nearly got away from me, imagining that we could somehow afford gymnastics coaching again, or maybe we were going back to Philly. That my parents were getting back together.

"Is Dad—"

The usual frown took the sun straight from her face. "Your deadbeat dad isn't coming to save you. Might as well put that fantasy right out of your head," she said, her tone unusually vicious. Seconds later, the clouds parted and the sun returned in her smile.

"We're going to a job interview."

"I thought there were laws against child labor," my smart-alecky mouth said.

I was glad when my mother thought better of slapping me in my smart-alecky mouth. But the hope on her face seemed undefeatable.

"Put on your Sunday best. We're going to Toms River."

I scrambled from the bed and dug out the dress I used to wear to weddings, christenings, and adult parties. It was a little tight, but I squeezed into it anyway. It was the same with the toe-cramping patent-leather Mary Janes. I wanted to do anything that I could to keep the smile on my mother's face for however long it was going to last.

❦

God must have been on our side, because the duct tape and spit for glue that held my mom's ancient car together lasted long enough to get us to the Jersey Shore. Even though the ocean breeze I could smell through the open windows made me relax for the first time in forever, my mother's face was pinched in concentration.

"What number are we looking for?"

I turned toward the windshield. The houses here were few and far between, the very opposite of Camden, where only weeds broke up the bricks and concrete.

"Eighteen thirty-three," she said, leaning even farther forward and peering through the glass.

I looked right, then realizing those addresses were even, turned in the other direction.

"That's it on the left. The red barn-looking thing," I said, jabbing toward the glass.

My mother made a big swing and pulled into a long, winding driveway in front of either a house or a barn. I wasn't sure which. I'd heard there were still farms somewhere in New Jersey. Did Mom want us to work on a farm? I tried to imagine myself milking cows. Ignoring the rumble that thought caused in my stomach, I had to acknowledge that a farm probably meant there was no food shortage. Beans and apples, I could pick, if it meant farm table over dumpster.

"Do you think this is it?" she whispered to herself.

"The address is right, Mom," I said. "Did you apply for a job as a stable hand?" I asked, looking at the thick white "X" surrounded by a square painted on a double-wide door. Horses would be a hell of a lot better than cows and corn. For a moment, I allowed myself the fantasy of being a horsey girl. I could probably get one of those cute velvet hats and train my horse to jump fences. Maybe I could get into the Olympics that way. Probably required less training than gymnastics. And if the family had horses anyway—

"There haven't been stable hands since westerns were on

TV, Isabella." My mother's serious tone jarred me from my thoughts.

Like that, the equestrian fantasy went on the heap with all the others—abandoned.

"Then why is it red with white trim and barn doors?" I neighed like a horse for effect.

My mom looked at her cheap digital watch. The gold one she'd gotten from Daddy for Mother's Day had been pawned months ago. The roaches that lived in the kitchen walls hadn't appreciated the sacrifice.

"We're supposed to be there in ten minutes. Let's go."

As if my limbs were made of molasses, I poured myself out of the car. Then followed her at a snail's pace.

"So why am I here?" I probed.

My mother's smile had disappeared with the miles between Camden and the shore. My questions, plentiful in those first fifty miles, had gone unanswered. Exhausted with curiosity, I'd let the ribbon of expressway lull me into a nearly catatonic state. Faced with meeting someone new though, I'd finally woken up.

"It's a live-in job," my mom threw over her shoulder as she straightened her white knee-length skirt above its matching stockings and strode forward.

I yawned, stretched, and tried to catch up with her, the shoes pinching my toes and slowing me down.

Live-in? She wanted to move a gazillion miles from Philly? I was ready to bombard her with all my questions, but hesitated when the front door opened. I did have *some* manners. Airing dirty laundry in public was not cool.

"You must be Maria Aconi," the man said, stepping out in

slippers to shake my mother's hand. A suit and slippers. I wondered who in the hell dressed him. He'd have been laughed out of my old neighborhood.

"I am," my mother said, pulling herself to her full height —which wasn't much. At twelve, I could already see the top of her head. Took after my dad in that way.

"And who are you?" The man's English was heavily accented. He looked Chinese or Korean or something Asian. I tried not to stare at what made us different as he nodded at me.

Awkward and completely weird were not enough adjectives to describe how I felt. "Um, I'm Isabella," I said, using my full name.

He thrust out his hand. I glanced between him and my mother, then took it in mine, doing my best adult handshake. His grip was firm and dry.

"I'm Wu Feng. We're from China," he said. "Shanghai. Have you heard of it?"

I looked between them again, but they were both looking at me. I was pretty sure Beijing was the capital but couldn't have said much beyond that if pressed. So I just nodded and pretended I was an expert on world geography. Maybe the next time I'd actually pay more attention *in* Geography.

"Great. So many people don't know anything about China. Come on in, both of you."

We followed him through a series of rooms. My eyeballs burned, in danger of melting.

The house could only be described by one word: wallpaper. The colors and patterns would give an epileptic a fit. Big swirls of purple and navy paisley in the entryway, dark-red paisleys and bold stripes up and down the living room wall, huge purple and pink flowers against a maroon background on a dining room wall. It continued on like that as we followed Mr. Wu.

Blue Oriental rugs, flowers on the elaborate furniture with wood arms and pleats and buttons and every decoration that could possibly be smushed together. I wanted to pull my mom outside and tell her the assault on the eyes alone should have been enough to make us bail.

Finally, we arrived at an office or den or something, and he offered my mom a seat in a fancy wooden armchair.

"How old are you...Isabella, was it?"

"Izzie," I piped in, then wanted to hit myself. I'd left that childish name behind in Philly. "Isabella," I corrected under my breath. When no one spoke, I remembered there'd been a question. "Twelve."

"Well, Izzie. It's important that I talk to your mom alone about the potential of you guys living and working here. Hold on a minute." He pressed a button on a box on his desk. When a crackle came in on the other end, he spoke in singsong but rapid-fire Chinese.

A few seconds later, a lanky boy with skater hair appeared in the doorway. He looked to be about my age, or maybe a year older like my brother.

"Wu Jian," Mr. Wu barked. The boy jerked up, standing tall and sweeping the hair out of his face. "This is Isabella," he said in English. Mr. Wu nodded his head, a small smile winging the corner of his lips, then he continued a long explanation in Chinese. The boy nodded solemnly.

"Follow him, Isabella." Mr. Wu's voice was a little softer with me, but the command was clear.

I was starting to understand that few people probably said no to Mr. Wu. He was nothing like the waiters at Joy-something, the dim sum place my father had taken me on the last birthday he'd still been with Mama. Those Chinese men nodded, and bowed, and gave soft-spoken answers to any question asked. Mr. Wu was one hundred eighty degrees from that. I was as sure as hell that no one asked him for more water or fried rice.

I turned to my mother, her warning about not going off with strangers bouncing through my head.

She nodded her head slightly. "I'll be right here."

Wu Jian stalked off through the door. I had to practically gallop to keep up.

The crazy-busy wallpaper and tacky furniture continued through a hallway. The kitchen, with its thick planks of diagonal wood paneling, was kind of a relief. The smell coming from the stove was amazing. Almost enough to make me forget the assault on the eyes that this house was.

Now, my mama was a great Italian cook, don't get me wrong, but this smelled just as good in a completely different way. My stomach, empty since the afternoon before, growled in compliment.

Wu Jian looked at me from under his big sweep of hair. I tried not to shrink against the wall in my dress. It was my last official party dress, and looked stupid. Seafoam green pleats, flowers embroidered against the chest I didn't have, and with a big bow tied across my butt. It screamed "little girl."

"You hungry?"

"You speak English," burst from my mouth ungraciously. Damn, I was going to screw this up for my mother. In the last minute, I'd gone from thinking this whole live-in housekeeper thing was the worst idea in the world, to not half bad. I might go blind, but at least I wouldn't die from bedbugs, rats nibbling away at me, or worse, starvation.

"Of course. Why wouldn't I?" he asked. His voice was hovering between low and high. If I'd known him better, I'd have totally made fun of him. Arturo's voice had changed last summer as he'd squeaked his way through to puberty.

"Um, your dad spoke to you in Chinese," I said.

"Mandarin."

"What?"

"Mandarin. It's the dialect. There are a lot of Cantonese speakers in New York and New Jersey."

Mandarin, Cantonese, it was all Greek to me. But I managed to keep my mouth shut this time around.

"I asked you a question," Wu Jian said. He looked at me frankly, dissecting everything. There was nothing I could do to hide the fact that my once-strong muscles had withered away to skin and bone—from losing my coach, my gym, my sport, and not enough square meals. It's why my twelve-year-old body fit into my two-year-old party dress.

"I could eat, Wu Jian," I said, trying to be cool as a seafoam green cucumber, but stumbling over his name just the same.

"Sit there." He pointed to one of the seats surrounding a huge green marble table. "I go by Jake, by the way."

"Okay. Jake." I nodded trying to give him my most adult and serious look.

Jake lifted the lid on a tall wooden stacked thing and billows of steam came out. He opened and closed a bunch of cabinet doors until he located dishes. He pulled out a couple of bowls and plates. He dumped them on the table in a noisy clatter.

I got up to wash my hands at the sink, drying them on my pleats when his eyes were turned. I didn't see paper towels and didn't want to have to ask. Instead, I started setting the table. I gave us each a plate, bowl, and what I think was some kind of cup. The ceramic was no less busy than the rest of the house, each dish rimmed in an intricate blue maze-like pattern.

He took each dish to the stove. In seconds, he came back with steaming rice, soup of some kind, and a plate of dumplings.

He lifted a teapot from the back of the stove and filled each cup with dark-brown liquid.

Before he sat, he pulled chopsticks and huge spoons from a metal cylinder.

Jake didn't say anything before he bent his head and shoveled rice into his mouth, then soup, then dumplings, then more rice.

I watched him carefully. Chopsticks I wasn't ready to tackle, but soup I could do. I slurped at the thick stock. It had everything and the kitchen sink in it, and was one of the best things I'd ever tasted.

"What's this?"

"Duck blood soup."

Jake's smile wasn't nice. Everything in his face said that

he expected me to up and run away. But having an Italian mama meant I was made of much sterner stuff.

"It's good." My smile was as snarky as his had been.

"Your heard me, right?" He put his chopsticks down and lifted his head fully, tossing his hair to the side, his newly revealed chocolate-brown eyes piercing mine. "I said blood."

"Have you ever had sanguinaccio or biroldo?"

"What's that?"

"Blood sausage. Sanguinaccio is salty. Biroldo is sweet, like with raisins and stuff. Unless you have a dead human in here," I jabbed toward the bowl with a single chopstick, "I've probably eaten it all."

I didn't say that a person who ate food from a dumpster didn't have the right to be picky. I'd watched my mom pick over dead rats, pull out living roaches from food, and serve it anyway. Instead, I did what he'd done, put my head down and ate.

"Aren't you going to have rice?" Jake asked, poking a chopstick in my direction.

In a Chinese restaurant, they'd at least have offered me a fork. I winced as I remember doing just that, asking for a fork and knife, the last time we'd gone for Chinese. Arturo had laughed at me for days. I'm not sure when my older brother had become an expert in all things chopstick, but I'd nearly slunk from the lunch with him and my father in mortification.

I could feel heat rising up my neck, warming my face, making me sweat in the suddenly overly warm kitchen.

"I can't use chopsticks. Okay? I grew up with regular stuff...knives, forks, spoons smaller than the bowls they go in,"

I said, waving the big ceramic spoon in the air above the bowl not much bigger than it.

With his right hand, he rested his chopsticks on the little ceramic holder I'd thought was some kind of broken napkin ring, then swooped his hair from his face again in one single practiced action.

Jake scooted his chair around the table next to mine. I braced myself for the laughter.

It never came. Instead, he reached around, took my hand in his.

Something like an electric current stole up my arm, raising the dark hairs there.

"Did you just joy buzz me?"

Jake's face screwed up in a look of total misunderstanding.

"Joy what?"

An awareness of a completely different kind came over me. Heat stole up from under the synthetic dress. I waved my hands, hoping to dispel his concern at the same time I cooled myself down.

"So..." I prompted.

"You do it like this," he said, maneuvering my finger like a master puppeteer. "Hold the top one in your hand like a pen or something. That's the moving one. The other needs to stay steady. You know what? Hold on." He left my side, warmth disappearing with him. He opened and closed a few drawers, then came back with red chopsticks joined at the top, shaped like a very long letter "M."

My face heated again. I wanted to rip off this stupid dress and sit here in my usual T-shirt and jeans. I looked down at my stupid black patent-leather flats, remembering that my new sneakers were sitting on my windowsill waiting for the sun to do its magic, bleaching them clean.

I sighed and sat more heavily. I wanted to run away from Jake and the weird feeling he was making in my chest. But I had nowhere to go. Not in Toms River. Not in Camden. Not in Philly.

"Are those for kids?" I asked.

"My mom got them for me when I was little, probably."

"Where is your mom, anyway?" I hadn't seen anyone else in the house since we'd come in.

"Nanjing."

He must have read my ignorance all over my face, better than his father had. I wondered if Mom should have studied a map of China before having the bright idea to drive across the state of New Jersey. I didn't know if her best skirt was going to be enough.

"Oh, that's nice," I said. It was my usual response when I came across someone new at school who was from some tiny town in Jersey or Pennsylvania I'd never heard of. Most people never questioned you beyond that. Jake was no different.

He scooted closer to me. I wondered if I was going to die of heat exposure. No one person had ever made me so hot, and itchy, and uncomfortable.

"Here," he said, wrapping my hand in his again. I took a deep breath and tried to listen to what he was saying. "These have like a little grip thing on them to help you pick up food."

We tried it with a dumpling first. Carefully, like I was playing a game of Operation, I pinched the thin skin of the dumpling and moved it from the steamer to the rice bowl in front of me, like I'd seen Jake do. It dropped in a single piece, not a tear. He let go of my hand and moved across the table. I aped him, picking it up again and lifting it to my mouth.

First, it was so good—pork, and some kind of soupy liquid, and—I don't know—a really good taste. Second, I wanted more. More food that wasn't ten days old and warm with rot.

All embarrassment at eating with the kid utensils disappeared as I filled my belly the way I used to during Sunday dinner with Mom and Dad and Arturo.

I tried to smother the pang that squeezed my guts, threatening to dislodge the food so comfortably settling there.

"You play *Phantasmagoria*?" Jake asked, as if I was a baby sitting at the adult table.

Food and chopsticks quickly forgotten, I leaned forward in the chair. Ever since I'd gotten my hands on a joystick at a friend's house years ago, I'd been dying to do some gaming.

"Your mom lets you play that?" 'Cause even if we could afford a computer, my mom wouldn't let me anywhere near anything like that. Good Catholic girls didn't play video games with all their gore and sex and violence. Father O'Connell's mass on that had gone on way too long.

When my mom had said that, barring me from my friend's house, I'd wanted to mention that good Catholic women didn't get divorces. Thankfully I hadn't left all my sense in Philly, otherwise I'd have been long dead and would have never met Jake Wu.

Meeting Jake Wu was starting to feel like a very good thing.

"She's not here." Looking around the kitchen, he leaned in conspiratorially. "I rode my bike to the mall with Dad's credit card and bought it. It's really good."

"Can we play?" I asked, not even trying to play it cool like I probably should. The way I'd learned to in school so kids wouldn't bother messing with me.

Jake shrugged. "Might as well."

He clearly was a student in the play-it-cool school as well. But when he glanced over his shoulder to make sure I was behind him, there was a tiny sparkle of mischief in what I could see of his eyes peeking through his too-long bangs.

I followed him from the kitchen through a bunch more rooms that would blind a bat and landed in a room with a huge color monitor bigger than the tiny thirteen-inch color television that my mom got in the divorce. Dad had taken the brand-new Sony Trinitron. From a cabinet, Jake pulled out a couple of joysticks. I tried to hide the little quiver of excitement that was shaking my limbs.

This was going to be fun. Something that had been missing for many long months.

I couldn't remember the last time I'd been on the verge of something good like this.

"Do you have brothers and sisters?" I asked, wondering where all the other kids were in this big house. There must be a slew of them living in different bedrooms, each with their own TVs and toys and games and stuff. Maybe there was a girl my age. My fantasy of playing with dolls I was way too old to like in public, and borrowing her pretend glitter makeup, nearly spun out of control.

Done plugging in things and arranging wires, Jake turned

to me. Now that I wasn't hungry or nervous, I could see that he was cute. Super cute when he smiled. My heart stopped for a minute, then started again.

"It's only me. One-child policy."

"What policy?"

"China only allows parents to have one kid."

"Seriously?"

"Yes."

"What if there are twins or something? Does someone kill the second kid?" I knew the question was probably stupid, but the idea of a government deciding how many kids you could have was crazy. Obviously, there weren't any Catholics over there.

"It's China, and not barbaric like that. Twins are fine. And if you have a girl, you can also try again for a boy."

"Why? What's wrong with having only a girl?"

"Let's just chalk it up to it being a different culture. Alright? Boys have a big list of expectations that girls just don't have. They have it easy in a lot of ways. Now, let's play."

Girls having it easy. I wanted to know more about that culture. Girls had it anything but easy as far as I could tell in my life. Maybe China had figured out a way for boys to have the babies and clean the house and do all the cooking.

I tried not to squirm when the opening sequence played with a half-naked couple in bed together, kissing. I was glad Arturo wasn't there with me. Last year, things had gone from alright to awkward with me and my brother. We used to laugh when people kissed on TV. Just before Mom and I had left Philly, Arturo and I had shifted from our usual seats to opposite ends of the couch, where we didn't have to look at each other at all. This was almost as uncomfortable, but in a different way.

Instead of closing my eyes and blocking my ears, I kind of wanted to be the woman on the screen, and for Jake to be that man. But I'd just met this kid. How could I have any kind of crush on him?

Hormones. That had to be it. The school nurse, who'd done the after-school sex-ed program I'd only gone to after I'd forged my mother's name on the permission slip, had said we'd get weird around boys.

I cleared my throat and shifted in my seat until the opening ended and we could click the icons on the screen.

We were halfway through the first puzzle when the screen suddenly paused.

"Wu Jian!" his father boomed, walking into the room like he owned the place, which of course he did.

My heart beat a rapid, unsteady rhythm, sure we were in trouble. Of *course* I'd gone and done the one stupid thing that would cost my mother this job opportunity.

I dropped the controls and jumped from my spot on the plush leather sofa.

"Sorry. I...uh..." I stopped, not quite sure why I was apologizing or what to be sorry for.

"If your mother accepts my generous job offer, you'll be living here. Wu Jian and I will show you the guesthouse," Mr. Wu offered.

Jake flicked off the screen as casually as if he'd been working on math homework, and not solving one of the hardest puzzles in the most forbidden game of the year.

Ducking my head as the last in line, I followed Mr. Wu, my mom, then Jake out of a side door. We walked through grass, down a dirt path to another red house. Someone here liked red—a lot.

This red one was like a regular-sized house. A stone circle thing sat to the right of the front door. Mr. Wu produced a key from a ring in his pocket, inserted it into a shiny new brass lock, and jiggled the front door open.

"It's small and needs a good cleaning, but here it is," he announced.

I was starting to think Mr. Wu didn't know from small. Small was the shithole in Camden we were calling home. Small was not a stone entranceway flanked by kitchen and living room on one side and three bedrooms on the other. I hated cleaning, but wanted to get on my knees and pull out a bucket and rag and start scrubbing. If we couldn't go home to Philly, then this weird compound with the Chinese family and this little house we could call our own seemed like the next best thing.

Mr. Wu winced, but I couldn't stop myself from bowing all the way from the tour of the grounds back to Mom's car in the gravel.

"Why were you bowing and scraping?" my mom asked the minute we cleared the gravel and were back out onto the paved road.

"Asian people bow, right? I saw it on television. One of those travel shows you like to watch."

"That was Japan, Isabella. Japan."

"What's the difference?"

"There's no bowing in China. They shake hands like everyone else."

"So are you going to take the job?"

"How do you know he was serious about the offer, Izzie? I've never done a job like that before."

"What's the job?" How hard could it be, I wondered. My mom seemed like she was capable of anything and everything, except maybe getting Daddy to come back, but Mr. Wu probably didn't care about that.

"Cleaning. Cooking. Driving young Mr. Wu from school to his activities."

"Oh my God, Mom. You're like a thousand-hundred percent qualified. That's exactly the same job you did for me and Daddy and Arturo, only no one paid you. This guy is offering cash money," I said.

I hadn't paid a lick of attention to money or how much things cost up until when Mama and I left Philly. Until then, I knew we weren't rich, like Oprah Winfrey rich, or afford-an-airplane rich, or even Mercedes rich, but I knew we weren't poor either. We didn't live in Strawberry Mansion or Fairhill, but we'd never been hungry. We had Sunday dinner and Christmas and even Coach Popescu.

Now we didn't have anything, and I wanted something again. If I couldn't have Dad or Arturo or gymnastics, then a house free of rats and roaches was high up on my want list.

"I did that because I love you. All of you," Mama whispered, interrupting my thoughts about money and how much I missed having it.

"Is Daddy coming back?" I asked, my voice the same whisper as hers. I'd only dared ask one other time, and my mama had gone berserk. Yelling and crying and generally making me regret being nosey. But it had been a year now. Any hope that our lives would go back to the normal I'd known for the first ten was fading fast. I kinda wanted to know if I needed to kill that hope right dead.

I counted two dozen Pennsylvania license plates before my mom opened her mouth to answer.

"No. They're moving back to Italy."

My guts practically plummeted through the cracked vinyl seat.

Italy.

My dad leaving, or kicking us out, was one thing. Another whole continent was something completely different.

I looked down at my stupid dress and wondered what in the hell I'd done that could have been so wrong. How had my father loved me one day and hated me the next? Because it had to be me. I knew dads walked out on families. That crap happened all the time. But Daddy had left Mama and me, but kept Arturo. Was it because I wasn't a boy? I'd thought I was his favorite, until I wasn't.

"Back? But we're American," I said, instead of asking if I'd ever see my father again. Other divorced kids got visitation, but I didn't.

"Your daddy was born in Gallipoli. His mama never left."

"Then we're moving to Toms River, I guess." Resigning myself to this second twist of fate, I let out a huff of breath and flopped back against the seat. I counted six Delaware plates in the silence this time.

"It's not ideal, Izzie. It's what I can do. You'll get to go to the schools there. Mr. Wu says they're some of the best in the state."

Something, anything had to be better than Camden. The door to Philly was closed tight and I didn't have the key. At least the food would probably be good in Toms River.

"Let's go pack!" I raised my arms and pumped my fists in the air. I'd have to have enough enthusiasm for both of us.

CHAPTER 4

NOW

ACCORDING to some magazine article I read, I was probably going to hobble my way through my seventies. For now, though, I wasn't ready to give up the heels, not when the corporate overlords were watching.

I turned my ankles this way and that, admiring the gleam of the crystals in the spotlighting of the sound booth.

Jake Wu glanced my way. His eyes drawn to the shoes. Rhinestones were best in dim halogen lights, exactly what shone above all of us. A stray thought hit as I admired myself.

Daniel would have loved these shoes.

Daniel would never see these shoes, I solemnly promised myself.

I had another thought then. I got out my phone and took a quick snap of my shoes and ankles and, before I thought better of it, texted the picture to Daniel. Maybe it would be just enough to get him off my back for a few weeks.

"Hey, watch it," an engineer warned me as he snapped his headphones back into place.

My feet were unforgivingly propped on the soundboard as I watched the umpteenth awards show of my career. Daisy was at the other end of the board, her finger hovering over the so-called Futterbutton. Named after some woman in Standards over at another network, who'd dominated the button that would stop any of the seven dirty words from being uttered on air for more years than I'd probably been alive. During this trial by fire, Daisy was learning that the seven-second delay was a girl's friend.

"I promise not to damage anything precious," I retorted, knowing full well the technician couldn't hear me. He was working desperately to keep a rock star's voice out of screech range, saving viewers from catlike wailing and bloody ears. That in and of itself was a full-time job. He didn't have time to police my foot placement.

Normally one of us from my department could do this job: make sure the network didn't get embarrassed, or worse, fined. The Screen Actors Guild Awards, Tonys, even Golden Globes were full of old actors who didn't dare utter a bad word, and young ones trying to show their gravitas.

Music awards were a whole other shot of tequila. Half the musicians were high or drunk or both. Liquored and lubed, they were liable to spout anything, and Daisy was too new to see the signs that an act was about to go off the rails. Her supervisor, Connor, had some work event with his partner. So it was down to me to make sure she didn't fuck up.

Except she would have to do the last few minutes on her own. The liter and a half of water I'd downed in the last hour had hit my bladder like a tsunami. Jake Wu had made my mouth unintentionally dry, and an entire bottle of Smart Water hadn't made it any better, or me any smarter.

I looked up at the monitors, while swinging my legs to the floor. "Daisy, you got this? I have to take a call from the network," I little-white-lied. I held up the back of my phone, waving for effect.

"Who's calling?" Jake asked.

What was calling was my flight response. Jake was triggering all sorts of feelings, flooding me with adrenaline.

"Gotta take this," I said, one foot out the door.

"They're closing with that hair metal tribute band, Revival. From what I hear, they're clean," Daisy shouted across the booth.

I peered over my shoulder at the flying permed hair and guy-liner on the four rockers. Poor things had to be over forty. Daisy could definitely handle it. The worst that could happen was that the pyrotechnics could set those Aqua Net backcombs on fire. And that, while a network disaster, was not a Program Practices problem.

I slipped from the booth, and ran-walked in four-and-a-quarter-inch heels to the ladies' room. Never had I felt so much relief. I swear all the juicing and electrolyte-loaded water and Jake Wu were going to be the death of me. I was about to open the stall door when my phone rang for real.

My *other* phone.

The relief from emptying my bladder was quickly replaced with a heavy leaden feeling in my belly. I looked at the New York City area code, the seven numbers that followed as familiar as my own.

I didn't need to scroll to see who was calling. Only a single person still called from that area code.

I'd made a mistake encouraging him with that text. I should have known he couldn't resist. He'd liked to dress me like a refined and elegant version of a Barbie doll, the one with the dark hair. I glared at the vibrating phone as if I had the power to made it disappear.

I have no idea why I still carried the stupid BlackBerry, but I did. Every year, a brand-new one arrived with my old 203 number. I recycled the old one and put the new one in my purse. I kept accusing Daniel of not being able to let go, but I hadn't quite put him out to pasture either.

"I did so love buying you shoes. You were very appreciative—"

"Daniel. I'm at work. Awards show. Can't talk," I blurted.

I needed to get him off the phone before he started waxing nostalgic about how I was the only woman who could fulfill his needs.

I could hear him fiddling with something in the background, then the sound of heavy metal filled my ear from his end.

"Damn, this awards show looks as vacuous as the women I meet."

"Every show can't be a documentary about the inciting incidents that sparked the first World War, or a primer on post-Cold War Poland." Daniel had been and probably still was a huge history buff. I'd gone to Owen College, one of the most well-regarded Ivies, taken a history class or two to keep up with him, but his vast knowledge put me to shame nonetheless.

"Well, this just got very interesting," Daniel said, his voice growing faint as it moved away from the mouthpiece.

"What got interesting?" He was doing it again. Reeling me in like a live fish. He'd often said that to me. That having me in his life was like fly fishing. He was patient like that though. He could wait. He'd waited for nearly a dozen years.

I wanted to swim away, upstream. I was no longer his for the taking. I pried the metaphorical hook from my mouth.

"I have to go, Daniel. You know better than anyone else that I have a job. I'm forever grateful to you for everything you've done, but I really think we have to cut off this communication." I tried to inject a note of finality in my voice, like I'd done every single other time I'd uttered that sentence.

Daniel paused a long time. The sound of the concert echoed from the sound stage through the phone, delayed by seven seconds. "Bella... Isabella Aconi, does this band sing about sex?"

I sighed, the age gap yawning between us. "Yes, I think it's the punch line to their perpetual joke. All their songs are about them not getting the girl. But, Daniel, I have to go. I'm training—"

"Ho-ho! I wouldn't lose my number too fast, my dear Bella. After tonight, I think you're going to need it."

"What?" I screeched.

Daniel never joked. I yanked my skirt down and slammed open the stall door.

"You may be unemployed in the next five minutes if you don't do something fast."

Foregoing handwashing, I hung up, tossed the phone in

my purse, and ran out of the bathroom as fast as I could on four-and-a-quarter-inch heels.

Yanking open the door to the booth, I saw it on fifteen different full-color, high-definition screens in all its glory.

The Penis.

The Revival bass player had no bass in his hands. That stringed instrument was in splinters in front of him. But the very large penis he *did* have was on display for millions of viewers to see.

Fuck.

This could not be happening on my watch.

Seven seconds. Daisy should have had plenty of time to black out the screen. Send it to a host or commercial or, worst case—test pattern.

Daniel's remark about the end of my career was leading me to believe that I wasn't going to be so lucky.

Backing out, I ran, then hobbled down the concrete corridor and followed the line of suits to the back of the stage. More wool than in all of New Zealand had crowded on the stage.

Chaos had a sound, and this was it.

CHAPTER 5

TWENTY YEARS EARLIER

"IZZIE, hurry up! Don't make me late on the first day of school!"

I twirled in front of the mirror in my new bedroom. Last year, I'd grown to hate the first day of school. I had no idea how uncool I was until I got to Forest Hill and all the kids made fun of me.

Forest Hill was a nice name for what turned out to be a really shitty school. When Mom came home and told me I'd be starting there in a couple of days, I wasn't exactly thrilled about what that meant for Dad and Philly, but I figured I'd make the best of it.

There was no best. It was the worst year ever. The Camden kids called me dorky and uncool. Their pants were baggy, both the boys and the girls. T-shirts were oversized. When it got cold, they wore plaid flannel. My cutesy boyfriend sweaters and flared jeans with flowers my mom had embroidered were not cool.

Everything I owned was the very opposite of cool. But

with no money for shopping, I didn't have the luxury of stuffing my crap in the back of my closet in favor of ironed jeans and T-shirts. Mom wouldn't spring for Timberlands. Not when my duck boots fit just fine.

So every day, I walked under the archway as kids threw stuff at me when no teachers were looking. The rest of the time, they called me the little Mafia princess.

I'd wished hard we'd been in The Family.

Last year had been hellish in more ways than one, and I did not want to make that same mistake. Not when we wouldn't be leaving Toms River for a while, as far as I could see. Mom was getting to do what she did best, take care of people, only for money. She was like a duck back in water after a very long drought.

"Izzie!" my mom yelled again before the sound of the front door slamming echoed through the house.

I pried my eyes away from my reflection, picked up my backpack—a clone of Jake's and sure to be cool—then ran outside.

The car Mr. Wu had given my mother was idling about fifty feet away in the driveway. It wasn't a Mercedes, but it was really nice inside, full of shiny wood and soft leather. Turns out Mr. Wu's company made cars. Chinese ones I'd never heard of, but he'd shipped one to New Jersey for my mom to use nonetheless.

People looked twice at the Chinese characters on the trunk, sometimes asking questions, but I was happy to wait while my mom explained about DynoAutomotive, if it meant getting in a car guaranteed not to stall, break down, or quit in the middle of the turnpike.

I pulled open the back-door handle. Jake Wu was already inside, in the middle, his backpack taking up one side seat.

"Move over," I said, starting to shove my bag into the car.

"Excuse my Izzie, Mr. Wu. Honey, you'll need to ride up front with me."

"Wait. Why?" Jake and I had been riding together in the back seat of Mr. Wu's cars since we'd moved in a month ago.

Mom had taken us for ice cream, to the mall, to the library, to the beach, and we'd always huddled together in the back seat. It was the only way we could conspire to get a banana split, buy a game neither one of us was allowed, or get the good fantasy books from the library's adult section, the ones with off-limits naughty stuff in them.

Frowning, I turned to my mama.

"C'mon," I started. I'd been planning to pick his brain on the kids who ran the school. No way was I going to run afoul of the top cliques on day one. No fucking way.

Mama silenced me with a look. "Mr. Wu expects a certain protocol," she said.

Reluctantly, I closed the back door and got in next to my mom. As the car tires crunched through gravel, I tried to put a positive spin on it. I mean, how many times had I called front seat when it had been just me and Arturo?

In the last few weeks, I hadn't even thought about sitting up front. Mr. Wu had said the back seat was the safest and I'd jumped in without a thought. With good air-conditioning and Jake at my side, it had been the most fun I'd ever had riding in a car.

It was cold up front when I finally got in. I fiddled with the vents to keep from growing icicles on my still damp hair.

"Leave that, Izzie. Mr. Wu needs to be comfortable."

I dropped my hands to my lap and looked at the trunks of the huge maples passing outside my window. Mr. Wu had welcomed us like family, I'd thought. He'd given us a house and a car. But we weren't family, of course. My mama was his housekeeper and Jake's chauffer. I was the poor kid from Philly by way of Camden.

Mama's breakfast of caffe orzo and zeppole was threatening to come back up as I tried to swallow my embarrassment at forgetting my place.

We were halfway down Old Freehold Road when Jake spoke.

"Can you pull over here, Mrs. Aconi?"

"You can call me Maria," she said for about the thousandth time. Over a prohibited weeknight dessert, Jake and I had tried to figure out why it was okay for him to call my mama Maria, but I had to call his dad Mr. Wu. He said in China, no adult was really referred to informally. So he still called her Mrs. Aconi. And of course, I called his dad Mr. Wu.

Slowly, Mama edged the big sedan to the side of the road.

I looked at Mama, then turned back to Jake.

He flipped his hair to the side, something he did when he was really going to look at you. His eyes met mine, crinkled up in a big old smile. He shoved his bag to the floor and scooted to right behind my mom.

I didn't need any further invitation. I popped the lock on the passenger door, unbelted myself, then slammed into the back seat. I didn't even take the side seat, but scooted across the coffee-brown leather to the center.

While my mom drove off, clicking her tongue along the way, I nudged Jake with my elbow. He shoved at me with his knee. Then I turned. We touched foreheads and laughed like hyenas.

My best and only friend in all of Toms River, New Jersey, was on the same page as me. I stopped caring about how I looked because no matter what faced me today, I wouldn't have to face it alone.

♥

I tried not to quake in my chunky Mary Janes and empire-waist dress as my bravado of twenty minutes ago fled. Mama had let me and Jake out of the car, blew me a kiss, and had driven the dark-blue sedan away. She had about a thousand errands to run, two houses to clean, and who all knows what else before picking us up. So I didn't mind too much that she couldn't stay for even a few minutes. Not that there were any other parents there.

Hundreds of students thronged the circular drive. I looked at the three dolphins screwed to the front of the brick school building and crossed my fingers behind my back, silently praying for good luck.

I'd long given up on the idea of going back to Philly. I had no idea why that wasn't going to happen, but I knew that door was closed as firmly as Mama's mouth when I asked about Dad. Camden, I wanted to forget. So that left this intermediate school and Toms River with the Wu clan as my only option going forward. I had to make it work.

"What classes are you taking?" I asked Jake. He'd fished

his schedule from a pocket in his large but mostly empty backpack.

In the four weeks we'd been kind of under the same roof, I'd never seen him nervous or fidgety. Now he was worrying the printed schedule smooth between the long, thin fingers I'd seen him play perfect piano with. The light-blue ink was already faded from the paper.

When he didn't answer, I nudged him again, bumping my shoulder against his.

"Jake?"

"Math. English. Earth Science. U.S. History. The usual stuff. Plus, I'm signed up for orchestra and some kind of art class."

"Did you take Programming? When I was looking at the booklet Mama brought home, it was like you could make your own video games. Seemed like something you'd totally be into."

Jake's laugh was weirdly uncomfortable. "My parents would never go for that."

"But they let you play the games, though." To me, they seemed very permissive about some things.

"With straight A's, an hour of violin every day, three hours of piano a week, and Saturday Mandarin tutoring."

Mrs. Wu, who was really Mrs. Li, was due back from her spring and summer in Nanjing at any time, I'd been told.

She'd sent a long list of new rules for Jake. I'd thought Mr. Wu was strict, but she'd taken things to a whole new level and she wasn't even *in* New Jersey. I was kind of anxious about what it'd be like when she did fly into Newark.

I worried that the days when Jake and I could hang out were numbered.

I was thinking about what it would be like to be Jake when a group of boys jumped off a school bus, jostling their way through the crowd. It only took me seconds to suss out that these kids were on the top of the middle school food chain. Great white sharks, African lions, grizzly bears, and these boys ruled the animal kingdom.

Each one was dressed cooler than the next. Not Camden cool or Philly cool, but a whole different level. This wasn't street-savvy fashion, but money.

"Who are they?" I whispered, leaning my head close to Jake's. He was rich and cool like them. I wondered if these were friends he'd kept from me, the not-very-cool daughter of his housekeeper.

I'd half worried that one day his real friends would show up and I'd be back to helping Mama dust our guesthouse or hanging out with the gardener. But that day had never materialized. Were these them in the flesh? They were probably down the Jersey Shore until Labor Day, seeing as how tan they all looked.

"Fuck me..." came from under Jake's breath.

It had to be the worst word I'd ever heard come out of his mouth. The murders in *A Puzzle of Flesh* hadn't even irked him. But his swear didn't have the sound of someone who wanted to reconnect with his friends after a long summer away. In fact, it kind of sounded like—

I didn't even get a chance to finish my thought before the tallest, best-dressed, coolest of the group emerged from the pack.

"Evan!" the remainder of the group collectively called out in support of whatever mischief Evan and Jake were about to get up to.

Slinging one arm around Jake's neck, Evan yanked Jake from the makeshift line. Knuckles scrubbed against Jake's scalp, mussing his carefully gelled hair. They called him some nickname that ended in Panda.

Pandas were from China. I rolled my eyes. So original.

Boys.

Dismissing them, I shook my head, then looked down to fiddle with the front zipper pocket of my new backpack. I'd jammed raspberry lip gloss in there when Mama wasn't looking. I was slicking on the tinted cream when Evan's friends moved to circle Jake. What had looked friendly was quickly turning into something else.

I tried to sort through it in my head. So his friends weren't friends or it was more stupid boy stuff. I'd seen it with my brother a million times. One minute they were laughing, then wrestling, then someone got punched, then more back slapping and laughing. I'd learned to ignore most of it.

I finished rubbing my lips together and screwing the cap back on the tiny pot of gloss when I turned back to the boys.

Uh oh.

This was anything but friendly. They were chanting fake Chinese sounds at Jake. They'd messed up his shirt and grabbed his backpack. One guy was opening the zipper. Suddenly, I knew just how Arturo felt when I'd started elementary school. He'd had a huge protective instinct a mile wide.

More than anything I wanted to rescue Jake, wrap him in

something to protect him, even though I was younger. If someone didn't do something, in two seconds, all the paper we had so carefully clipped into his green binder would be all over the circular drive.

Tucking my fingers in my mouth, I whistled like my father did when my brother and I were arguing.

Evan and the gang stopped what they were doing to stare at me, like half the kids in line who'd turned around. Hundreds of voices quieted to nothing.

"What's up, shorty? Why the noise?" Evan asked.

"Izzie Aconi," I spat in my best Robert De Niro/Corleone voice. "Shorty's my dad's nickname."

I gave Evan a second or two to think about that. He didn't look as dumb as his associates. When he didn't say anything, I rethought that.

Finally, the kid with the darkest hair pulled Evan away from Jake.

"What the fuck, Cole?" Evan asked, his even features screwing up into a frown.

"Shorty Aconi ain't no joke. He just got out of prison for some shit, but they say he's put dozens of guys in the bay."

I watched kids whisper to each other. I wasn't a lip reader, but it didn't take mad skills to see the words "Mafia" and "Godfather" on the lips of first one, then the next, like a giant silent telephone game.

"We just moved this summer. Jake's my neighbor. We're tight like family," I insinuated, wrapping my index and middle finger around each other like stripes running up a barber pole.

"Where you from, Shorty?" Evan asked.

"Philly. Ninth Street area." That part at least was true.

"Why are you here?"

"My dad had to return to Italy for...work." I forced a hesitation, making my family's connection to the mainland seem way more sinister than it really was. "He thought it would be safer for us if we were out here by the shore. Until things calm down between the families," I said. "He took my older brother, though. Never too early to learn the business."

Nobody said a thing, and in seconds, the large front doors were pushed open and the kids surged forward, sweeping me and Jake along with the current.

Large signs were erected above long tables in the big hallway, one for sixth grade, one for seventh, and one for eighth. A couple of teachers manned each.

Before I could join the youngest kids in front of the far-left table under the dolphin-shaped banner, Jake pulled me aside.

He moved his hair over. His deep-brown eyes looked at me without the hint of humor that had reminded me so much of my brother in the last month. "Don't tell my dad, especially about the Wimpy Panda part."

"Tell him what?" I asked, playing dumb. If Jake had any brothers or sisters, he'd have known that silence and secrets were a given.

"About Evan or the other kids," he continued, leaning closer. His intense look made me warm and shivery at the same time. I rubbed at my upper arms, trying hard to ignore my hormones. Jake, thankfully oblivious, continued, "I told Baba everything was just fine at this school. He thinks America is the best country in the world."

I could see the problem. Jake wanted to stay in New Jersey. It's why he tried so hard to follow his dad's rules, and those his mom laid down from the other side of the earth. Mr. Wu had only sort of hinted at it, but the message was more than clear. If Jake didn't follow the rules, then he'd have to go home to China. No more video games. No more skateboarding. No more fun.

"You gotta do the same for me," I whispered.

"Do what for you?"

I lifted my eyebrows, trying to get him to see that I was serious too. "Keep my secrets."

Jake looked me up and down, then shrugged the single shoulder without the backpack strap. I could see in his eyes he saw me as no more than a little kid. It kind of hurt my feelings.

"You don't have any."

"Ice cream from the freezer after my mom and your dad go to bed. Video games that have," I lowered my voice, "sex and violence." My mama wasn't exactly at mass every day doing the sign of the cross or praying the rosary, but she still did believe a lot of what the pope had to say.

I could see in his eyes the moment he got it. The moment he realized that we could be a great team, the way brothers and sisters ganged up on their parents. "All right, so we don't rat on each other."

"No rats." I nodded, my voice serious. "Pinky swear."

He shook his head and wrinkled his very cute nose, wide where mine was pointy, in a way that told me he didn't understand what I was talking about.

"It's a tradition," I pronounced.

I pulled his schedule from his right hand and extended my pinky and thumb. I nodded at him, urging he do the same. In a few seconds, he mimicked me.

I wound my pinky around his and pushed our thumbs together until our little fingers broke apart.

"And that?"

"Was a one hundred percent American-style pact."

"Kind of like all for one and one for all."

"Except we're short one musketeer," I said. We both laughed.

Everyone cleared a path as I went to the sixth-grade registration line. I didn't even have to wait my turn. Being the daughter of a made man had its privileges. I couldn't wait for lunch.

CHAPTER 6

NOW

"WHAT IN THE hell just happened back there?" Jake Wu yelled into the crowded dressing room.

"Blue happened."

"Blue? Who? What?"

Jake had been an "A" student of American pop culture. His ignorance surprised me. Maybe China was really walled off like people said.

"Indigo Hawk goes by Blue. The bass player for Revival decided to play a different sort of instrument," I said, hoping for a laugh, a snicker, something to break the tension in the room.

Creatives. No sense of humor.

The writers and producers on the network shows thought of the suits, those of us in corporate, as the enemies of originality, creativity, and a whole bunch of other adjectives they loved to throw at us in table reads or over meetings about show notes. But as I've told all of them time and again, I was the port in the storm.

The grumpy old men who ran this place would make the network fifty percent Andy Griffith and fifty percent Angela Lansbury, given half the chance. It was my team that let writers and producers take chances, push that envelope, be as edgy as they could be within the confines of network television.

For the second time in a week, I was overrun with executives. The dressing room that had gone unused earlier in the evening was now filled with crotchety old white men with a sprinkling of cantankerous old Chinese men, me and Jake.

"When we hired you," my boss started, a man who I saw twice a year at most, and in golf clothes one time and a tacky Christmas-themed outfit the other. "When we hired you," he repeated, "we had two requirements. Two things that could not happen at this network. No George Carlin and no Janet Jackson."

No swearing and no nudity, he was saying. They were the two transgressions that could bring down the wrath of the FCC on our heads. And for nearly half a decade, I'd done just that, protect the network. Those eighteen hundred days of perfect behavior had been swept away with this one transgression, not of my making.

"It's not like we administer a drug test before performers come onstage. Not a single one of them would pass any kind of screening anyway," I said a bit defensively.

Just then, the door opened wider and Blue, the now fully clothed Revival bass player, and his management pushed into the room.

"Hey, man, I'm not a druggie. I have a medical marijuana

prescription," the aging rocker said. "My bud-tender gave me a pre-roll of Green Crack. Must have been super potent."

"So potent you unzipped your pants?" I asked, flicking my eyes toward his now-zipped acid-washed jeans.

"Yeah, well. I was kind of in the moment. Made me horny as shit. This babe put her tits on the stage—" Blue started.

"Okay, that's enough," I cut him off. "Rehashing isn't going to do anything. Thanks to Ms. Jackson and the moral majority, we're looking at a fine of at least..." I tried to do the calculations, but by brain wouldn't work through the multiplication. It was still mired in...the Penis.

"Three hundred twenty-five thousand dollars per station," Jake said.

"Hopefully that won't happen." I pasted on a megawatt smile. "This was more a Bono incident than a Janet Jackson," I argued, albeit weakly.

Bono had used the phrase "fucking brilliant" after winning an award. Probably because of Bono's coolness factor, the FCC had let the network off with the equivalent of a slap on the wrist and a warning that, next time something like that happened, there would be a fine.

Best-case scenario, CBT would get off with a warning. Bono's comments had to have been longer than the nine-sixteenths of a second the singer's nipple had been exposed.

I surveyed the balding, jowl-laden heads. They weren't buying what I was selling.

Shit.

I'd done my job scrupulously for five years. The push-the-envelope shows were garnering all the ratings and critical praise, a combination that didn't happen all too often. All that was forgotten in an instant.

"I'll be here all weekend getting out in front of this," I said.

Jake fingered the phone in his hand, calculator app helping *him* with math. "We're talking a possible fine of nine million dollars, Isabella."

"Let's not jump the gun. No one's filed an indecency report. The FCC hasn't called. Let's go home, get a good night's sleep, and meet in the morning. By then I'll have a draft letter for the owned stations and affiliates."

I'd spend the next however many hours using up every last bit of my Ivy League degree throwing three- and four-syllable words of apology and contrition into those letters.

Everyone looked in their hands or in their pockets as a phone trilled. But it wasn't the iPhone we'd all been assigned from the network. It was the distinctive tone of the Black-Berry that I should have shut off once and for all. That I should have chucked right into the Pacific Ocean the last time I had the chance.

"You going to answer that?" That was Jake. He looked at me expectantly.

I snagged the phone from my purse and jabbed at the tiny buttons, ignoring the call. I stood.

"As I was saying. Tomorrow morning, eleven o'clock. Fifth-floor conference room. Until then, gentlemen."

I gathered my phone and purse, turned my back, and walked the hell out of that room.

I knew when to cut people off, and it was that time. If I'd stayed, it would have been untold hours of tape replays and recriminations over something that couldn't be changed. Because if there was such a thing as a time machine, I'd turn the clock back a good twenty years, not merely twenty minutes.

While walking to my car, I searched the recesses of my mind. The Janet Jackson fine had been a shade over half a million. A drop in the bucket for a network raking in billions, and if Woo DynoMedia took the hit, it wouldn't even make a ripple in the Chinese economy. Sure, the FCC had raised fines since then, but the current commission was made up of all men, with penises. Gender allegiance would probably help quite a bit.

I felt a whole lot better as I walked to my car—alone.

The sordid underbelly of being network brass? No perks.

Networks were cheap as hell. CBT was no different. The few months we'd been owned by Woo hadn't loosened the purse strings.

There was no limo to get me from Broadcast City to the theater and back. Just my car. Trying to ignore the pain radiating from my cramped toes, I took mincing steps to the valet stand. Then I remembered. I hadn't valeted that damned car. Some memo had come down the pike talking about cutting costs, and even getting someone to park your car was like sending up a big red flag and asking for a department audit.

Once I'd located the parking elevator, I traded my near stilettos for pink ballet flats. There wasn't any reason to dress to impress in a parking lot.

There were few cars left even though it was still early in the evening Pacific time. Everyone who was anyone had gone to an after-party or had gone home to gossip about what they'd seen.

I'd tried to play it cool in that impromptu meeting, but I knew that my office would be flooded with postcards come Monday. There was likely already a line outside every office supply store in middle America.

Every morality-policing, religious fundamentalist group would be scribbling furiously tonight about how we'd somehow corrupted their children, half of whom had their own penis, and ruined their chaste, genital-free night that had otherwise been filled with gyrating hips and suggestive lyrics. Their grip on irony was nearly as good as Alanis Morissette's.

Fob in hand, and about ten feet from where I thought I'd left my car, I pressed the button, making my parking lights flash, the telltale lights and beeps pointing me in the right direction.

"Isabella?"

I nearly jumped a foot in my flats. After years of working as a Julie, I hated when people snuck up on me. My breath hissed out when I saw who it was.

Daisy.

She was leaning against her tank of a Mercedes, agitation shaking her foot. Her dark hair, normally the sleekest bob I'd ever laid eyes on, looked as if she'd worked her fingers through it a thousand times since the broadcast.

"I didn't know Laura Ashley had cocktail dresses," I said archly. It was totally unnecessary, but I couldn't help poking the girl a little bit.

"How did you know it was Laura—"

I couldn't stifle the bark of a laugh that came from my mouth.

"Oh my God, I was fucking kidding. Only you, Daisy."

For once, she didn't let my ribbing get to her. The worry lines didn't disappear from her face. She got closer to me, her blue eyes earnest under her pinched eyebrows.

"What's going to happen?" she asked as if the sword of Damocles were going to fall from the concrete slab above us.

"What I think you mean to ask is, 'am I going to be fired?'"

"Yeah, that." She fiddled with the gray-black pearls at her neck. Leave it to Daisy to have pearls in more than one color. I had zero doubt they were anything less than the real thing. Like Jake, she was one of those kids from one of those families where pearls, and cars, and millions of dollars were as common as chains that turned your neck green, and bus passes, and mounds of debt were in mine.

That said, I decided to throw her a bone.

"I haven't reviewed the tapes yet, but I don't think anyone could have seen that coming. One minute it was all bass, the next, penis."

Worry lines that would probably become a permanent fixture on her face ten years from now, smoothed out.

Even without four-inch heels, I wasn't exactly short. Nevertheless, I pulled myself to my full height and leaned a little bit into her space. "But, you're not going to skate on this. Have a memo to me as soon as you can on all the steps you took to keep indecency off the air."

"I'll do my best," she said, sticking an actual key into the door handle of her ancient car.

"Look, you need to do more than your best. I need to come out of this smelling like a very rare rose. Because if I get fired, the rest of you will fall like dominoes."

Daisy looked at her watch. "I'll have it to you in an hour."

"Good girl." I wanted to pat her on the head, but I refrained. Instead, I walked the five or six spaces to my own car.

With another beep, I unlocked my car and lowered the hard top. The sharp red leather upholstery buoyed my spirits. Lots of people said that money didn't make you happy. I was intent on doing a personal experiment. So far, I wasn't convinced the naysayers were right. I slipped into the seat of the little Mercedes. It fit me like a glove, making me smile.

Thirty traffic-choked minutes later, I knew why Daniel traveled by helicopter when he was in Los Angeles. Back at my office in Broadcast City, I got right to work. Even though I craved a bottle of wine or a few shots of something hard to wash this day away, it would have to wait a few hours. Daisy's memo came quickly and I only needed to spruce up her apology a tiny bit.

It was eleven o'clock when I finally thought it safe enough to turn off my computer. There was a lot of damage control yet to be done, but not on this Friday night.

I felt around under my desk for my flats, grateful I would not have to try to jam my feet back into those "fuck me" pumps. When some of the other, older girls had said one day I'd no longer be able to run in stilettos, I'd thought they were total punks, but now that I was three years past thirty, even I could see that those days were coming to an end.

No matter. I could still pull it out when I needed to be six feet tall and look men in the eye.

The hairs stood up on the back of my neck as I turned the key in my office lock. The first and most important lesson I'd ever learned when working as a Julie was to be aware of my surroundings.

So as not to appear completely nutso, though, I turned slowly, as if my nerves were made of steel. The year we'd lived in Camden, I learned that fear was a weakness. The strong would prey on you in a heartbeat.

When I was done with my slow revolution, I met the eyes of the person stalking me.

Jake Wu.

"Don't you have somewhere else to be?" I asked. I'd exorcised him from my life and thoughts long ago. But that didn't mean I wasn't affected by him creeping around the domain I'd so carefully constructed for myself.

He leaned against the mauve-colored wall between TV show posters, as if he belonged there instead of me.

"The deal with Father was that I could straddle between daytime and evening programming, even stick my foot into news, but I'm being sidetracked by having to put out fires in Program Practices."

I took a deep breath, one that would keep me from playing defense. Instead, I went on the offense.

"Since you don't quite fit into the org chart here, I'll give you the CliffsNotes version. The editions of the awards show that will air later or be repurposed for streaming have been edited to remove the genitalia, but still remain within time limits. We've got interns scouting the web for the next ninety-six hours looking for illegal copies of Revival's performance and we'll issue takedowns as they come up. Now I need to get home and get some sleep before tomorrow's meeting."

"What time is that again?"

"I'm sure you have something better to do."

I turned on my half-inch heel and stalked to the elevator. When the car arrived, I stepped on, gratified that Jake hadn't followed me. Hopefully, I wouldn't see him again for a while. I'm sure he'd be wooed away by Programming. Taking pitches from nervous producers and deciding which shows would get the green light was a lot like playing God.

Few with a healthy ego turned down that opportunity, and he had a more than healthy ego, being as good-looking as all fuck, and rich and powerful to boot. Next week, Jake would probably snag himself the world's biggest office and wield his newfound power from there, far from Program Practices.

I felt half-sorry for CBT's current Senior Executive Vice President, Programming, and head ass, Kevin Manning. Almost.

As the gleaming doors slid shut, I shook my head ruefully. Nope, I didn't feel sorry for Kevin. One asshole deserved the other. If I didn't have a full-time job in Program Practices and a minor crisis to manage, I'd have pulled up a chair ringside to watch the two men butting heads. There wasn't enough popcorn in the world for that show. Too bad I was busy.

I lived a long L.A. city block from Broadcast city, and decided to leave my car in the lot and walk home instead of driving the half mile around the corner. It wasn't like I'd be doing something other than going to work on Saturday morning.

While I was waiting for the interminable light at the corner of The Grove Drive and West Third Street, my phone beeped. My work phone. The light turned as I debated whether or not I was off the hook for the night.

The debate was very short. Once at my building gate, I pulled the corporate-issued iPhone from my purse and swiped the screen to get to the inevitable voicemail.

The return phone number was unfamiliar, but I anticipated I'd be getting a lot of messages from all sorts of CBT executives over the next forever.

"Do you think Programming is overrated? Dad thinks that with my traditional Chinese sensibilities, maybe I should take a swing through Program Practices, see if I can set this ship right. I'm sure you'll find me an office."

No, "hi," no "bye," just an announcement that I was already half-fired.

"Miss Aconi, you okay?" the elderly guard asked, tipping his hat in my direction. I was probably wearing my dismay all over my face.

"Fine, Gerard. Buzz me in, please."

He pressed a button in his little guard booth, and the man-sized gate swung open.

My steps to the elevator and down the hall to my penthouse were slow. I found my key and slipped it into the lock. It turned easily and I stepped into my two-story apartment, taking my first breath of air not constricted by those around me.

I locked the door and dropped everything on the floor,

making a mess for once. I stripped off my clothes and walked up my narrow staircase naked as the day I was born. Not caring a whit about the drought California was facing, I stood in the shower, letting the eight well-placed jets shoot pulsing water at me until my skin turned pink and tingled.

Wrapping myself in the robe I'd hijacked from a luxury hotel in Bali years ago, I lay down on the bed and let my mind go blank. It was a long time later before I got up the courage to retrieve my phone from downstairs.

There was only a single new text message. I swiped.

I kind of liked your office. If you don't mind, I'll camp out there for the next few days. It'll be like old times.

I didn't have to pretend I didn't know who it was any longer. It had been signed this time, un-ironically and unapologetically: *The Wimpy Panda.*

CHAPTER 7

EIGHTEEN YEARS EARLIER

"GOOD CATHOLIC GIRLS don't wear nail polish," Mama shouted.

"Good Catholic women don't get divorced," I muttered under my breath as I turned toward the hallway.

"Did you say something?"

"No, Mama," I said in my full voice.

"I didn't think so." She turned on her heel toward the living room. In seconds, I heard the blaring sound of a car commercial come from the TV. Maybe if we just headed on down to the Route 37 auto mile, all our problems would be solved.

I slammed the door to my room as hard as I dared. How was it that Mama didn't think fourteen was old enough to wear nail polish? It wasn't like I was going to go to school with dragon-lady nails or anything. I just wanted a little bit of sparkle on my fingers and toes like the other girls.

Mama had zero idea how much work I'd put into being queen bee over the last year. Half the girls—wannabees—

worshipped me. The other half feared my dad would kill theirs and didn't dare cross me.

I'd played off the conservative clothes and no makeup pretty well. My father, I said, was a devout Catholic. He'd kill me dead if he saw me in a short skirt or so much as a smear of lip gloss. Mama had confiscated that first pot long ago.

I'd made a big deal about me being the one to push going to public school, as if my parents would have me locked up in a convent in Italy if they had their way. But the act was getting old.

A supposed a badass like me needed to engage in more... badassery. That meant defying school rules with too-short skirts, even shorter belly-button-revealing sweaters, and makeup. Despite the school regulations prohibiting it, even the least-popular girls were wearing mascara, colored gloss, and Johnna Rossman had a belly button ring that winked at you every damn time she raised her hand in class. I was starting to think she volunteered so much on purpose to rub it in that her parents let her put a diamond in there.

A pebble pinged against my window and shook me from my sulk. I jumped off my bed and ran to lift the sill. A second rock hit me in the neck.

Jake was standing off to the side, just out of view should my mother look over her shoulder and catch him outside. I didn't think she'd look though, Oprah had her attention. He had his hand over his mouth, barely able to contain a laugh at his direct hit.

"That's not funny," I hissed. "You could have taken my eye out." I tried to keep my lips thinned and my expression fierce, but it wasn't meant to be. In five seconds, I'd picked up the errant stone from the carpet next to my bed and tossed it back at him, giggling behind my own closed hand as it pinged him in the forehead.

"C'mon," he beckoned.

I glanced at the pink alarm clock on the white table next to the canopy bed. Mrs. Li had everyone, except me, on a tight schedule. There was a printed copy of the Wu family's comings and goings attached to our refrigerator. Mr. Wu was napping before businesses opened in eastern China. Mama had her hour break before dinner. Jake had his own hour by hour plan. The other live-in employees, the Perezes, didn't work Friday.

"Aren't you supposed to be studying Mandarin right now?" It came after school homework, but before piano.

"Mr. Chin is in China," he said. I'd forgotten that his tutor was out of the country for a few weeks. Probably to spend time with his own wife and kids. Mr. Wu was big on family. I'd heard him offer to bring Mr. Chin's wife and kids over to America. The tutor had refused, instead going back a few times a year.

"That doesn't mean a thing." I knew that Mrs. Li didn't care about that kind of detail. I was sure Mr. Chin had been obligated to leave a long list of detailed lessons for Jake to complete while he was away.

"It means that there's no one to tattle about me skipping out. C'mon, I want to show you something." Under his hair, Jake's eyes sparkled with mischief.

He knew he had me. His naughtiness was contagious. Had been from that first moment we'd pulled out joysticks to play *Phantasmagoria*. For someone whose whole life was ruled by a long list of musts and shoulds, he really did know how to make almost anything fun.

I dropped the contraband nail polish into the drawer of my bedside table and slammed it shut.

Mr. Wu owned a great deal of land in Toms River, which was really called Dover, officially and all that. Mama said that not only was this place on Freehold Road seven acres, but that Mr. Wu owned another three hundred farther down the parkway. He had a plan to bring Chinese cars to America and needed the land to build some kind of assembly plant, Mama said. Seemed to me that America already had a bunch of Japanese cars coming over and wasn't looking for more Asian cars, but what did I know about business?

What I did know was that this six acres and change was huge. There was the Wus'. Mama called it the main house. Our house, she said was called a guesthouse. Rich people put their guests up nice, if that was true. Then there were a few more buildings where Mr. Wu kept a bunch of different cars, and another where Jana and Randy Perez sometimes stayed over. Mama called them groundskeepers.

Mr. Perez did a lot more than mow the lawn, though. He fixed everything that needed fixing and kept the cars running besides. They weren't always around, though, Mr. and Mrs. Perez. I think Mama said something about them having family in a place called Stone or Brick or something that didn't sound as much like a beachy place as the rest of the towns around here.

Even though I knew better, I took Jake's outstretched hand and climb-hopped through the window. It was a good thing Mr. Perez had taken off the screens the week before but hadn't put in the storm windows yet, otherwise I'd have to have given Mama a million excuses as to why I was going out and wasn't in my room doing homework like Jake.

Living with the Wus had turned Mama into a stickler about school. If Jake could study twenty-four seven, then there wasn't any reason I couldn't study half that much. My grades were better, but my attitude was worse. Mrs. Li sucked the fun from life like a huge mean vacuum.

"Let's make a run for it," Jake decided once I was standing next to him in the damp patch of weeds and gravel.

Hand in hand, we sprinted across the open lawn, past the pool, which had been covered for the winter, toward the woods. We were both breathing hard as we collapsed against the trunk of the biggest beech tree I'd ever seen.

"Think anyone saw?" I asked. Mama had warned me time and again about staying away from Jake and out of trouble. I'm not sure if she knew half of what we got up to though.

"We're clear. Your mom will be in my kitchen soon. My mom went to New York."

"What's she doing there?" Mrs. Li was in New York City a lot. She shopped for dresses and shoes and purses, but I could never really figure out why. It wasn't like she had a job or anything. I mean, did a woman need really shiny shoes to go out with friends to buy yet more shoes?

"Shopping," Jake said, confirming my suspicion.

"So what's up?" It could be anything. In the last year, he'd taught me how to climb a tree, find my way in the woods. We'd sucked at trying to build a snowman, though.

"It's in the shed." He pointed back towards the cluster of buildings in the middle of Mr. Wu's land.

"We should have run there first."

"It would have taken too long to explain it standing next to your window."

"So what do we do?"

The plan was simple. I would run first, since no one would be too upset if I was outside playing. Mama would only yell that homework came before dinner. If Mr. Wu saw Jake, though, there'd be hell to pay. I was to turn the combo lock three times, like the one on my school locker, then lift the hasp and wait for him by the snow tire collection inside.

I nodded my understanding, repeating the combination in my head a few times to commit it to memory.

"Ready, set, go!" he called, and I darted this way and that from the woods, across the lawn, to the low one-story shed. Even though the October afternoon was cool and getting cooler, my hands were sweaty with nerves. Took me three tries to remember to turn past the second number before notching in the third.

With a click and a jerk, the lock opened. I pulled at the heavy wood door and slipped inside. The shed was the size of a four- or five-car garage. All manner of stuff was stored in there. The Perezes' garden tools shared space with window screens, furniture covered in dust cloths, huge steamer trunks, and the tires. Remembering my instructions, I hid next to the three-tiered racks of rubber.

Minutes later, the creak of rusty hinges let me know I wasn't alone. I held my breath on the off chance it was someone other than Jake.

"Bella?" He was the only one who called me by that nickname.

I came around from the side of the rack. "Sorry. It could have been Mr. Perez or even Mama."

"I thought you told me she was afraid of the spiders in here."

"She is, but if Mr. Wu needed something and no one else was here, I think she might have tried to come in."

Jake pushed the door shut and slipped a tiny bolt into a hole in the doorframe. With the door closed, we were in near darkness. The only light were diagonal slashes of sun coming down through small rectangular windows near the pointed roof.

The second Jake's eyes met mine in the shed, nervousness about going against the house rules changed into something altogether different. Right then, I wondered when he'd stopped being a stand-in for my long-lost brother, Arturo, and when he'd become important to me in an entirely different way. My eyes flickered away from his and down to his lips.

I wanted him to kiss me.

The thought slammed into my head, nearly making me lose my balance and knocking me down. Suddenly, desperately, I wanted a paper bag to breathe in before I hyperventilated like I'd seen girls do at school. Instead, I held my breath for a really long time.

Jake came closer, standing directly in front of me. A thin dime wouldn't have fit between our bodies, not with my new breasts pushing toward his chest. I had to crane my neck to see his face. He'd shot up over the summer. He was a full head taller than me now. His too-long hair brushed against the top of my own head, nearly making me jump out of my skin.

I hadn't known until that moment that I even had nerve endings up there. I looked into his eyes, sucked in a lungful of air, blew it out then nodded. He clasped his hands—the ones that were, like his feet, slightly too big for his body—around my waist. I couldn't help the shiver that whispered through me. I clenched my thighs together trying to stop it.

In what felt like hours, I gathered my thoughts and said, "What did you want to show me?" I was happy that my voice sounded normal and not like that of a stupid seventh grader with the world's biggest crush, which was what I'd suddenly become.

"It's over there," he said, jerking his head toward the far corner, deep in shadow. For some reason I didn't understand, Jake's parents kept all the Chinese language newspapers his mom brought back from her trips to New York City. There was a giant pile of them, unreadable characters spilling vertically down the newspaper to the fold.

Abruptly, he let go of me and walked to the far side of the shed. Like a loyal puppy, I followed.

He lifted some of the newspapers. I squinted to see what was underneath.

"Oh my gosh! Those are so cute, what are they?" I asked, looking at the little squirming animal bodies that were tucked into a hole the mom had probably dug into the middle of the paper pile.

"Mice? Rats?" He looked at me for confirmation on all things American. I shrugged. Then he said, "I don't know. I saw what I think was the mom running in and out from my bedroom window. When she had an entire apple in her mouth, I figured she must be feeding more than herself."

"What's going to happen to them?" I asked. They looked nothing like the vicious things competing with Mama and me for food in Camden. They probably had a whole other kind of rodent out here by the shore. One who wouldn't dare steal the food from a rich person's kitchen.

"They'll grow up in a few weeks and move out into the woods, I guess. I don't know where they go for the winter."

I reached my finger to touch the soft-looking brown hair on one of the babies.

"Don't!" Jake snatched my hand back, but kept hold of it.

I didn't let go either, but turned to him. "Why not?"

"I asked Mr. Potter about them." Mr. Potter was an Earth Science teacher at school. "He said that New Jersey rodents carry all sorts of insects and diseases that could make us sick."

"Does that mean we should tell Mr. Perez to get rid of them?"

"I don't think so. It's not like we have any pets or farm animals here or anything. As long as we don't touch them, I think we should be okay."

I dropped his hand and moved to what looked like a couch. I lifted the white cloth and sat on the red and gold seat. Jake lifted the newspapers, taking another look, then dropped them again. He came and sat next to me.

I wanted to run, bolt, sprint away from my feelings because I had no idea what to do with them. Mama had said that I was too young to like boys, but I should stay away from them nonetheless. The school nurse had talked about biology, intercourse, and pregnancy during Health class. Neither one of them had told me what to do with the yearning in my heart.

Following my feelings, I let my hand creep across the couch cushions until it met Jake's. He grabbed it and we held hands. His was hard and soft and rough and smooth. When his thumb brushed against the back of mine, I thought I'd jump clear out of my skin.

His touch made me think of hugs, and kisses, and all the stuff I'd read about in one of the books that the girls in school passed around, the spine falling open to the good parts when it was my turn.

We sat that way, silent, for a long time. The only sound I could hear was the wind rustling leaves outside and my own heartbeat pulsing in my ears.

"I'm glad you came to New Jersey." The rustling sound wasn't leaves maybe, but Jake turning toward me. His knee touched mine. Even through the jeans his mom only allowed him to wear at home, I could feel his heat.

"Me too." I squeezed his hand tighter.

"I like you, Bella."

I nudged his knee with mine, letting him know without words that I felt it too. All of my insides were pulling, leaning, yearning toward Jake, but I was so afraid because I didn't know what acting on those feelings looked like. I took a deep breath, shored up my bravery then turned.

I looked him directly in the eyes. Like mine, his were brown, but I could see so much emotion swirling in them. The same fear and doubt and hesitation that was paralyzing me was stopping him, too.

It was at that moment that I wrapped myself in the same false bravado that I used to get through school. It didn't have to be only used for evil. Like a budding superhero, I realized that I could use my power for good as well.

Lifting my left hand, I let it push his heavy hair back. His whole face, with his forehead bare, looked vulnerable.

I leaned in closer and closer until I could feel the whisper of his breath stir the tiny hairs on my face. Closer, until I could smell the scent of those little candies he liked. The ones wrapped in red paper that his mom had brought from China. Closer until my lips almost touched his. I tilted my head one way. He shifted his the other.

Then the rattle of the door made me jump about ten feet in the air.

In milliseconds, I was off the couch and crouching by the tires. Jake was at the door, lifting and unlatching the small bolt he'd locked.

"Wu Jian, what are you doing in here?"

It was Mrs. Li. As always, she looked like a TV talk-show host. Her hair was cut perfectly. Even when she moved it never got messy, moving like a curtain of silk. Her beige suit was buttoned tight, the matching belt with its pearly square buckle was cinched at her waist. Her white stockings never had a run or a hole, and shoes the color of picked-clean bones didn't have a speck of dirt. It was like she hadn't walked across the huge lawn, but had somehow materialized there right before our very eyes straight from her walk-in closet.

"I was showing Jake," my use of his Americanized name was deliberate. I wanted her to know he was one of us now. China was his past. "I was showing Jake," I repeated, and I prayed for God's forgiveness for consigning one of his creatures to death as I said it, "uh, this rat that just gave birth."

I darted across the room and lifted some of the newspaper stack. "They're mighty cute."

She turned to Jake. "Wu Jian," were the first words she spoke, and the last I understood. The rest descended into an onslaught of Mandarin. Over the last year, I'd gotten used to all the Chinese spoken around me. Mrs. Li understood and spoke English, though I'd only heard it once or twice. Mostly she let Mr. Wu speak for her, to us at least.

Even if she didn't quite believe me about the rodents, I could tell from her tone that she wasn't happy that we were out there, that Jake wasn't studying, that there were rats near her house.

From the pointing of her manicured fingernails, I knew the little mother and babies would be lucky to survive the night. I sent up a Hail Mary.

Jake didn't say much as his mother laid into him. I looked back and forth between them. No one was looking at me, so I decided it would be a great time to get back to my own homework and whatever chores Mama wanted me to do.

As quiet as a mouse, I stepped first one foot, then the next toward the door. I figured I'd snake around Mrs. Li, then book it to the guesthouse.

The toe of my sneaker was halfway through the door when something like a vise banded around my upper arm.

"Not yet," Mrs. Li said, her English as clear as a bell. I stopped in my tracks.

She didn't let go while she continued speaking to Jake. In a few minutes, his head bowed in contrition, he shuffled out of the shed. My eyes practically bored holes in the back of his head, but not once did he look back at me.

Mrs. Li marched me from the shed. Despite her perfect manicure and flawlessly clean suit, she picked up the lock from the ground where I'd dropped it, and in seconds, had it in the loop and the door locked up like it was Fort Knox and there was gold in there, instead of old furniture and baby mammals.

Even though she wasn't holding on to me anymore, I didn't think I'd been granted permission to walk away, so I stood stock still, expectation sour in my belly.

Two different scenarios played out in my head. Either she'd get me in trouble with Mama, or even worse, get Mama in trouble with Mr. Wu. I was trying to decide which would be the lesser of the two evils when she stuck her very cold and bony hand under my chin.

Though her accent was thick, her words were clear. "My son will overtake DynoAutomotive in some years. He will need to study very hard. Your mother is a housekeeper, so you don't have big ambitions. You must respect my son needs this time in America to study, not play."

She removed her hand and nodded in dismissal.

I ducked my own head and made my way slowly to the guesthouse.

Everything she'd said had been true. Jake was expected to run a company. My mother was *only* a housekeeper and cook for the Wu clan. Tears clogged my throat anyhow.

Everybody—my mom, my dad, our teachers—said that anyone in America could be anything. According to Jake, that wasn't true for China, but we were here, right in New Jersey in the heart of the United States. I swallowed hard at my disappointment in believing in something that might not be true. Maybe Mrs. Li was right. Maybe moving to this rich town wouldn't make any difference in how my life turned out. People like Jake would run the world and people like me would clean it.

I walked back in through the front door, into silence. Mama wasn't inside anymore. It was going to be dinnertime for the Wu family soon and she needed to make sure it was on the table precisely at seven.

I closed the door behind me and walked down the hall to my room. It would have been a thousand times better if Mrs. Li had told on me instead.

CHAPTER 8

NOW

NO WAY WAS I giving up my fucking office. What was I supposed to do, swap out for the tape-storage room we half cleared out whenever we had interns? Hell if that was going to happen.

I jammed my phone into the speaker, debated between bands, and landed on the all-time classic, Nirvana. It wasn't time to mess around with experimental alternative music. With the remote in my hand, I had to crank the volume to ten before I could drown out Blue and his penis, Daniel and his hold on me, and most of all, Jake turning up like the Ghost of Christmas Past.

Wet hair flinging water everywhere, I danced as if I didn't have a care in the world. For ten whole minutes, I was able to give myself up to the music, then noise, loud and persistent, invaded my space.

Weezer's *Make Believe* had just started. In that pause before a song begins, I heard it again. Banging.

Jesus.

Penthouses in Los Angeles didn't have the same exclusivity as they did in movies about New York City. There wasn't a restricted elevator that traveled to the top floor, dropping me off in rarified air. It was more like I had a top-floor apartment with a small second floor that housed my bedroom and bathroom. The apartment was a gift from Daniel. A perpetual gift that kept on giving.

Well acquainted with my penchant for loud music, he'd somehow arranged it so neither the building management nor neighbors ever bothered me when I needed to decompress. There was someone new who hadn't gotten the memo. I'd seen boxes a week ago and hadn't thought much of it. In a transient city like L.A., people came and went all the time. I'd learned not to get too attached for just that reason.

With a sigh, I turned off the music and stalked to the door. I nearly tripped over my bags before I could twist the two locks that had come standard and the third lock I'd had installed to make sure Daniel respected my boundaries. Door separated from jamb and I peered into the hallway I shared with the other top-floor inhabitants, not seeing anyone.

I almost closed the door when a shiny leather shoe prevented it. I looked up to see who in the hell would do that. Mafia princess Aconi was going to have to make an appearance.

Jake.

"Are you stalking me? I hate to have to bring you up to speed on American labor laws, but working for CBT doesn't mean I'm a slave or indentured servant or something. The minute I walked off the lot, I was off the clock. No locking me in the building or anything."

His eyes traveled from the top of my ridiculously tangled hair, past my gaping robe—which I then pulled together with urgency—to my bare feet. They weren't quite ballerina feet, but were starting to show the results of the abuse Jimmy Choo and Christian Louboutin heaped on them.

"Bella."

"Isabella," I corrected.

"Isabella, then. This is fortuitous."

"Four syllables. Your father's tuition to Woodward Tillman Hall didn't go to waste after all."

"Are you going to invite me in?"

"I'm indisposed at the moment." I tucked my robe tighter around my nudity and retied the belt to avoid my own wardrobe malfunction.

"We lived together for six, nearly seven years. I've seen it all."

I didn't point out that he hadn't "seen it all" in New Jersey, but Connecticut, during a night I'd rather forget.

I backed away from the door, slamming it the moment he slipped in, nearly catching his stupid suit jacket on the knob.

"Watch it. Mom had this tailored."

"Singapore."

"I feel like I ought to give you a prize."

"If you're here to talk about your stupid office thing, I'm happy to let you know that suitable accommodations equal to your contribution to our department will be made."

"I was here about the music."

"Revival? I know you didn't have Google in China, but now that you're here, I'm sure you're resourceful enough to figure out how to get whatever information you need about the band."

"Not that music. I came by to ask you to turn down *yours*."

"None of the actual residents have ever complained."

"That's not true."

I hated this about the Wus. They loved to turn things around, shake the ground under my reality. I reverted to the behavior that had saved me more than one time during my tenure in Toms River. I didn't say a word.

"Your newest neighbor is lodging a complaint," he said. Jake released the three buttons of his suit jacket, and took a seat on one of the ottomans that marked the space between my so-called living and dining rooms. Any other person would have looked awkward perched on the mid-century furniture, but not him. He looked like a fucking model for scotch or some kind of urbane liquor with the recessed lights reflecting off his shiny black hair, his broad chest straining at the confines of jacket and shirt, his full lips tilted in a half smile.

"I haven't met him...or her."

"But you have." He held out his hand and I took it without thinking. "Jake Wu. I'm in four-ten."

I tried to drop his hand, but he didn't let go.

"Four-ten," I repeated stupidly.

Next door.

My mind went right to the not-so-friendly apartment managers. I started working out schemes that would allow me to trade one generic penthouse apartment for another. Calling Daniel came to mind but I immediately dismissed it.

It had been hard enough getting him to pay for this one. He wasn't exactly like an ATM. Everything with Daniel was give and take, and I wasn't in a giving mood.

I snatched my hand back. It had gone all warm and tingly while I stood there trying to integrate my new reality, a skill I'd honed to perfection since leaving Philly.

"If you'll excuse me." I ran up the short staircase and closed and locked the door to my sanctuary. My robe had to go. I hung it up in the bathroom. Traded it for a sports bra, serviceable underwear and a tank top. I flicked through some hangers in my walk-in before settling on a sleeveless T and boyfriend sweats. I shoved my feet into my broken-in Stan Smiths and went to check the damage in the bathroom mirror.

Not great.

With wax, I smoothed back my hair into a sleek ponytail. Tom Ford pencil in hand, I drew in my eyebrows, lined my eyes and declared myself acceptable. My mission, should I choose to accept it, was to find out what Jake's sudden appearance in Los Angeles meant for me.

As I slicked on a little gloss, I calculated the cost of asking Daniel for one last favor, should my television career go south. I wasn't trained for much else, that was legal anyway. Tamping down my panic about career alternatives, I flicked the lock open and went downstairs.

Jake had abandoned his jacket, loosened his tie, and helped himself to Dutch gin from the freezer.

"Top-shelf stuff, this." He lifted the ice-cold spirit to his lips and took a sip.

I got my own drink and sat on the second ottoman. My heart

clenched with the familiarity of it all. Back when we'd been friends—best friends all those years ago—we could sit together, the silence filled with first relief at having found each other, then yearning, then love. Later frustration, at so much of what had happened in the world around us that we couldn't control.

The herd of elephants in the room were trumpeting, announcing their presence. I'd learned not to avoid the elephants.

"Why are you really here, Jake?"

"The neighbor thing was an accident, I swear."

"Your family likes nice things. There aren't but a handful of these kinds of apartments in the city. You picked the one closest to the network. Makes sense."

"You always did like your music loud."

"I can't feel it unless I *feel* it."

"You loved that Led Zeppelin concert. I still can't believe our parents let us go by ourselves. Unless…"

"Yeah, unless they wanted us out of the way for a night." Elephant number one, poached.

"I never pictured you in a place like this."

"Where did you see me ending up, Jake? Because I didn't plan to take your mother's advice and work as someone's servant."

"Of course not. You have to forgive her traditional ideas. You have to forgive your own mom."

"I don't have to forgive her anything."

"You don't think?"

"I'm not my mother. She's an adult. She was an adult long before me. I have no control over what she does."

"Why can't you try?"

"If this is why you're still here, you can leave," I said.

I was not. No, I was never going to pretend about my mother or defend what she did. It always came to this—me on trial for my mother's actions.

"I've let you stay this long because we did know each other once. We were friends once. But if this is going to devolve into our parents' shit, I'm out. I got out when I went to Owen. Washed my hands of it. Put it behind me. Whatever other clichés you can think of."

"Who's paying for this apartment?"

"My finances aren't your concern."

"That was Daniel calling, right?" He lifted his glass. "Dutch liquor. Seven-thousand-dollar apartment. Doesn't take Agatha Christie—"

"That's it. Get your jacket." I stood and slammed my drink on the coffee table, not caring that the spilled liquor would probably strip the finish from the wood and leave my apartment smelling like Pine Sol.

"Why?"

"Because I'm an adult. I'm not dependent on you or your dad anymore."

He raised an eyebrow. "Aren't you?"

"There are other networks. More than there ever were. I can keep tits and ass off one channel as well as I've done it on CBT. The Wus no longer control me. I'm not Maria Sofia. I'll never be like her."

Oh so slowly, he put on his jacket. Drained his drink. Walked to put the glass in the bar sink.

"You're exactly like her, Bella. Trading your body for a house, money, designer stuff."

I could no more control my hot Italian temper than I could control a runaway horse. My slap left a pink mark on his perfect face. His hair, waxed to within an inch of its life, didn't even move.

He didn't flinch. Didn't say a thing. Just stepped through the door and closed it so softly behind him, I could barely hear it catch.

Jake Wu...Wu Jian...was a lot of things, but a liar wasn't one of them. When everyone around him was as duplicitous as shit, he stayed true to his own strict moral code. I'd never been able to say the same.

Like mother like daughter.

CHAPTER 9

EIGHTEEN YEARS EARLIER

AS WE EMERGED from Penn Station, someone muttered something about the Bridge and Tunnel crowd. For once I didn't give a shit what anyone was saying about me or Jake.

Through my mittens and his gloves, I couldn't feel a thing, just the pressure of him pulling me aside when we got to the top of the escalator. He slid a glance toward me and we put our foreheads together like we used to when I first moved in.

"Bridge," he said.

"Tunnel," I retorted.

We both laughed for a good couple of minutes. I pointed as best I could with four fingers stuck together toward the signs directing us to Madison Square Garden.

"How did you do it?" I asked for the thousandth time.

And for the thousandth time, Jake shook his head and shrugged his shoulders.

His dad and my mom, the two strictest parents in Toms River, had let us come to New York City by ourselves.

When I'd begged to go to the Led Zeppelin concert on Thanksgiving weekend, I thought for sure my mother would say no. It was her favorite word. She said it for nearly everything I wanted to do, from wearing makeup to spending time with friends she didn't approve of. And she didn't approve of a single one of the girls from Toms River Intermediate North. They were all too rich and too wild for her tastes, as if hair spray, nail polish, and chewing gum made them the whores of Babylon.

When she'd said, "yes, if you can convince Jake to take you," I nearly fell on the floor. I might have *actually* dropped my backpack and slid down the wall to the wood floor. I had waited maybe five minutes before I ran over to Jake's house to tell him the good news.

I didn't care that I looked like a tourist as I took in the big wall mural showing what the station had probably looked like when my mom was a kid. What I didn't do was jump up and down at my excitement at seeing a band live and in person. Led Zeppelin had been the background music of my life in Philly.

"I hope you like it," I said to Jake as we got closer to where the ticket takers stood. My dad had always played Led Zeppelin in his weekend music rotation. He used to dance with me and Arturo. We'd throw around our hair, strum air guitars. We'd had such fun back in those days. I mean, life was fun now with Jake in New Jersey. It was just different.

"You okay?" Jake asked.

I had stopped moving. Was standing stock still in a crowd of thousands.

"Sorry," I said. I was no closer to unraveling the mystery

of my dad than I'd been those first months we'd spent in Camden. I'd almost stopped fantasizing that he was going to come along and swoop me up like a prince in a fairy tale.

In the darkest of night, though, when I couldn't sleep because of the noises of unseen animals rustling in the trees and grasses, I wondered if he'd ever loved me. He'd said it a thousand times that I could remember and a thousand more I couldn't. But if he really loved me, how could he walk away without a backward glance?

I still hoped that even if I didn't get to see him regularly, he'd show up one day and surprise me with tickets to a vacation in Disney World, though at fourteen I was getting a little old for that dream.

"You still want to do this? We don't have to. It's New York. Dad gave me a few hundred dollars. We could do anything."

I squeezed his hand, hoping he could feel it. "Nope. I'm good. Great in fact. Let's go."

For two hours, I stood and sang and nearly shouted myself hoarse. Every so often, I looked at Jake. His hair was a little bit shorter these days. Still too long, but not covering his eyes the way it used to, though I still couldn't see his ears.

When the last chords of "The Song Remains the Same" reverberated through the arena, Jake pushed back his hair and looped it behind his ear on the side facing me, making his vulnerable-looking lobe visible to me.

I knew at that precise moment that I loved him. Not like, not a crush, but love. Mama would say I was too young to know my own mind, but I did—know my mind, that is.

After the concert, we walked around a bit in the city,

stopping at a diner to have coffee and pie. He had cherry. I had pumpkin.

When we stepped out under the fluorescent restaurant sign, it wasn't quite raining, but the air was thick with mist. The night couldn't have been any more magical. I didn't want it to end, but agreed with Jake that we didn't need to push it too far by coming home too late, otherwise a day like this might never come again. And I, at least, wanted to experience this magic again and again.

The bus, once it crossed the bridge back into Jersey, was quiet and dark as most of the partygoers fell asleep. We sat side by side, and I felt like I'd burst into a million tiny pieces any second. I wanted to blame it on the coffee, but the reality was that I wanted Jake to know how I felt. Wanted him to love me back.

It had been a year since his mother had caught us in the shed, and we were as close as we ever were, but he'd held himself back from me. I hadn't heard that he was dating anyone in the high school, but the connection I felt between us was a bit one-way at times.

I pulled off my mittens and tucked them into the pocket of the seat in front of me. When a streetlight passed through the length of the bus, I saw that he had his hands knitted together tight, jammed between his knees.

"Jake?"

The rustle of hair against the seat told me he'd turned in my direction.

"You're not asleep? It's after midnight." His voice was rough, hoarse, already changing from that of the boy I'd met to the man I imagined he'd one day become.

"I..." I trailed off, no idea how to say what I wanted. Mama's sole dating advice had been to stay away from boys. Somehow Jake had skirted her vigilance.

I lifted my hand from my thigh, pulled up the armrest between us, and grabbed at both of his.

"Oh, Bella," he whispered in one second. In the next, we were holding hands. My arm was on fire. Everything, from the hair standing at the back of my neck down to my toenails, tingled and flooded with warmth. I turned my head toward him. I could feel his breath stirring the hair around my face.

We sat like that, breathing each other's air for the space of a dozen heartbeats.

"Bella." It came on an exhale.

"Why do you call me that?"

"It means beautiful."

I checked my seat to make sure I hadn't melted into a puddle of goo right there on the New Jersey Turnpike.

"Do you think—"

"That you're the most beautiful girl I've ever known? Yes, Bella. Yes."

I don't know who leaned in first. Light swooped over us and my lips found his. There was nothing at first but anticipation, then the briefest touch.

The hand that wasn't holding mine cupped my jaw, drawing me closer a fraction of an inch at a time. He pulled away for a brief moment, as if to give me time to change my mind. But I didn't want anything to change except for there to be more.

This time I was the one to lean in. To press against his mouth. This time, he pressed back, taking charge of the kiss.

His hand left my jaw, caressed my ear, then buried in my hair. I imitated him with my free hand. He paused, sucking in breath, then parted my lips with his.

French kissing, the girls at school called it. Heaven was what it was.

For the remainder of the bus ride, but not long enough, we kissed. It was too much and not enough all at the same time.

Like we'd promised Mama and Mr. Wu, we got into one of the taxis that were forever sitting at the park-and-ride lot and directed the driver to take us home.

I didn't let go of Jake's hand. Not when we got off the bus, not when we got in the taxi, and not when the cab dropped us off at the foot of the gravel driveway.

The clock at the bus stop had read one thirty in the morning. It had to be close to two now. I couldn't have slept even if a dozen mattresses and a dozen feather pillows had fallen on my head.

"Are you tired?" I asked as we stood, not moving toward our two separate houses.

"Not the least bit," he said. "You want to watch a movie?"

"What movie?" I asked.

Jake's smile grew bigger, and I got it then. Watch a movie was code for make out. I kicked myself for sounding like an eighth grader.

"I would very much like to watch a movie with you, Jake Wu. Where?"

Taller than me by several inches this year, Jake leaned down to kiss me again, and I didn't give a rat's ass about movies or locations, though I realized we couldn't stand outside all night. The mist was getting heavier by the minute and feeling a lot more like rain.

"Shit," I said, then covered my mouth. "I forgot my mittens on the bus."

"I'll keep you warm, don't worry," he said, lifting our joined hands and adding his other on top of them.

"Your house," he concluded after a long minute. "You said your mother sleeps like a rock. My room won't work because Dad gets up in the middle of the night half the time to make calls to China. I've seen him stick his head in on the way down to his office."

"The guest room," I said, jerking his hand and pulling him up the driveway. The guesthouse had three bedrooms. Mama used one. I had the one next to hers. But across the house was another that I think she'd saved in case Arturo ever visited. We would be safe from parental detection there. I hadn't seen any of our parents in that room for more than a few seconds. It had been my sole job to dust and vacuum it on weekends.

When we got to my front door, I fit the key in the lock. It turned smoothly, nearly silent. The door opened without a squeak. I was suddenly very grateful that Mr. Perez was really good at his job.

Shushing each other but laughing anyway, we tried to tiptoe down the hall. Halfway there, my feet stuttered to a stop. Nerves replaced the certainty I'd felt only a few minutes before when we'd been standing outside. He was in high school now. I wondered if he expected more than I was ready to give.

"I only want to kiss you, Bella," he whispered as if

reading my mind. "Hold you for a while before I go back to my house." His words were exactly the reassurance I needed.

With my back to the door, facing Jake, I reached behind and turned the knob. My nerves were back and I was giggling again. The clouds had covered up any moonlight, and I flicked at the switch that would put the bedside lamps on.

Feeling bold, I wrapped my arms around Jake's neck, wanting to continue what we'd started on the bus.

His palms shoved me back and I had to work to catch myself from falling. My brain scrambled for a second as I tried to figure out what I'd done wrong.

"Dad?" Jake said in Mandarin.

Not making any sense of that, I turned around.

Jake's dad's naked ass was facing the ceiling.

My hand flew to my face, covering my eyes.

Oh, my, God!

Jake's dad was sexing up someone in my house! Why had my mother let him do this? She'd probably had no choice; it was the Wus' house, really.

It was gross, his old-guy butt. My mother should have put her foot down, told him that he had his own perfectly good house where he could do that. Mrs. Li was back in Nanjing and wouldn't have known a thing. She'd left just this afternoon. My mother had driven her to Newark, I was sure. It's why Jake and I had been allowed to take the bus instead of getting a ride to the city.

Rapid Mandarin flew between Jake and Mr. Wu. I heard the rustle of covers.

"Isabella Beatrice. What in heaven's name do you think you're doing?"

There were only two people in the world who used my middle name, and one of them was in Italy.

Dropping my hands, I turned. Mr. Wu was standing next to the bed, the maroon-and-navy-striped comforter wrapped around his middle. His smooth chest—nothing like Daddy's hairy one—was completely bare, as were his feet.

Sitting up against the padded headboard, sheets pulled up to her chin, was my mother.

"Mama?"

"How many times have I told you, Isabella, that boys only want one thing? You promised me that you'd stay a virgin as long as you were under my roof."

"I wasn't going to sleep with Jake, Mama."

"Then what were you doing with that boy coming into this room?"

My head swam like I'd drank a bottle of chianti on top of not having slept. Why were Mama and Mr. Wu naked? I looked between them and decided not to ask that question.

Instead, I asked, "What about Daddy?"

Mama's snort was unladylike. I'd have earned a sharp look, if not a pop in the head, if I'd made a noise like that.

"Francis Aconi." She spat his name. "Don't you ever speak that man's name in my house again."

"He's my daddy, Mama. When he's done being mad at you, I'm sure he's going to come back for me. Take me to Disney World like he promised. Maybe I'll even get to spend the summer in Italy with him and Arturo."

"Get your head out of the clouds, Izzie. Francis Aconi isn't any kind of father."

"Daddy *is* my father, Mama. I know you divorced him or he divorced you or whatever, but he'll always be my father."

"Izzie—he was never your father."

My head swam. It was too much, too fast, from too many directions. "What?"

"Francis Aconi isn't your flesh-and-blood father. When he figured that out, he was on the first plane to Gallipoli so he could sit at his mother's knee and bitch about me. That man never took responsibility for one damned thing."

"He's not...my dad?"

"Never was. And you can stop all that talk about Disney or whatever, because Francis Aconi is never coming back."

I tried to swallow down the bitter bile rising in my throat, but I couldn't. Instead, coffee and pumpkin pie erupted from my mouth and all over the guest room's pristine beige carpet.

CHAPTER 10

NOW

I HUNG up my landline as I canceled the last of my appointments. Saturdays were normally reserved for the maintenance and upkeep of Isabella Aconi. I had a round robin of standing appointments for highlights and lowlights, brow threading, waxing, manicures, pedicures, shopping with my stylist, and a massage to start.

The corporate mouthpieces in human resources would have you believe women could succeed on brains alone. Maybe that was true somewhere like Detroit or Silicon Valley. To claw my way up, I not only had to do impeccable work, I had to look flawless while doing it while all the time hiding that I was nothing more than a scholarship kid. They wanted you to be one of them. I paid a lot to pretend I was.

Done with what rearranging I could do, I slipped into a silk, below-the-knee pencil skirt, a casual light-blue T-shirt in linen, and gladiator sandals. Despite being called "suits," most of the network executives in L.A. dressed down, no Brooks Brothers or Hugo Boss. Didn't mean their jeans would cost less than a car payment, though. Casual dress was a mirage of a different type.

Twenty minutes later, I joined Alexandra in one of the screening/conference rooms the network sometimes used for focus groups or pitching small groups of ad execs.

"Do you have it?"

She looked terrified, as if I had asked for her firstborn child, then gathered herself. Her expression became neutral. If she cleaned up, she'd have my job one day, or maybe an even better one in a department someone actually respected. But I wasn't her mother and was tired of trying to fix her, so I didn't say anything about her frayed jeans or five-dollar flip-flops.

"The disc you asked me to put together?" she said finally. "Yes, I have it. I stayed up all night in the editing suite."

So that was why the poor girl looked a bit rough. She had hair sticking out in all directions and her clothes looked sloppier than usual. I'd have to try to remember to get her a Burke Williams spa certificate. I made a mental note to myself because even I knew, as bitchy as I was, that having your assistant buy her own gifts was a shitty thing a lot of bosses did. It was the kind of thing that didn't win you loyalty points, and those I was going to need in spades.

"Put it in," I said.

She went to some cabinet, pressed a bunch of buttons. A hidden drawer emerged, featuring an electronic console that could take nearly any kind of disc or plug you could throw at it.

For fifteen minutes—the average attention span of an

entertainment executive in Hollywood—her compilation played.

"Perfect," I said, because it was. "Rewind it, or do whatever so it starts at the beginning when I hit the play button on the remote."

Alexandra fiddled a bit, then handed me the small plastic controller.

"You ready?" she asked. I couldn't let her deer-in-the-headlights look affect me. I had a job to keep. She'd learn soon enough that without appearing confident, people in this town would eat her for breakfast.

I reached under my seat, found the hydraulic pedal, and lifted the chair at the head of the table, where I'd already put my water glass and copies of Daisy's memo. The leather backrest was an inch taller than those surrounding it. It would take a bigger asshole than me to try to usurp the seat of power.

"Let them in."

I tried not to smile when I saw Jake, impeccably outfitted in a different bespoke suit—either he'd change how he dressed, or his new employees would. He swerved past my chair, one he'd expected to be vacant for him, and took up position at the other end of the table.

The rest of the table filled in with some people I knew, the head of the legal department and two underlings. Lawyers traveled in packs like that. Other execs were from Business Affairs; Kevin Manning from Programming, looking as nervous as all get out; and the guys who ran Special Programming, which was all reality and awards shows. The power players sat at the table, while the assistants, including mine, sat in low-backed rolling chairs lining the walls.

"Gentlemen..." 'Cause they all were at the big table. On this one day, a roomful of penis-havers was going to be a blessing, not the usual curse. "Gentlemen, good morning. In a moment, Alexandra Hughes, my assistant, is going to pass out a memo I've put together outlining the steps this department is going to take to mitigate the damage Revival's bass player, Indigo Hawk, known as Blue, has done to the network's reputation, as well as what we're going to do differently going forward to assure nothing like this ever happens again."

I took a deep breath, let that sink into their heads. Let them know I was not only in charge, but calm. Panic has undone many a person. Certainly had messed with my mother, ended my life in Philly as I'd known it. Had she stayed as cool as a cucumber, my father would never have been the wiser. I could have joined the ranks of the ten percent of children being raised by fathers who were clueless as to their kids' biological origins.

I shook my head clear of that stuff. The past was unchangeable. The future I could still manipulate.

"I've taken the liberty," I continued, "of putting together a short visual presentation that will put last night's performance in context."

Alexandra had another remote in her hand, this one darkened the lights. I pressed play on mine. What followed was a montage of FCC violations other networks had committed.

From Bono to Janet Jackson's musical performances. After that, it segued to a teenage orgy scene from a police procedural. The so-called offensive and lurid images flickered on screen. Then there were scenes that had pushed the envelope network TV was forever trying to live on the edge of, with all the bare male asses Alexandra could find.

What was it about old-ass actors lining up to show their crepey butts on screen? It's a club I was glad I'd never be a member of.

The montage closed with the actual half-second clip of Blue's penis, which, when shown against that backdrop, looked like a tiptoe through tulips.

When Alexandra again put the lights on full blast, each person had a stapled memo packet in front of them.

"Gentlemen, going forward, we're going to be even more diligent when live shows come on the air. I propose increasing the time delay from seven seconds to fifteen. That should give anyone enough time to..." I hesitated a second. I wanted to say censor, because that's what we were. Book-burning, sex-shaming censors, here to save Americans from themselves. But the liberal elite hated to think of themselves in that paternalistic fashion. I course corrected. "...edit what goes out across the airwaves."

The minute I closed my mouth and took my seat, the questions started. These men could be stand-ins for supreme court judges. They did the big blowhard thing, chest pounding and trying to demonstrate for all around the length of their—uh—ties, and superior knowledge of anything and everything.

"What about the Family Viewing Council or Mother Knows Best?" the Programming exec asked.

"What about them, Kevin? Ninety percent of the shows on our network were on their shit list before Friday. There's one reality show and one comedy they haven't come down on. During the upfronts, it was a point of pride that CBT was pushing the envelope. When you push it, sometimes it opens. I promise you, we'll seal it back up tighter than a nun's asshole."

"Will you respond to them?"

"Their formal letter to the network or the postcard campaign sure to rain down more than El Niño? I'll leave both to Legal."

Three lawyer heads nodded in unison. The last thing they wanted was me shooting from the hip.

An old Chinese man I didn't know stood up. "And the fines? We'll have to take a loss next quarter if the FCC is half as punitive as they've threatened to be after Howard Stern and Bubba the Love Sponge."

Before I could open my mouth to tell the man that Howard Stern probably had a regular wire transfer to the FCC set up, Jake stood. Our eyes met for the briefest second before I had to look away.

My sleep had been fitful the last couple of nights. Probably would have been just from the appearance of Blue's penis alone, but having Jake in my apartment had shaken me up way more than I wanted to admit. All yesterday's bravado had fled. It was a good thing we weren't one-on-one, because I would have folded like a cheap suit. Once again, I'd have felt inferior to all his wealth and power.

Mortification churned in my belly. I want to kick myself —hard—every time I think back to when I thought I was in love with him, back when I believed in love.

"We think you've done an excellent job of putting last night's...incident...into context."

I lifted my head. Met his eyes, mine full of shock, I'm sure. I couldn't read him. Probably hadn't been able to read him in twenty years.

Silence permeated the room. People had stopped shifting in their chairs as heads swiveled between Jake and me. I'm sure I wasn't the only one expecting yelling and recriminations, not this calm acceptance.

"Thank you," I said, caught flat-footed. "Alexandra Hughes did an excellent job overnight."

"So she did," Jake observed. He remained standing. I think everyone else was doing the same as me, waiting for the other shoe to drop.

"What about the fine?" Kevin asked. "Whose department is covering this?" He looked at me and winked. "Of course your budget doesn't cover it."

I nearly laughed at his use of the word budget. We got office space, newish video equipment, and all the red pens we would ever need. We didn't have the lavish budgets to spend on stars or trailers or productions that other departments had.

"Nope. Our money goes to salaries and pencils, Kevin. Past fines have been paid from Legal and Programming. I do hope that the FCC will minimize the fine, given that it was a live show and not scripted entertainment gone too far."

That started a ten-minute squabble between Special Programming and Legal that didn't end until Jake cleared his throat.

"As a show of good faith, Woo DynoMedia will cover the fine. No one will have to sacrifice their budget."

I gasped.

Out loud.

I couldn't help myself. My hand didn't fly up to my mouth fast enough. Corporations sucked money out of networks like profit-center vacuums. It was never the other way around.

Self-preservationists that they were, the drones from Legal, Business Affairs, and Programming scrambled from the room before Jake could change his mind, or anyone from Woo DynoMedia could change their minds and close the checkbook.

"Isabella?" Alexandra had either asked a question or uptalked. With her generation, it was impossible to know.

"Wait for me in my office." When the girl wilted like a flower starving for rain, I relented. "Go home. Get some sleep. I'll see you on Monday, okay? Thanks for all your help."

She picked up discs and leftover paper and ran from the room like the hounds of hell were chasing her.

It was Jake and me and twelve feet of conference table between us. I glanced at the clock above his head. I could probably reschedule my pedicure. I'd definitely spring for the extra shoulder, neck, and foot massage today. I couldn't see any other way to get these kinks out. Kinks that were getting tighter with each passing second.

"Isabella," he said, before I could escape. "Bella."

"Don't call me that."

"Why not? It used to be my nickname for you."

"Jake, I have to go. Appointments and all that." I shrugged, trying to be casual and failing. Why did he have to come back after that first day? I'd been on my A game then. It was nearly impossible to keep it up at that high level.

"I want to talk to you," he said, as if we were old friends.

"Thanks for covering the fine. Really great of you and your dad."

"I didn't do it for the network."

I stood and gathered my stuff. I didn't want to hear a single thing more. Pasts belonged just there, in the past. Mine was playing far too prominent a role in my present.

"Great. Well, I'm glad that you're starting your reign... um...tenure off on the right foot. You've bought yourself a lot of goodwill with that." I strode toward the door.

"What about you, Bella? Have I gotten into your good books?"

After he left Toms River, his English tutors had always been British, because our slangy American English had never been good enough for his parents.

Good books.

Sounded like he was right out of south London with that one. When we were kids, I used to help him with all that. Keep him from sounding like a stuffed shirt. He hadn't found a down-to-earth friend to keep it real. Too bad.

"My books are filled, Jake. We do best when we stay away from each other. I'll get you an office, then I think it would be best if we don't have anything to do with each other. My deputy, Connor Quinlan, has been in this department even longer than I have. I'm sure he can and will happily answer any questions you might have."

"I think there's one he couldn't answer." Jake strode

closer. There wasn't anywhere for me to run except out the door, and I wasn't yet that big a coward.

"What's that? I've got a couple of minutes." The glance at my Rolex was lengthy and deliberate. It was the kind of hit that even the socially inept recognized.

"Can we try again?"

I was as glad as hell I was wearing gladiator sandals and couldn't fall off my heels, because I surely would have.

"Have you lost your mind? Did you eat blowfish or something over there in Asia that altered your brain chemistry?"

"We once loved each other, Bella. I haven't met another woman who can replace you in my heart."

I looked around the room.

"Have you green lit a hidden-camera show? Am I your first victim—I mean guest? 'Cause then this might be funny."

I wanted this to be some kind of practical joke. Otherwise nothing made sense. What rational person thought they could just waltz back into someone's life after...stomping on all the goodwill, and my heart to boot, on the way out?

"I wouldn't joke about this, Bella."

"You and me...we were a disaster, remember? You took my heart and trampled all over it."

"I'm not giving up. I expected you to act like this. Knee-jerk reaction. I'll give you time to think about it. Let it settle in."

"Well I am. Giving up, that is."

I stalked out. Maybe I was prize of the month at the billionaire's club. I wanted to take myself out of the running.

CHAPTER 11

SEVENTEEN YEARS EARLIER

"WHERE ARE YOU GOING? Did you do your homework?"

I glared at my mother. Not your regular teenage glare of frustration. More a glare of contempt. I had no idea who she was anymore.

"Are you going to tell me who my real father is?"

She turned away, shuffling toward the television and her usual date with Oprah Winfrey.

I turned my back and went into my room. Ever since Jake had gone to boarding school at Woodward Tillman Hall midyear, I lived in my room. I slammed my door for good measure and shrugged off my backpack. Rain splattered, melting last week's snow.

Droplets of water streaked down the windows, making what was usually clear, blurry.

I'd often wondered if Jake's parents had sent him away because he was the only honest person among us.

Starting the moment that Jake went away last January, I

asked Mama and Mr. Wu for a computer. Newly solicitous, they'd promised I could have anything I wanted. A brand-new turquoise clamshell iBook arrived on my desk a few weeks later. My mother called it a belated Christmas present. I knew it for what it was, a bribe to keep quiet.

For over twelve months, I'd kept my part of the bargain.

At least I had email. It was the only thing keeping me sane. Jake and I sent messages at least once a day. Even better, though, was that I'd found Arturo online, and now we emailed as well.

I was about to pop open the laptop to see what Jake had sent today, when there was a knock on my door.

I closed the laptop to keep the spies from the truth.

"What?" I pulled at the door so hard it banged against the wall behind it. Instead of my mom, it was Mr. Wu standing there.

"Come outside with me, Isabella."

I sighed, plucked my raincoat from the hook hanging over the door and followed him past where my mother was sitting and out the front. I closed my eyes, ready for the lecture that was about to follow. The talk about how my mom was my only mom and how I should forgive them their trespasses. How his marriage was in name only or some shit. How it wasn't really my business.

I watched daytime soaps. I knew all the excuses.

Mr. Wu came to a stop in front of his garage. I nearly hit him because I'd been looking at my feet. The garage, huh? Maybe he'd started a car company because he was one of those people who could only have a serious talk while driving. I braced myself for the hour I'd have to spend listening to tires slap on wet pavement.

"Your mother says," he started. I looked up into his eyes, able to pull my hood back because the rain had stopped. Here we go. "She says that you're turning sixteen in April."

"Sure, yeah, April first," I found myself saying, all the while wondering what in the hell being sixteen had to do with anything. Was he going to send me away to boarding school too? Did he think he was entitled to my body like he was my mother's? Ideas bounced around my brain like a pinball in an arcade machine.

Something clicked, and the farthest garage door started to roll up. Inside was a cherry-red SUV. Didn't look like anything I'd seen on the turnpike, though. Must have been one of the new DynoAutomotive models from China.

"That's a nice car," I blurted out.

"It's yours," he said. Mr. Wu extracted a set of keys and a plastic fob from his jacket. He lifted my hand from my side and wrapped the keys in it. "Why don't you check it out?"

"I, uh...okay," I stammered.

Forgetting about my anger at him for taking advantage of my mom, I stepped closer toward the garage. I pressed the pictogram that suggested an open door. The car gave a pleasant beep as the locks popped. I walked right next to the passenger-side door and opened it. Stepping on the running board, I launched myself into the seat.

The car smelled heavenly. I rubbed my hands against the toffee-brown leather. It was soft and looked like it would be a comfortable ride.

I hadn't noticed that Mr. Wu had come into the garage. I jumped when he touched my arm.

"Get in the other side. You'll be driving it. You have to get used to sitting in that seat."

I took his hand as he led me down, then let my fingers trail across the hood as I walked around the front toward the driver's side door. I adjusted the seat, bouncing on it a bit until I was comfortable. I moved the rearview mirror like I'd seen my mom and dad do a million times.

"Start it up."

"What?"

"Cars are for driving. Today's your first lesson."

I stuck one of the keys in the ignition and turned. Nothing happened.

"Lesson one, make sure the car is in park and put your foot on the brake."

I did as he said and, in seconds, the engine came roaring to life. Roaring may have been an exaggeration. It was more of a quiet purr. I could barely hear it at all, but I could feel the vibration of the engine under my thighs.

"What now?"

"Hear that bell?"

I nodded. There was a persistent and faint chime every ten seconds or so.

"Fasten your seat belt. My company has designed this car so that the bell rings whenever the belt is not...attached. So always wear it."

"I pinky swear."

Mr. Wu turned to me like I'd spoken Martian. It was the same look Jake had given me the first time I'd said it to him.

Uncomfortable, I turned back to the windshield.

"What I mean is that I promise to always wear my seat belt."

"Keep your foot on the brake. Move the shifter from D to R."

One minute I'd been sulking in my room, and the next I was driving. *My car.* Even Jake didn't have a car. I couldn't believe it.

We drove around Toms River for a bit.

"Turn right on Lakewood Road," he said.

I did. It was a bigger street than where we lived. Two lanes going in each direction. I think I nearly caused a crash five different times. Mr. Wu didn't bat an eyelash.

"This isn't too bad," I said at a red light.

"Most of the population gets a license. They can't make it too hard, can they?"

When the green light came, I pressed the gas. He was right. I felt light with newfound confidence. Driving wasn't some mystery. It was something I could master, like being popular at school.

Then it hit me like lightning. I'd be a kid with a car at school. I couldn't wait to spring it on the girls at lunch tomorrow. It would be a way to keep me permanently on top.

Mr. Wu pointed toward the entrance to the parkway. My heart sped up. I'd been confident, but this was a lot.

"I'm not sure."

"The only way to learn is to do it."

"I don't want to kill us."

"I won't let you." He pointed his finger. I followed the line of cars onto the entrance ramp.

"Oh, God," I wailed. The cars in front of me were moving fast, as were the ones behind me, not to mention those I was supposed to join on the Garden State.

"Stay calm. Keep your foot on the gas. Press harder. Look at the mirror." I looked in the rearview; the line of cars was intimidating. Horns were starting to blare.

"Not that mirror. The one out of your window. Now, when there's a space, ease into it."

I tried once and nearly sideswiped a white sedan of some kind. The honking behind me intensified. I couldn't see anywhere to pull over and catch my breath.

"What do I do?" I whined. I wasn't ready for this. My own father—or not father—would never have done this to me. He said the parents who threw their kids into the deep end of the pool or pushed like Coach Popescu were the worst of the worst.

"Try again. Keep pressing the gas, you're slowing down. Merging is easier when you go fast."

I tried again and missed. The third time, I was able to pull into the traffic. I didn't hear much of what Mr. Wu said after that. It required all of my brain cells and then some just to stay in my lane for the four or five minutes we drove.

"Now we're going to exit."

"Where?"

"When you're ready."

I tried to calm down my heart, but it wasn't easy.

"See that sign? It says route sixty-six, east. We'll take that one."

I looked at every one of the three mirrors about a dozen times as well as over my shoulder. Following Mr. Wu's instructions to the letter, I got us off the Garden State and into the parking lot of a new mall that had just opened.

My hands were shaking, my palms sweating. I peeled off the raincoat because everything was wet on the wrong side.

"Let's take a break," Mr. Wu said.

If it hadn't been Mr. Wu, what followed would have been like a fairy tale. We went into an electronics store. I came out with a brand-new Nokia in iridescent pink. If I thought the car could cement my place as queen bee, this would make me supreme ruler of all time.

He spared no expense as he let me pick out any clothes I wanted. The latest Air Force 1's were mine for the taking. The North Face jacket I'd admired on a senior, he bought two, one in black and the other in baby blue. Timberlands were added to the haul. I have no idea how much he spent, because as good as my math skills were, I lost count. He had to have a valet bring all the stuff to the car. I didn't even know malls had that kind of service.

I drove home feeling like a princess.

"Happy birthday," he said, when we finally pulled up to the trio of barn-red buildings. "It's early. But I didn't think there was any reason to wait."

Spontaneously, I threw my arms around him and hugged tight. I'd missed having my dad so much, and for an afternoon it was like I'd had one back.

"I've enrolled you in the classes necessary for the license test. You should have your license in a couple of months," he said.

"Great. Thanks. I mean, I can't thank you enough."

"You know how you can thank me?" He'd taken my

hands in his at this point. His grip was hard. I couldn't have pulled away if I'd wanted to. I wasn't yet sure if I needed to.

"No. How?" I forced the words out from my clenched stomach and chest. Here it was. Nothing came for free. I hoped the price wasn't going to be too high.

"Be nice to your mom. She loves you."

I could do that—or at least pretend really well.

"Okay..."

"Also, once you get your license, you'll be driving yourself to school, okay? There's extra work in the house I'll need your mom for in the mornings."

He didn't wait for my agreement on that. He closed the door behind him quietly and quickly. In the middle of a pile of glossy, shiny shopping bags full of stuff, I was starting to think that he'd done an amazing job of buying more silence.

CHAPTER 12

"I GOT IT!" I typed into the ICQ box on my laptop. The Humanities paper I was supposed to be working on was open in the main window. Not that my mother would come in here, but I liked to be prepared just in case.

"Your license???" Jake typed back five interminable minutes later. We always instant-messaged at four thirty every day. I tried not to think about what would keep him away from his computer at the exact time he knew we IM'd.

My mother had showed me brochures from Woodward Tillman Hall when Jake had been sent there to—and this was with the world's hugest air quotes—expand his connections and opportunities. The pictures had been full of sporty, fit girls who looked comfortable with being rich. Not like me, the daughter of the help. Even I knew I could sometimes look like I was trying too hard.

My answering "yes" had about a thousand exclamation points.

Jake: I still can't believe he bought you a car.

Bella: I know, right?

There was another delay. One of his roommates had probably walked in and done some kind of dude handshake that required a lot of back slapping and the use of the word "bro."

Jake: Has he asked anything about us?

Jake was a topic that never came up any longer. I was sure Mr. Wu had thought it solved and tied up neatly in a bow when he'd shipped Jake off to Connecticut a short month and a half after the Led Zeppelin concert. It wasn't too far off to imagine him in his office using his fountain pen, crossing us off a list of Chinese characters representing Jake and me and puppy love.

Bella: He has to know I got the laptop to email you. Then again maybe not. Your dad's not a detail guy.

Jake: Did he restrict where you can drive?

Bella: Nope. He gave me a credit card, though. For gas and other stuff. I've taken the girls to dinner at Bennigan's a couple of times. He hasn't said anything.

Jake: Dad's never said anything about my credit card either. As long as I bring home straight A's, I can do whatever I want.

That one hit me in the gut. I had hoped that Jake would hate Woodward and beg to come back to New Jersey. Connecticut agreed with him, though. He didn't have either Mrs. Li or Mr. Wu checking on how many minutes he was on the piano, or quizzing him on classic poetry from the Tang Dynasty. It was me who was quiet for a bit as I tried not to let my jealousy rear its ugly head. I plastered a big fake smile on my face before I put my fingers on the keyboard.

Bella: Glad you like it there.

And not in hell with me here in Toms River, I didn't type. Not here, where I rang the bell before I came into my own house. Where I knocked and made sure to jingle my house keys loudly, and walked like an elephant to announce my presence if I were in the Wu home for any reason. Especially when Mrs. Li was out of town, which seemed to be more and more these days.

Jake: It would totally freak out your mom and my dad if you drove up here wouldn't it?

Bella: LOL. It totally would. But what could they say?

Jake: Probably nothing. We hold all the cards.

Bella: Totally American slang.

Jake: You're not my only source.

Bella: You know what? I'm coming.

Without waiting for a reply, or for him to talk me out of it, I closed ICQ.

Why not? Why the hell could I not do what I liked? Everyone else did.

I pulled open drawers, jammed in the perfect clothes for a weekend in Connecticut—puffy jacket for cold nights, Timberlands for hiking. Candy-pink sweats for lounging around in his dorm room. Ready to go, I grabbed the car keys.

The falling darkness outside slowed me down.

I looked at the time on the brand-new Michael Kors watch I'd charged to Mr. Wu. It was five o'clock on a Friday. Rush hour traffic would kill me. I cooled my jets for a minute and thought about it rationally, not letting the ants in my pants make me do anything really, really stupid. I took a deep breath then sighed—maturely, I thought, proud of myself. Saturday morning would be smooth sailing. It would have to do.

I opened the laptop again and signed on to the internet. Ignoring the ICQ notification blinking in the lower right-hand corner of the screen, I used MapQuest to plot out a trip. It would take me exactly three hours. If I left at ten, I could be at his dorm by one.

Having second thoughts about my impulsive packing, I jammed the duffle back into my closet. I'd tell my mom I was going to the mall with friends or to do SAT prep. I waffled. SAT prep would go over much better. Then once I got there, I'd make a call saying I was staying over with friends. With a cell phone, the issue of Caller ID wouldn't trip me up.

It was a done deal. A solid plan. No one would miss me.

I ate dinner and breakfast without a single argument with Mama. I was my most charming teenage self, gossiping about girlfriends and fashion at one meal and SATs at the other, even though the excitement of my plans made it nearly impossible to sit still and eat a whole meal.

When Mama went to prep Mr. Wu's lunch and clean whatever needed cleaning, I showered, pulled my hair back in a tight ponytail, swiped on some gloss and slipped into my brand-new hot-pink Juicy Coutures. I'd only shown Mama the front of the outfit. Somehow, I don't think she'd have liked the rhinestone "Juicy" that glittered on my butt.

Cover story unquestioned, I threw my backpack and duffle in the back of the SUV. Except for nearly sideswiping a tractor trailer truck when I fucked up the merge onto the Tappan Zee Bridge, the driving went pretty good.

I was in Meriden exactly at one. I got off I91 and slowed down on Main Street. Spying a public library, I peed, fixed my face, then came back outside to study the town. It was typically quaint New England that looked exactly like the brochure Mama'd had. Brick buildings, Greek columns, town, state, and American flags flapping in the cool spring breeze.

I turned this way and that until I saw a brown and navy sign affixed to two posts. These people needed to learn about signs from us down in Jersey. These all blended into the background, which seemed like the opposite of what a sign was supposed to do. A little reflective paint wouldn't have killed them.

I stretched, then got back in the car. I rolled through the wrought iron gates and down what had to be the main drag of Woodward. Girls in red T-shirts all shouting Woodward and matching navy-blue sweats darted from place to place. None of these girls had the least bit of makeup on.

Someone needed to give them lessons in the basics of mascara, eyebrow pencil or at least a little lip liner, because their eyes and mouths were nearly as pale as their skin, a total no-no unless you were straight out of the shower. And even then, that's what tattooed eye and lip liner were for.

As soon as I turned eighteen, I planned to have all that work done, along with laser hair removal. Presentation was everything.

They'd learn soon enough, these girls. Even Mama didn't leave the house without lipstick and her lids lined.

Never mind all that. I pulled to the side of the ribbon of damp black tar and pushed down the button. The window purred. I stuck my head out.

"Hey, you there."

A blonde girl, messy ponytail swinging, looked over at me, slowed the pumping of her legs and arms but still didn't speak.

"Yeah. You. Hey, I'm looking for Baxter Hall. Can you point me in the right direction?"

"It's in that cluster of buildings over on the left." She pointed to a tight knot of two-story brick buildings with lots of windows, but no columns.

I smacked my hand against the door. "Where do I park this?"

"There's no parking at the houses. Maybe turn left and left at the corner. There's a lot there the faculty use during the week. It's probably okay."

"Thanks. What's your name? I'm Isabella. Here to see Jake Wu. Chinese kid. You've gotta know him."

"Cricket. Jake's a nice guy. We do love our international students here at Woodward," she said. Girl didn't have any kind of accent. I didn't ask if Cricket was her real name. Didn't seem nice to make fun of her after she'd done me a solid.

"Thanks, Cricket. I'm here for the weekend. Hope to see you around." She'd be the first in the makeup chair, but before I could offer, she was running again, throwing me a wave over her shoulder. I parked where she'd said and walked around for a good five minutes, bouncing between brick and wood-sided buildings before I found the tiny white and blue plaque that signaled Baxter Hall.

There was no buzzer on the door, not that I could see, anyway. I waited a minute, and walked in when someone walked out, just like you'd do in any city building without a doorman there to spy on you.

Inside Baxter, there were four or five kids lounging on overstuffed sofas in what had to be some kind of dorm living room. A couple looked up when I walked in. The girl half elbowed the boy half, and he turned to me. In less than a minute, they were all staring at me.

"Isabella Aconi. Looking for Jake Wu."

They looked back and forth between each other before one could make up their mind to answer me.

"He's on the second floor. Room eight," a girl said. Another one in sweats with no makeup. I breathed a sigh of relief before taking the stairs two at a time. I wasn't going to have to worry a lick about these girls. The Crickets of Connecticut were zero competition for the Bellas of New Jersey.

I banged on the white door with the black eight screwed to the wood. Having sufficiently announced myself, I twisted the doorknob. Of course it was unlocked. Connecticut and all that. I walked in.

Three beds—one pristine and two unmade—greeted me. The smell of boys' sneaker funk hit me in the face. Damn. Since there wasn't anyone there, I stepped over lacrosse equipment littering the floor and pushed up a window. Smell got better immediately.

Mama would have had a heart attack at the state of this.

No matter how poor we'd gotten or how squalid the Camden apartment, there hadn't been a speck of dirt anywhere. Mr. Wu's house was spotless. Even if there hadn't been more going on, he'd never have any reason to fire her from that job.

Shaking my head, I poked around. The bed nearest the window was Jake's. The Mandarin book alongside English literature were enough clues to solve the case.

Briefly, I wondered if my visit would be a surprise or even welcome. Then I shushed my inner doubts. Of course it would be welcome, at least. Why wouldn't it be? We were young, in love. Weren't we supposed to be impulsive and a little reckless too?

I considered going out to try to find him, but the campus looked huge. My Timberlands were not made for walking through the woods. Instead, I plucked a book from the windowsill. I opened *The Age of Innocence* to talk of an opera house.

"There's a present in your bed," a male voice hooted.

My eyes snapped open at the unfamiliar noise. Shit, I'd somehow fallen asleep.

I sat up and the book that had put me to sleep clattered to the floor. For long seconds, I wondered where in the hell I was.

I turned to see four boys staring at me like I was an alien landed from Mars. Instead of a girl in pink Juicy Couture. Jake was at the back of the pack. He came forward when all four of them fell into the room. I squinted, wondering if I was still dreaming. I swung my legs to the floor.

"Coleton Lehman, you asshole. What are you doing here?"

I'd annihilated Jake's tormentors and hadn't thought much about them since I'd dictated who dated which girls. No boys wanted to be on my bad side, that was for sure. Johnny and Chas were a year ahead of me at school, still douchebags, but not to anyone I knew. I'd heard Cole had left, but it wasn't like his absence had left a vacuum or anything.

"Playing lacrosse," he said.

"Fucking A. I assume you're not shitting on Jake. I wouldn't want to have to come up here and whup ass."

"Whup ass?" One of the other two boys imitated me, then three of them laughed.

"I can bring it." I thrust my hand toward my chest. "I wouldn't laugh so fast if I were you."

"You hungry?" Jake asked, breaking away from his friends and coming to stand by the bed.

I stood, hoping my makeup hadn't smudged. I'd waxed my hair into place, so I was pretty sure my ponytail was still going strong.

"Starving. I haven't eaten since breakfast."

"Let's go get something to eat, then."

"I've got the car." I tossed the keys into the air for good measure. I followed him through the dorm and out the door. He didn't hug or kiss me. Despite that show I'd put on upstairs, I didn't have the guts to initiate anything. Instead, I made a great show of beeping the alarm and unlocking the door with a flick of my finger. I didn't want my disappointment to show or the sudden emptiness to make a bigger hole inside me. Maybe the Crickets of Connecticut kept all their kissing and hugging behind closed doors.

"What's good around here?" I asked while backing out of my parking space.

"Italian."

If I hadn't been buckled in, to avoid that damned warning bell if for no other reason, I'd have fallen out of my seat, I was laughing so hard. There was the Jake I knew.

"Seriously. What else? Please don't say Chinese."

He didn't laugh at my joke. Abruptly, I became silent. I hoped he'd been joking about Italian. Honestly, I assumed he wouldn't eat it anywhere except at my mother's table. He'd eaten all her fresh pastas and gravies and breads for years. Nothing in any restaurant compared to what Mama could make in his or our kitchen.

"There's a burger place that's really good." His voice was wooden.

I'd kind of been hoping for something romantic, then got a quick look at myself in the rearview. Should have changed clothes. I might have if I hadn't fallen asleep. I had a banging dress—the kind with a wire hoop around my neck and mostly with no back—in my backpack.

Nah, it was me and Jake, he'd seen me in pajamas and ripped jeans, clothes didn't matter. Neither did the food. What mattered was that we were together without Mr. Wu or Mama to come between us.

"Point and I'll drive."

Ten minutes later, I'd parked the car and we'd sat down at one of the many empty, dark wood tables, but he still wasn't saying much. Jake this quiet made me a bit nervous. I wondered if I'd gone over the top with Cole.

Nah. I shook my head. He'd been an asshole to Jake for a

year before I came in and knocked some sense into him and his buddies. He'd been grateful back then. Nothing had changed.

"I didn't really think you'd come," he said after he dropped his menu to the table with a thud. It fell open, askew.

"Why not?" I closed the menu, lined it up with mine as if arranging this bit of plastic and paper with metal corners could fix what was wrong. I continued, "I wanted to see you and I have a car. And a license. It was a total no-brainer."

"How long are you planning to stay?"

"What's up? You sound like you're behind a motel desk," I said. Changing my voice to sound older, how I imagined Cricket's mother would handle the question, I said, "I'm planning on checking in this afternoon. I'll check out tomorrow. What's your checkout time?"

He didn't laugh at my joke. He used to think everything I'd said was funny. His, "What did you tell your mother?" put a damper on my fun.

"Since when do you give a shit what Maria Sofia thinks? I told her I was staying at a friend's. All of that is one hundred percent true."

"What about when my dad gets a gas charge for New York or Connecticut?"

"You said yourself, he doesn't check. I'm not going to worry about fifty or sixty dollars in gas. I wanted to see you. We haven't been able to have a minute alone since forever." At the beginning of last summer, Jake had gone straight from Woodward to China and back. I'd waited for him to come home on one break or another, but he was always spending them at someone's house. Mr. Wu, he'd said, thought it was important he spend more time with others like him.

And less with people like me was the part not said.

Jake ordered a beer and something he called pork wings. Seeing as pigs didn't fly—or else my father would be back in Philly—I just went with it and ordered the only normal-looking burger on the menu and sweet potato fries for myself.

"That's it? You aren't going to try the pulled pork or something?"

"I know what a burger's like. I'll stick with that." I grabbed his hands, leaned across the table like the coconspirators we used to be. "I can't believe you ordered a beer."

"It's near a school," he said. He pulled his hands back. Wiped them on his khakis. "They never card."

We talked about stupid shit during dinner while Jake drank three beers and ate his so-called wings. I picked at my burger. It had enough toppings and sauces to threaten an explosion. I didn't want any of it all over my cute new velour.

After the waiter had taken Jake's empty plate, and I declined a doggy bag, I leaned across the table again.

"What do you have to do to get your roommates out of your room for the night?"

He took a cell phone I knew nothing about from the pocket of his khaki pants and dialed.

I was still trying to make peace with khaki pants on a Saturday and a phone for which I didn't have the number when he threw some cash on the table, stood, and started walking out.

Guessing that was my cue, I followed behind, wondering if the beers had somehow rubbed off on me.

Everything was off-kilter. Crooked somehow. And I hadn't had a drop of the beer or stout or whatever fancy name he'd called it. We were quiet on the ten-minute drive back to the school. I was trying to figure out how to integrate the old Jake I'd known and practically lived with, with this new beer-drinking, khaki-wearing boy.

After I'd poured all my concentration into parking and not hitting other cars in the now nearly full lot, I wondered if things were somehow different between us. Of all the things I'd imagined on the three-hour drive, us being different with each other wasn't one I'd bargained for.

I'd seen us as kind of a Romeo and Juliet. In love but separated by family circumstances. Him sent away to Meriden. Me imprisoned in Toms River. But from the look of things, he'd gone all sporty and frat boy. He was a rich kid in a pretty nice environment full of other rich kids. I was the poor church mouse who should be grateful for the roof over my head and car under my ass.

He jumped out of the car, slamming the door. I did the same, just a beat out of step. It was chilly out here. The little bit of warmth the sun had made was long gone. I crunched along the gravel behind him, fighting the urge to...

Fuck it.

I turned around and walked back toward the car. My shit was still in there. I pressed the key thing and it blooped its welcome.

I hoisted myself up into the seat and started the car again. I turned up the heat and then the CD player. Nirvana filled the cab. So much for a dramatic exit. I had to turn on the overhead light to figure out how to put the car in reverse. This was only the second time I'd driven at night; the first time having been ten minutes before.

Before I could shift the stick to the "R," there was a bang on my window. I pressed the down button.

"What, Jake?"

"Where are you going?"

"Home. I obviously crashed whatever you've got going on here. I figured I would do you the favor and head home."

"You can't leave at night. Drive in the dark."

"Why not? The expressways are open. Certainly the toll booths are twenty-four hours. Why shouldn't I turn around and go back from where I came? I'll take with me the lesson not to surprise people. Only come when you're invited."

"Turn off the car."

I did, and Kurt Cobain was silenced. Jake pulled at the door handle and I practically fell out of the car and into his arms. He pulled me in, kissing my hair. I turned my cheek to rest against his chest.

"Bella," he whispered. It wouldn't matter what he'd done before or said after. From that moment, I was his.

CHAPTER 13

SIXTEEN YEARS EARLIER

JAKE'S TRIPLE was mercifully empty when we got there. He'd carried up my bags and promised that we wouldn't be disturbed.

He flicked on a single floor lamp between his bed and the bunk bed and locked the door. Up until this moment, I hadn't been the least bit nervous.

Now I was.

I watched him as he went over to the shelf between the beds, and popped a CD into the boom box. The opening notes from Creed's "With Arms Wide Open" filtered into the room. All the other sound, kids laughing, toilets flushing, showers running, all of it faded. Jake turned to me, threw his arms open. I went to him.

We clung to each other.

"I'm sorry," he whispered into my hair. "So sorry, Bella."

I sniffed back tears. My best friend was here. All was forgiven.

"You can't let my dad or your mom get between us," he said.

They'd left me alone, but probably had put all the pressure on Jake to back off. Probably because he was the boy. I knew my own mind, though. I wanted him as much as I knew he wanted me.

He rubbed my back as we slow danced in lazy circles to the ballad. The song changed to something less familiar, and I dared to look up into his eyes. His thumb came up under my bottom lid and wiped away a tear. I didn't dare speak, otherwise I would cry.

My breath caught in my throat. His nickname for me came out in a whisper against my lips before his mouth touched mine. The time we'd spent apart disappeared like smoke.

Before tonight, every kiss we'd shared during the few stolen moments we'd had between the concert and him being shipped up here, had been tentative, slow. We'd been exploring each other during those weeks.

We'd moved beyond that, now. I gripped him tight, my hands moving from his neck to wind around his waist. He kissed me—hard. Without hesitation, I opened for him. He tasted like Jake, and beer, but mostly Jake. I'd had to drive three hours all the way to Connecticut to find my way home.

After that, neither of us could unzip, unbutton, unlace, or unsnap fast enough. In my bra and panties, I disentangled myself from him and lay flat on my back on his bed. He came to me and sat on the edge, facing me.

My eyes flickered from his down to the one strip of clothing he still had on. There was no hiding the hard-on that tented his jet-black briefs. Those two areas of intense color, his hair and his underwear, set off acres of golden skin I'd always been half envious of. I could become as dark as him, but only after hours on Ortley Beach. He'd been lucky enough to be born that way.

He flicked at the hair fanned out behind me.

"Are you sure about this?"

About what, he didn't have to say. We were both virgins. This night could change everything about us and between us. I turned toward Jake and propped myself on my elbow. I'd imagined this moment a thousand times and a thousand ways. I may have been nervous. But I was sure.

"I love you," I said in answer.

"God, you're so beautiful, Bella. The name, it still suits you."

His hand traced under the strap at my shoulder until he found the clasp in the back and flicked it open. I lifted my other shoulder and he pulled the scrap of pink fabric away from me. It dropped to the floor, taking up the space vacated by the lacrosse stick and pads.

We locked eyes and laughed. I knew what he was thinking. It was the same thing I was: I'll show you mine if you show me yours. Without speaking, we both took off our underwear.

Jesus, holy mother of God. Mary would need to pray for us, because he was the hottest guy I'd ever seen and I was about to become a sinner.

Tentatively, I reached forward and traced his collarbone to the place in the middle. He swallowed hard and I could see the beginning of the Adam's apple he'd one day have. All the sports at this place must have agreed with him, because he was heavier with muscle everywhere.

"I want to touch you, too, Bella," he said. He lay next to me and we explored slowly. I shivered when he touched one of my nipples and weighed my breast in his palm. He gasped when I ran the tip of my finger along the underside of his cock.

Our mouths came together then. My body hummed with desire and craved something, but I wasn't exactly sure what I wanted. Not enough that I could tell it to Jake. Not that I'd have had the guts to ask. Did girls do that? Ask for boys to touch them in certain places? Embarrassment shot heat through my body at the thought.

Every time he got close to my nipples or rubbed my back in a certain way, I couldn't help but clamp my thighs together. I shifted, feeling a lot turned-on and uncomfortable in my own skin at the same time.

Breaking the kiss, Jake said, "I'm going to get a condom, okay?"

I nodded. He went across to a desk, riffled through the drawer, and came back with a black foil packet in his hand. He sat on the bed, opened it, and pulled out the rubber. He rolled it tight onto himself and lay down next to me again.

"I want you," I murmured. It's what I'd heard someone say on one of the soap operas my mother sometimes watched.

He got the hint and rolled on top of me. I opened my thighs a little.

"More," he said, bending one of my knees up so my foot was flat on the bed. He grabbed himself in his hand, pumped a few times, then rubbed the sheathed tip of his cock between my folds. I had to bite my lip because that felt incredible. Better than anything yet.

He did it one more time. I bit my lip harder, tasting blood. But I couldn't stop my hips from moving, shifting, restless again.

He did it one last time before plunging into me.

Pain like a flash of fire tore through me. I tried and failed to elbow my way up the bed.

"It hurts the first time, Bella. I'm sorry."

I knew he was right. I'd read that in one of the books that had circulated among the girls. I'd need a moment to adjust, then it was supposed to get a whole lot better.

Slowly at first, then quicker, Jake moved over me, in me. It wasn't a whole lot better, but it wasn't worse, either. He'd pumped into me a whole bunch of times when suddenly it *was* better.

God, this. *This.* This is what people started wars for.

The good feeling continued, then Jake gave a grunt and it was over.

"It felt too good," Jake said, looking down at me, his hair, longer than I'd ever seen it, hanging like jet-black curtains around his face. "I couldn't stop."

"It's okay," I said, even though I still had that squirmy, unsatisfied feeling in my belly.

Grabbing himself near his pubic hair, he pulled out of me. The condom looked worse for wear.

"Did it rip?"

He looked down at himself, shrugged. "Yeah, are you okay though?"

I had no idea what I was supposed to be okay about. I

know I didn't want to rock the boat, though. Not when every-thing was finally alright between us again.

"I'm fine," I answered. "It'll be fine."

He stood and found some tissue at the bottom of a desk, rolled the condom in it, cleaned himself up, and balled it all for the trash.

"Do you have something to sleep in? You should put something on."

I took the duffle he handed me and pulled out the lace tank and matching shorts that didn't seem as sophisticated as when I'd bought them from the department store last week.

"We should get some sleep. There's a big brunch tomor-row. You should come. You can meet the rest of my friends."

Jake snapped off the light, got under the covers next to me and turned away toward the window.

"What about your roommates?"

"There are some overnight guest rooms for when day students stay. Or they could crash in someone's room who's away for the weekend. Don't sweat it."

In minutes, I could hear his soft snores. I looked at the clock. It wasn't even nine thirty yet. Frustrated, I slipped my hands between my legs and imagined Jake touching me there until pleasure liquefied my bones and I wasn't antsy anymore.

I curled against his smooth back, tucking my knees behind his, and after a long time listening to the dorm grow quiet and the crickets grow louder, I fell asleep.

I'm not sure what woke me, but I was shivering, cold and alone. I slammed shut the window I'd opened the day before and waited five, then ten minutes for Jake to come back.

When my bladder couldn't wait any longer, I stumbled to his door and opened it to an empty hallway. The faint sounds of other students moving around me slipped under their closed doors, but I didn't see anyone who could direct me to the bathroom. I turned right and gratefully found a room labeled "Women" before slipping in. I quickly relieved myself then washed my hands under the cold tap water. When it finally ran warm, I pulled a few paper towels from a dispenser and wiped at the smeared makeup on my face.

I froze when I heard voices on the other side of the door.

"Oh, snap. She's like the very definition of 'around the way girl,'" one boy said.

"Nineteen-ninety called and it wants its song back," Cole responded.

I placed the voices. It was Cole and one of Jake's roommates. I wondered who they were talking about. The other guy seemed like as much of an asshole as Cole.

"Fuck you," the roommate said. "It's true. Cole, I thought Toms River wasn't ghetto."

"Isabella is *not* Toms River," he responded hotly.

I gasped, then put my shaking right hand in front of my mouth. I couldn't believe it. They were talking about *me*. I looked up into the mirror. My face had gone tomato-paste red.

"Got there a couple of years ago," Cole continued. "Story is that she's either a Mafia princess or daughter of Jake's housekeeper. Never got the straight scoop on that."

"Man, that's dope. I vote for housekeeper's daughter. They should have a tab for that on sultrynewcummers dot com."

I recognized the popular porn site. The male half of my high school probably visited it once a week, then liked to talk about it all over school.

"I know, right? I had to go out and kill it. Jake never fessed up that he had pussy on the premises. Now I know why he wasn't desperately trying to hook up in school," Cole said, like he and Jake had been the best of friends in New Jersey, even though I knew that role had been held by me.

"Guys. C'mon."

It was Jake talking. He'd been there all along. I'd thought it was a bunch of rich assholes making fun of me. I started shaking with anger and humiliation. All the time, he'd been there.

I should never have gotten out of that car a second time. Not after he'd paid more attention to his beer than me at dinner.

"What? Oh, we're sorry, man. You're the one who told us this was a one-time hookup just to get her to go home. That she wasn't the kind of girl to bring home to Mama. My dad says that's the kind of girl to hit it with early."

"Was it good practice?" Cole asked. In my imagination, he was holding out his fist for Jake to bump.

There was a long, long pause before Jake spoke.

"Got my dick wet," Jake said.

They all howled like he'd won the lottery or some shit. Of course, not a single one of them bought a dollar ticket like Mama did every week, rain or shine. They'd already won the lottery by being born into rich families.

"You guys gotta shut it," Jake hissed. "She could come out in the hall at any moment."

"Gotcha, man. We're out. See you after brunch. It's not like she'll ever be back in Connecticut anyway."

"Unless she goes to Owen."

They howled again, the sound fading down the stairs as if the idea of me in the Ivy League was world's biggest joke.

I ran to his room, grateful it was empty. He must have followed his buddies out or went to someone else's room, because he didn't come in. I changed into jeans and a sweater as fast as I could with shaking fingers and blurry eyes. I didn't wait for Jake to come back and stomp on my heart some more. I took what I could carry in my hands and beat a path to the car.

I cried for the first two hours of the drive. Then stopped at the New Jersey border.

Once the tears dried up, I'd never seen life more clearly.

CHAPTER 14

IT WAS TOO bad they didn't sell pregnancy tests at the gas station. Even though I hadn't heard squat from Mr. Wu, I'd started to be stealthier in my charges. If I'd been pressed on this particular drug store purchase, I'd have said I was buying tampons or something. Female problems were the kind of thing that made men stutter, turn around, and leave a girl alone.

Unfortunately, it had been a couple months since I'd needed any kind of period stuff.

My door opened a crack, Mama's head poked in.

"Are you ready?"

I didn't say a thing, only nodded. Dressed in my comfiest sweats despite the warming June weather, I picked up my tote bag filled with fashion magazines and maxi pads, then followed my mother out the door.

"What time is the appointment?" I knew the answer, but I just...I don't know, wanted something to reassure me that this, all of this, was really happening. That I had to go and sever my last link to Jake.

"Eleven," my mother said as she eased the car onto the highway. I looked at my watch. It was nine thirty.

"Do you think I should call Jake?" I was still mad as hell at him. But if there was one person I wanted by my side, holding my hand more than any other, it was him. It was still him. Even with what had happened, it would always be him.

"Honey, that's the one thing I think you shouldn't do."

"Why?"

"What's he going to do? Leave school and come to New Jersey? Hold your hand? Tell you how much he loves you?"

Angry tears flooded my eyes, because that's exactly what I wanted and couldn't have.

After I'd driven home from Meriden, I'd checked my laptop first thing, before I'd even dropped my duffle bag from my shoulder.

The ICQ light had been blinking green. I was flooded with such relief that my knees buckled, forcing me to sit in my desk chair instead of falling. But that relief was short-lived.

"Now isn't a good time for visitors," Jake had typed, some twelve hours before I'd even gotten in my car. "Spring break is only four days at Easter."

That was it. No "I love you." No plans for the weeks before he'd be shipped off to China for the summer, a new thing his mother had pushed and gotten her way on.

I'd been so stupid not to read that. Read everything there was to read into that. Or the fact he had a phone I didn't know about. As soon as Mr. Wu had left me alone with my new cell, Jake was the first person I'd called on mine. But that hadn't gone both ways.

Maybe I *had* been nothing more than "pussy on the premises" and now that he'd moved schools, he'd moved on. Then I'd gone in all Jersey and pushed myself into the rarified air of Woodward Tillman Hall. That name said WASP and money, and second-generation Italians need not apply.

"There's a lot you have to learn about men, Isabella." My mother's tone was full of reproach. From her, of all people.

"You're the expert?" My question was well above the usual whisper I'd normally have reserved for this kind of thing.

As a rule, I wouldn't have had the guts to say that, but if having my period didn't make me a woman, getting pregnant surely did. Plus, I figured she wouldn't risk bashing up Mr. Wu's car with an impromptu slap throwing off her driving.

"I'm not an expert, but I do know more than you."

"So much that you're with a married man?" Up until now, my mother's relationship with Mr. Wu had been the one blemish on life in Toms River. I loved our little house, being queen bee at school, and Jake. Most of all, I loved that my mother's job had given me Jake.

I'd convinced myself that my mother was somehow deluded. It was becoming crystal clear that we'd moved into a nest of vipers who saw us as prey.

"Feng and his wife have an understanding," my mother explained patiently. "They're together because of the business. They practically had an arranged marriage. Their families go back centuries."

"So does that make you a concubine?" shot from my mouth before I could think better of it. I couldn't believe this stupidity was coming from my mother. It's like she hadn't soaked in *anything* from watching all those years of *Oprah*. Any woman with half a brain knows the guy *never* leaves his wife.

"I wouldn't be so judgmental about something you don't understand. I'm not the one going to a clinic in Princeton."

She had me there. I was pregnant. She wasn't. Whatever was going on with Mr. Wu—and I really tried not to think too much about that—she didn't look like she was having any more babies.

"I didn't mean for it to happen, Mama. We used protection. It was only my first time," I blurted out. I'd been keeping so much a secret, it was a relief to be able to tell someone the truth—that I hadn't been stupid, it had just *happened*.

"Quite the charm, then. Didn't even get to a third time. I've told you, *cara mia*, that boys like Jake are only after one thing."

"You've been saying that since I got my period, Mama."

"Facts haven't changed in thousands of years. Jake got the one thing from you, didn't he? Then he disappeared, right? No talking to you on your computer."

"How—" I'd thought the computer and talking to Jake was our little secret.

"I know you think I'm not that bright, Izzie. That I'm only a housekeeper who's with a married man. But you're no scholar, either. You didn't want that computer to become an honor student or anything. It was about a boy. It's always about a boy until it's about a man. We're the same, you and me."

We weren't the same, not at all, I screamed, but only in my head. I was feeling bold, not stupid.

"We're in love, Mama," I said. She had to know that this was the difference. I wasn't sneaking and lying and cheating. I was just a girl in love. A girl who thought her boyfriend loved her back. A girl who had been dead wrong.

"In love? Phooey," she spat. "Jake doesn't love you. He never calls. He went to visit friends over spring break. Didn't even pretend to want to come back to New Jersey. He was curious. You gave it up and now his curiosity is satisfied. He can get on to whatever in the hell interests him next. Fast cars. Video games. Other richer, prettier, smarter girls."

"It wasn't anything like that," I whispered through the emotion clogging my throat. I couldn't swallow down the self-pity, but I couldn't vomit up the pain either. I didn't want her to be right. But the facts were in her favor. Those days when we'd held hands or when he'd first kissed me, that all seemed like a lifetime before today.

"It was everything like that, Izzie. I'm going against God and the Pope to take you to this place. Never did I imagine on the day you were wearing your communion dress, that I'd one day be driving you to a clinic. But violate one sacrament, violate them all, I guess." She shrugged, like my eternal damnation was all but assured and we'd be in adjoining cells in hell. "When this is over, we're going to get you a prescription for pills, or maybe even one of those arm implants that last for years. Because I can forgive this once, but not twice."

When we got to the clinic, I walked in on legs weaker

than the noodles my mother spent so much time stretching and drying. Mama nearly shouted my name through a few holes in a thick Plexiglas window. I worked hard to turn my brain off. Not think about the little baby, a bit of me and a bit of Jake, nestled inside me. Not think about the next few hours and days ahead.

I'd spent all last week working myself up to having a literal vacuum stuck inside me. I imagined the hose of the floor unit Mama used every day plunged inside me without any painkillers.

It was the Catholic guilt talking, but if I'd just stayed a virgin like I promised, I wouldn't be here ready to have my body torn inside out.

There wasn't a vacuum, a nurse with short hair and nails assured me soon after we arrived and got situated in a little procedure room. I nearly wept in relief when she told me they didn't use them on patients like me. Maybe there was for other people, I didn't ask.

Instead, the clinic offered one pill, turned out from one of those tiny paper cups into my outstretched palm. This was after they talked to me for an hour about how I'd gotten myself into the predicament that had brought me there. I tried to answer as best I could, but the nurse must have gone to a school that had taught her the birds and the bees, so I didn't elaborate. Didn't every woman who came in here get pregnant in exactly the same way? But I did what I had to do, jumped the hurdle for the pill.

I lay on a bed in a tiny room, an IV attached to my arm after I'd swallowed it with a tiny sip of water from the same miniature paper cup. Mama sat upright in a small metal chair, her purse propped on her lap like she could pop up and run out at any moment.

I wanted Jake. I still wanted him, but right now she was second best and would have to do.

"I think they have a clinic all the way here in Princeton because it's full of fast college girls," my mother tsked after the first half hour.

"Princeton is a really good school, Mama." I lifted my head a little, her silhouette muted in the darkened room. "It's one of the Ivy League."

"What do I know from Ivy League? Are you still thinking of college? Rutgers maybe? Without gymnastics, you won't be getting a scholarship to anywhere fancy."

That hurt like a kick in the gut, although maybe it was the pills that were causing my stomach to go sideways. Why did my going to college have to be tied to being an athlete, which I definitely wasn't ever going to be again? Why couldn't it be just because I was a smart girl with a bright future? Who had decided that the no-makeup-wearing Crickets of the world were no worthier than me?

"I want to go to Owen." It was the first time I'd dared say it out loud. After that weekend in Meriden I'd started thinking about Owen for the first time. I had to be worth more than what was between my legs.

"Owen. Isn't that in Connecticut? You know Jake will be gone from there by then."

"This isn't about Jake, Mama. This is about me. I deserve to have the same things that rich kids have. They aren't any better than me." I want to be more than some man's house-keeper, and concubine went without saying, but the specter of that thought was there between us nevertheless. I was judging her, and she knew it.

"How much is this Owen?"

"Thirty, forty thousand," I said, hope in my voice. I know Mr. Wu paid Mama, it would really be slavery if he hadn't.

"That's not bad, I thought college was a lot more." I didn't have any idea how much she'd saved over the last few years, but Mama should have made bank by now. Other than clothes and food for me, there wasn't anything to buy. Hope burgeoned. If she could pay, all I'd have to do is get in. "So about ten thousand a year?" she asked.

"That's for *each* year," I said, my hope dwindling with each word she spoke.

"Did you win the lottery and not tell me?" Mama laughed, the first deep, genuine belly laugh I'd heard from her in years. Of all the things I'd ever wanted her to laugh about, this wasn't one of them.

"No, Mama," I started, my voice drop-dead serious. "You know, when I was up at Woodward, those kids made fun of me behind my back. Like I wasn't the kind of girl who could do more than open her legs. But I know I'm more. *You* know I'm more."

I motioned for the pink spit cup and Mama passed it to me. The contents of my stomach erupted all over the kidney-bean-shaped plastic.

"This is just the beginning, Izzie," she said, taking the cup and tipping the whole thing into some red hazmat bin. She washed her hands in the little sink.

"Of what?" I croaked.

"Life with men."

The rest of Mama's wisdom was cut short by another wave of nausea. Leaving me alone in the dim room, Mama disappeared into the hall. Sometime later, a nurse gave me a shot and my stomach stopped spinning like the earth had gone off its axis. Even though my stomach was in line, it still felt like my life was out of control.

CHAPTER 15

FOURTEEN YEARS EARLIER

WHILE ZIPPING four pencils into a slim Hello Kitty case that I carried ironically, I scanned the score sheet from October's exam.

Thirteen-seventy.

My mom had thought it was a great score. My college counselor had said the same, all the while listing lots of second-tier liberal arts colleges and top-tier state schools I could consider.

But thirteen-seventy wasn't good enough for Owen. Next to my score sheet was another fact sheet I'd kept tucked in my desk drawer. It was the newest version of the Owen Freshman Class Profile. The majority of last year's newly admitted freshmen had scores of at least fourteen hundred.

Today was the last exam of the year, my last chance to increase my score by sixty points, if not more.

Applications for regular decision were due in January, less than a month from now. I'd already been turned down for early admission, so I had to throw my hat in the ring along with tens of thousands of other applicants. The only thing I could change was my score. It was too late to volunteer a thousand hours building a house for the homeless or train to become an Olympic-level athlete. All that was left was what I could do with my brain.

I zipped my pencil case into my purse. Glancing at my watch, I figured there was just enough time to pour some of my mother's espresso along with a healthy shot of milk into a travel mug for quick energy and hop into my car. Late kids wouldn't be admitted to the test. That was the number-one rule.

The kitchen was unusually quiet when I stepped in to get the coffee that would fuel me through the long morning. There were no little cups of espresso on the counter. I laid my hand on the side of the copper machine. It was ice cold.

Mrs. Li was in town for her usual holiday shopping spree, so there was no way Mama would be at Mr. Wu's house before eight o'clock. Mrs. Li didn't like to be disturbed during her first days home after the super-long flight from Asia. But even then, Mama should have been up making my breakfast.

I looked at my watch again. It was coming up on seven thirty. I didn't have time to worry about this.

A loud groan came from Mama's bedroom.

I stood, paralyzed. She wouldn't have brought Mr. Wu here, would she? That was a breach of an unspoken rule. The time Jake and I had walked in on them had been the last time anything had happened in our guesthouse. Whatever was going on between them, *if* there was still anything, happened far away from here.

The groan came again, louder this time.

Even from my very limited experience in this area, I didn't think that last was the groan of a satisfied lover. Sounded a lot more like a dying cow.

I dropped my bag and coffee mug and beat a path back down the hall, but detoured to her room instead of mine.

She was lying on top of the covers, half-dressed, like she'd started to put on her clothes but had quit halfway through. Her black pants were zipped but not closed. Her white blouse was done up, but the buttons and holes were mismatched by not one, but two, like she'd put it on while drunk.

"Mama?"

She stirred at the sound of my voice, but rolled away from my touch. I'd not shaken her enough to make her wake up. I pushed her shoulder a bit harder.

"Mama!"

She rolled onto her back with a heaviness I'd never seen from such a small woman. Panic welled up in my chest and held my head in a vise grip, making it hard to think. I remember Mama coming by my room last night, saying something about turning in early and the flu. But I'd been cramming down some last-minute practice questions and hadn't heard half of what she'd said.

Mama's face was flushed a dark mottled red. I didn't want to admit this to myself, but for a quick moment, I thought Mama looked like she was dying. I tried to push the thought away, but couldn't.

What if my mama had more than the flu? She'd been kind of sick and run-down a couple of weeks now, and after a long night of sleep, she was worse, not better. She'd worked on the house, then came back and collapsed into bed. No *Oprah*. No dinner for me. She'd said she was getting better.

Here, now, it didn't look like better.

What if Mama had cancer or some such? I'd be an orphan. Homeless. If Mama died, what would I do? Go to Italy and beg my non-biological father's forgiveness? Beg him to love me again like he used to?

Maybe Arturo would help me. We were blood relations. Though he was in university now and probably didn't have the money to put up his half sister.

I pushed away the disastrous thoughts and shook Mama again.

"What do you need, Izzie?" she croaked. "Aren't you supposed to be at the high school?"

"I need for you to go to the doctor."

"It's the flu, I'll be fine."

"Mama, you've had 'the flu' for three weeks."

"Bad strain this year. Heard it on the six o'clock news."

"Let me get you some water."

"Okay, *cara mia*, my throat could use that."

Once in the kitchen, I poured water from the Britta pitcher in the fridge into a plastic tumbler that wouldn't break if Mama dropped it. I took it to her and she sipped, then gulped it down, leaving the cup dry. She lay back down looking a tiny bit better. But water wasn't some magic healer. It wasn't going to make her better.

Even if the diagnosis was bad, and Mama was going to die, we needed to hear that from a doctor. From someone who could maybe give us medicine that would help. Or hope for a recovery. I looked at my watch again. I had five minutes to make a decision. It was SATs and my last shot at Owen, or my mama.

Even if Mama didn't choose me most days, I chose Mama.

❤

"It's a good thing you brought her in," the nurse said as she rolled the small plastic wheel to adjust the fluid going into Mama's veins.

"Is she going to be okay?"

"Probably that flu going around. Men complain the most, but women get it the worst."

"I think my mom worked up until last night, cleaning."

"We always do, hon. Let me see where the doctor is. I'll get him in here as soon as possible."

"Thanks."

Mama was dozing, so I dropped my backpack to the floor. There was nothing in it but pencils and a forty-eight-ounce bottle of Gatorade. I didn't have a thing to occupy my mind. Take me away from wondering what in the hell I would do if I didn't get into Owen. If they hadn't liked me the first time, I wasn't holding out much hope. There wasn't much else I could add to my admission packet to make myself look better at this point.

"Where am I?" Mama's head rolled back and forth on the too small pillow. Her eyes fluttered open, unfocused. After some blinking, they focused on me like lasers.

"Mama. You're in the hospital. You wouldn't wake up, so I brought you to the emergency room."

She pulled at the IV. Thank goodness she was too weak to get it out.

"I've gotta get back. I didn't make lunch for Mr. Wu."

"Mrs. Li can make lunch for Mr. Wu, Mama. You're here because you won't be making breakfast, lunch, or dinner for *anyone* if you don't get better."

"I'm fine. Aren't you supposed to be somewhere this morning?"

"Maria Aconi?" The name tumbled from the lips of a doctor who didn't look a day older than thirty. That could be me in a dozen years if I got into Owen. Kids from the Ivy League could go anywhere. Be anything.

"That's my mother, here." I pointed to the bed where Mama was trying her best to sit up.

"Mrs. Aconi, please don't move. Let me." The doctor reached for some wand and Mama's head and back rose up, along with her bed.

"I've got to get back to work," Mama said.

"Mrs. Aconi, I'm Doctor Gray. Marshall Gray. You came in with some unusual symptoms, so we've taken a number of tests."

"Flu?"

"If you don't mind, Mrs. Aconi, I think your daughter should step out."

Cancer. It had to be that. Some kind of fast-acting brain tumor that would kill her dead. I half wanted to stay, but I leaned over to gather my backpack, putting off the bad news for a few minutes. Preserving my imperfect life, such as it was. A life with Mama in it.

Before I could move three feet, Mr. Wu burst through the door. He was more CEO than Mr. Rogers, though. His navy suit, white shirt, and red tie made him look like he was going to testify before Congress, not visit his housekeeper in the hospital.

Doctor Gray didn't miss a beat. "Is this your husband?"

"No!" all three of us said in unison.

"My mom works for Mr. Wu," I hurried to clarify.

"I appreciate your concern, Mr. Wu, but I need to discuss test results with the patient."

"He can stay," Mama said. To his credit, Dr. Gray didn't bat an eyelash, though I did.

"Mama, this is personal. Patients are entitled to keep their medical stuff confidential."

"What your daughter says is true, Mrs. Aconi. I can't share information without your consent. I think it'll be better if I talk to you first, then you can share—"

In the time Dr. Gray had been talking, Mr. Wu had made his way to the side of the bed. He held both of Mama's hands in his.

"Mrs. Li must be at home," I said, glaring at where they were joined. My hopes that nothing had happened beyond that one time were dashed on the shores of gloom.

"This does not concern Mrs. Li or you, Isabella," Mr. Wu said. His words were like a slap in the face.

"I'm her only living relative," I said. That wasn't exactly true, but I was the only person who was going to be by her side no matter what happened. The judgmental relatives here and in Italy had written her off once the truth about my paternity had become known. If they knew about Mr. Wu, they'd probably have her excommunicated so she could never be buried in the parish graveyard.

"Dr. Gray, did you say?" My mother's whisper quieted us all. "Please tell me. My daughter and Feng can stay."

Dr. Gray looked like he'd rather be anywhere but here with us, but he took a seat on one of those rolling stools and soldiered on.

"Can you confirm that you've been suffering from a fever and sore throat."

"Flu symptoms," Mama said, then nodded.

He snapped on blue latex gloves and lifted the sheet. He pressed four fingers of each hand into her stomach over the powder-blue hospital gown.

Drawing in a quick breath, Mama hissed it out when Dr. Gray's hands came away from her skin.

"Abdominal pain?"

Mama nodded this time. I think the pain made it too hard for her to speak.

"Have you had pain or burning when urinating."

Mama nodded. She'd never mentioned that to me. I tried to lock eyes with her, but she wouldn't meet my gaze.

"For a couple of weeks, maybe."

"Heavy period?"

"Yes, but I should be due for the change, right?"

"Maybe, Mrs. Aconi, maybe not. Depends a bit on family history."

"Okay."

"We did a full blood panel upon admission. The test results indicate that you've been infected with gonorrhea, mainly effecting the nasal and larynx areas."

Did he say gonorrhea, like the STDs we'd learned about in school? Mama had a sexually transmitted disease?

My butt hit the chair, squeezing the air from the vinyl padding with an audible squish.

"By law," Dr. Gray was saying, "I'm required to notify the state and county health authorities. A social worker will be in to see you shortly. Someone from the Ocean County Health Department will notify your recent sexual partners, so they can get the necessary treatment. Often carriers are asymptomatic.

"The nurse will be in any moment to give you a strong antibiotic that we'll administer here. An intramuscular shot of ceftriaxone, as well as one tablet of azithromycin orally. You should be able to go home in a few hours. You should feel better in a couple of days."

Dr. Gray patted my mother on the shoulder, tipped his head at us, hooked the chart on a peg on the wall, and walked out of the room. As if he hadn't left a huge fallout in his wake.

I gave Mr. Wu the death stare. I wished that my father was in the mob and I could call him or an uncle to put some cement shoes on this guy.

"Get out," I shouted to Mr. Wu.

He dropped Mama's hands and stepped back.

"Get out! Haven't you done enough? You heard the doctor. Mama could have gotten some brain infection and died because you can't keep your dick in your pants. I think you need to go home and tell your wife in case she has 'the flu' too."

"I can explain," he whispered to Mama.

She held out her hands, ready to accept whatever bullshit he was about to lay out.

"Just go." I shoved at his shoulder, trying to move him. My hands slipped right off the suit jacket. I cut my eyes to him. "I'll stay with Mama. I'll bring her home later. Tell Mrs. Li that she's going to need another few days off."

He ducked his head and backed out of the room without a word.

"We can leave, Mama," I pleaded, my voice hoarse with desperation. "I'm going to graduate in June. I don't need to go to Owen. I can go to Rutgers. You can move up to New Brunswick with me. Or I could apply to the Camden campus. We could share an apartment. You could find a job in Philly. I think you'd make a great assistant for a lawyer or CEO or something."

"I love him," was Mama's reply.

It was like she hadn't heard a thing I'd said.

"Mama, he gave you a disease! He's cheating on his wife and he's cheating on you. How can you love someone like that? They're probably going to make you take an HIV test too. He could have given you something that could kill you! No one who loves you would do that. He'd leave *me*, Mama, your only daughter, without a mother. Mr. Wu doesn't think about anything but Mr. Wu."

"I can't leave, *cara mia*. Where would I go?"

"Mama, weren't you listening? You can stay with me at school until I graduate. It's only four years. Then I can get a job that will take care of the both of us."

"He's not like Jake."

I cursed the flop my belly did at the mention of Mr. Wu's son.

"What does Jake have to do with this?"

"I know you loved him and he treated you badly. But Feng is not like that boy. He genuinely loves me."

"Then why doesn't he leave his wife? Marry you? Make you head of his house instead of the woman who cleans up his wife's toilet?"

"You don't understand."

"Then explain it to me, Mama. Is this what you want for *me*? To be some rich man's plaything? To do with what he wants, with no promise of love or a future?"

"He loves me in his own way. It's very hard for him. You don't understand."

"Mrs. Aconi." A woman dressed in tweed strode in briskly, folders and black Bic pens in hand. "Dr. Gray explained to you the health procedures that must be followed in cases like yours."

Mama nodded.

The social worker finally introduced herself, then filled in Mama's pertinent information on a form she'd officiously clipped into place on her brown clipboard.

"I'll need the names, addresses if you have them, and phone numbers of the men or women with whom you've had sexual contact in the last six weeks."

"I'm not sure," Mama said.

"I'm sorry. You're not sure of which part?"

"I don't know the names of the men I've been with in the last six weeks."

"Are you stating that you don't have first and last names of your most recent sexual partners?"

"That's what I'm saying."

"Perhaps you'd like to have...your daughter, is it?" I nodded. "Leave the room so that we can talk freely."

"No need." Mama shook her head. "I'm sorry, but I won't be able to help you."

"Our notification is anonymous," the worker said. "We will not name you. We need to inform him or her that they may have been exposed and need to get treatment."

"Sorry."

"If you're the victim of domestic abuse, that's another matter, and we can make arrangements for your safety, but we still need that information."

"No one has hit me. I can't help you. Isabella, can you please find the nurse so that I can leave. The doctor said that I could be discharged as soon as I took my medicine. I want to get better in my own bed."

I pulled Mama's coat from the little pressboard closet in the corner.

"I'm sorry I can't help you, miss. I'll let you get on with your more important cases."

With a huff, the social worker gathered up her folders and pamphlets and pens and stalked from the room without so much as a backward glance.

Into the quiet, I heard the giant clock above the door ticking. It was four o'clock. The SAT was long over and my last chance at Owen had gone with it.

I'd chosen Mama over Owen, and she'd chosen Mr. Wu over me.

CHAPTER 16

FOURTEEN YEARS EARLIER

NOTHING FUCKING CHANGED. I tapped a pencil furiously on my desk, its tip peppering the top with stipple. Dr. Gray practically dropped a nuclear bomb into the middle of Toms River and everyone acted exactly the same.

Zero fallout.

Mr. Wu went on CEOing and Mama went on cooking and cleaning for the cheating rat bastard who'd never heard of a condom or safe sex. I hated having to think of my mother used in that way. I mean, her throat. I couldn't get that mental picture out of my head. I wanted to scrub my mind with bleach.

Instead, I took a couple of messages from the Ocean County Department of Health and left hot-pink Post-it notes on our fridge. I wanted so bad for them to talk her to her senses. I'm pretty sure Mama never called them back, though.

With a sinking pit of hopelessness in my belly, I sent in my application for Owen—two weeks before the New Year's Day deadline. I'm sure we all prayed for salvation from our respective problems. At least I know I did. Owen was my only chance at getting the heck out of this hell not of my making.

Recklessly, stupidly, foolishly, I didn't apply to a single other school. I had to prove it to Jake and his asshole friends at Woodward. I had to prove it to myself that I was good enough for the Ivy League.

Sadly, six nights before Christmas, I was in my room—where I'd been hiding out for two and a half weeks—messaging my friends. School was out for the holidays and I was trying to get some kind of party together. I needed something, anything, to take my mind off Owen and the countdown to graduation a long six months away. Whether it was Owen or trying my luck at getting some kind of job, I was getting the hell out of Wu country.

The problem with not having our own house was that we couldn't have parties. Not really. Not without revealing the lies I'd told for the last six years. But no matter who I messaged, they couldn't host a party either.

"Get dressed," my mother said behind me.

I probably jumped a mile in the air.

"Jesus Christ, Mama, what about knocking?" I said as I spun around and flattened my laptop in one smooth motion.

She pursed her lips hard but did not say a single word about taking the Lord's name in vain. When she opened her mouth to speak, it wasn't a rebuke, but a request.

"Put on a nice dress. That velvet one would look good. Heels, too."

There were no secrets anymore. She'd been spying on me. My shoulders slumped.

"There's no party, Mama. All of my friends are with their families this weekend."

Mama frowned. "Mr. Wu's party. That's where we're going."

"The help isn't invited," I said, and turned back to my desk and mentally shuffled through my closet. Maybe I could use my fake ID to go to a bar. Have a drink. Meet someone who didn't think they knew everything there was to know about me.

The exasperated breathing let me know that Mama was still there.

"This year, he has asked us and Mr. and Mrs. Perez to come." Her voice was reverent, like the president had asked us to have dinner at the White House or something. The Wu house was no White House.

"When? Today? Because a last-minute invitation is a brush-off in nice wrapping and a pretty bow."

"Just put on the dress."

I turned around and noticed Mama for the first time. Gone were her usual dark pants and long-sleeved shirt. All five feet of her looked beautiful in a white strapless dress. It flared from the top in asymmetrical A-line style. It hung on her amazingly. Her hair was up in some kind of twist thingy. She looked about twenty years younger.

It wasn't such a mystery what my real dad or Francis Aconi or even Mr. Wu had seen in her, despite her or them being married.

I stood and reached out to stroke the dress. She slapped my hand away before it reached the snow-white fabric.

"Is that silk?"

"Yes, it is."

"Where'd you get the money for that? I hope you haven't spent my first semester's book money."

"It's a Halston. A gift from Mr. Wu and Mrs. Li."

Yeah, right. That had to be the biggest, fattest lie ever. Maybe the dress had been a make-up gift. I snorted in disgust. Mrs. Li was not scouring the racks in the city looking for designer dresses for the help.

"I know they're not your favorites, Izzie, but they've invited us all for Christmas dinner and dancing, so get dressed."

"'Us all' who?"

"You, me. Mr. and Mrs. Perez, the rest of the people who usually come. Their friends from the club, her friends from the city, the DynoAutomotive managers." She waved her hands dismissively. "None of that matters. Just get dressed."

"When, Mama? When is the party?"

"In an hour."

"You could have warned me. You know, like told me earlier."

She didn't say anything while I pulled off my sweats to jump into the shower. We both knew it went without saying that she hadn't told me because I would have disappeared. I'd have found at least one friend willing to shelter me for the night. But she needed me there as a buffer, to make believe that this was just an employee Christmas party, and not her flirting with Mr. Wu and danger.

After the hospital, I'd put my foot down on Mr. Wu. I had patently refused to step foot in that house again unless she was bleeding and dying.

Mama or Mr. Wu wanted me there for some reason, though. Maybe there was something beyond me acting as a buffer. I didn't want to know what that was. I was content to find out when I needed to know. Mama's steely gaze let me know that refusal would lead to World War Three. We didn't need any more bombs.

In twenty minutes, I was zipped into the dress I'd bought for the high school winter formal. Mama stood behind, adding finishing touches to my hair. I poked dangly crystal earrings into my earlobes. Mrs. Li would be wearing diamonds.

When I blotted my lips and pronounced myself done, my mother fiddled in a tray of odds and ends, then lifted a gold chain from the palm of her hand and not so ironically fastened her best gold cross, the one with a single pearl in the middle, around her neck.

Without coats or shawls, we went out into the cold, shivering while we tiptoed across the gravel. We stood behind other guests and, when it was our turn to step through the door, followed a hired butler into the house. The coil of apprehension in my belly loosened a little at the sight of the tuxedoed man. At least my mother wasn't expected to work tonight like she had in all the years past.

I can't believe how many of these parties I'd been to. When I used to think it was fun to sneak food and leftover champagne with Jake while my mother worked her ass off, Mr. Wu and Mrs. Li swanning about never touching a dirty dish. I'd been so fucking oblivious to the differences between us. My current self wanted to go back to that naïve twelve-year-old and slap some sense into that girl, tell her to open her eyes and see these people for who they actually were.

"Oh, I forgot to tell you, Jake's going to be here."

If there hadn't been a knot of people behind me speaking rapid Mandarin, I'd have turned tail and run.

I did not want to enter a roomful of people I'd come to despise.

Not five seconds into the crowded room, its purple cabbage rose wallpaper made even more ugly with clashing red and green decorations, I spotted him in a receiving line.

I felt him more than I saw him. A jolt of electrical awareness raised the hairs fallen from the back of my updo. Even after everything that had happened, I wanted to be nowhere other than in his arms.

Cursing myself a bigger fool than his mother or mine, I lifted my head and shoulders with confidence and did some swanning of my own.

Like magnets, our eyes were drawn to one another's. He didn't have long hair anymore, so I could see his eyes widen in surprise. Jake must have run out of friends or excuses to stay away from New Jersey. Either that, or Mrs. Li had summoned him home to stand at the end of their three-person receiving line, preparing to take over the role he'd someday inherit.

For the last couple of years, I'd tried hard to pretend Jake didn't exist. And with him spending summers in China and the rest of the time at Woodward, then Harvard, it had been almost easy.

Even Mama had tried, for my sake, to pretend he'd never taken advantage of me, but sometimes she'd found herself repeating some of Mr. Wu's stories of his accomplishments at college. I always cut her off, because rich, privileged kids finding success wasn't a matter worthy of mentioning.

Mama steered us toward the three-person receiving line.

"Lovely to see you, Isabella," Mrs. Li said, holding the tips of my fingers limply for a second before dropping them like a used tissue.

"You as well. Hope you're enjoying the holiday season. It's good that you can come home and finally be with your family." I made my voice saccharine sweet. "Mr. Wu gets so lonely—"

"Isabella," Mr. Wu boomed, while he vigorously patted me on the back and steered me from his wife. "I hear you've applied to Owen. Good for you. Two Ivy Leaguers in the family can't be a bad thing."

I nodded and pulled away. Family my ass. If we were all a family, it would be the most fucked-up, incestuous family ever worthy of Ricky Lake *and* Maury Povich.

When exactly did Mama and Mr. Wu discuss my life? While she was dusting around him while he was making his uber-important transpacific phone calls? Or did she wait until they were in bed together, discussing the future they would never have?

I closed my eyes for a long second, blotting out images of my mama in bed with this man, and of his son, cut from the same mold, in front of me.

"Bella." Jake made my name two long syllables, nodding at me.

I kept my arms stiffly at my sides and my mouth firmly shut. His use of my nickname made my knees weak. He smelled heavenly to boot. Some kind of citrus cologne wrapped around me and practically pulled me to him. My ankle buckled slightly and he extended his arms to stabilize me.

I stepped back as if he had shocked me with a thousand bolts of electricity.

The satin-collared tuxedo and black-and-white-checked Vans he wore over his bare feet should have looked ridiculous, but of course didn't. It made me want him to be mine again.

I didn't linger. Instead, I turned toward the bar because I was being stupid. He had never been mine.

I took a tall flute of champagne from the bar. I scanned the room, practically daring anyone to take it from me. In two swallows, I gulped it down, then did the same with another. I glanced at the chunky rhinestone watch that didn't look as good with my dress as the Vans looked with Jake's suit. Eleven minutes. That's how long I'd been here. It already felt like forever. How long before I could make a clean exit?

"How do you know the Wus?" a man asked me, materializing at my elbow and handing me a third glass of bubbly.

My usual Mafia-girl excuses flitted through my mind, but I was tired of being that girl.

"My mother works for him," I said, pointing toward her with my half-empty glass. She and Mr. Wu had their heads bowed together. His hand was at her elbow. Mrs. Li was a few feet away, looking as if she's swallowed something extremely bitter.

My head was a bit fuzzy, making it difficult to process

what I'd just seen. Instead, I turned to the man next to me and focused on what he was saying.

"Beautiful. Like mother like daughter." He had that look that men had given me for the last three years. The one that said he was thinking about what I looked like naked. For once, I didn't mind.

"And you?" I really looked at him now, taking in his waxed dark hair, midnight-blue eyes fringed by dark lashes. He sported enough stubble to darken his jaw and make him look a little bit dangerous.

"Tennis at the Dover Country Club." He stepped around so he was standing in front of me. I liked that he blocked everyone else from my sight. "Todd Sheridan." He shook my hand two beats too long. "I haven't seen you there," he said after he let go. "I'm sure I'd remember that." He touched the teardrop tip of my earing, setting it swinging.

I laughed. He took a sip of his drink, something in a short glass that looked stronger than wine, then smiled like he was the wittiest man ever. But I'd laughed because I'd never been to a country club in my life. Jake had told me about taking swimming and tennis lessons there. He'd always said it was boring as hell and stuffy to boot. Now I'm thinking he did that to make me not feel bad about missing out.

"Too busy with school." I purposely left the "high" out of that statement, but Todd was no fool.

"Where are you?"

"I've applied to Owen for the fall."

He stepped back a hair. I could tell he'd thought I was older. It made me think he was less of a creep than I'd originally suspected.

"Good school. I'm a Dartmouth man myself."

I finished the drink and placed it on a tray of a passing waiter before picking up another.

"Maybe you should slow down on the champagne. You're probably not used to drinking, being that you're underage and all."

He's fishing. Rather than dangle the bait on the hook, I told him exactly what he needed to know.

"I'm of age in Europe, Canada, and New Jersey if we're not talking wine and spirits." I lifted my brow in what I hoped was conspiratorial camaraderie.

He laughed and lifted his own glass in a toast. "Touché and cheers."

The clink of the crystal had the most pleasant sound, far better than the noise the glasses made when Mama and I toasted in our kitchen.

"I'm Isabella by the way," I said, holding out my hand.

"Todd, again," he said, catching my fingers. It wasn't exactly a shake because he didn't let go. This time I didn't push away my feelings. I was shocked that there was a tingle there. Awareness I hadn't thought possible with someone who wasn't Jake crept through me. I gripped Todd a little tighter to show him that whatever he might be feeling was very much mutual.

"There's a family room just over there," I whispered.

The little matchstick implant in my arm hadn't had much of a chance to get a workout. The champagne had me feeling just bold enough to try Todd out.

"I'd love to get off these heels and hear more about Dartmouth. There are two weeks left if I want to apply to other schools."

Todd took two fresh glasses of the dark liquid he'd been nursing, and followed me past knots of guests to a closed door. I turned the knob and we were plunged into darkness. I expertly wove my way to a Tiffany lamp on a far table. I snapped it on to the lowest setting.

"I could turn it up, but the wallpaper may blind us," I mock whispered.

Gratefully, Todd laughed. Sinking back into one of the plush love seats, I eased off my heels and tucked my legs underneath me so that I was turned toward the only other seat. Taking the hint, he lowered himself next to me, depositing our drinks on the round table that sat between us and the matching love seat catty corner.

"Dartmouth's in New Hampshire, right?" I asked, as if Ivy League schools were the most intriguing conversation topic ever.

"Hanover." He nodded, handing me my drink and taking a sip of his. "Colder than a witch's tit this time of year."

"Maybe I'd be warm if I had one of those long green-and-white-striped scarves." I took a sip of the liquid. It burned a bit going down, but heated me from the inside out.

"I don't know if you'd be warm, but you'd be incredibly beautiful."

I ducked my head, feeling like I'd fished for that compliment and caught it on a hook.

"You didn't have to say that."

"But it's true. The incoming freshmen at Owen are going to be incredibly lucky." He leaned even closer. The furniture creaked slightly below us. I wanted to be kissed. By someone who wasn't Jake. The hand that cupped my neck was warm. I shivered a bit, took another sip, and set my glass on the coffee table directly in front of us.

"Cold?"

"Warming up," I said, leaning toward Todd.

His blue eyes closed as he placed his lips on my cheek. I breathed in the cool, minty scent of this man. I itched everywhere, my skin stretching tight. I reached a hand back behind me and snapped off the light. Moonlight replaced the artificial.

Todd pulled back a hair and I stuck my hand inside the black jacket. Body heat and cool, starched cotton were in sharp contrast. I pushed him back against a throw pillow and kissed along his hairline, brushing my lips against his jaw like he'd done to me. Stubble tickled at my nose and mouth.

Todd's intake of breath made me bold. I pulled up my dress so I could straddle his hips with my knees. In seconds, my body was on fire.

We stopped fooling around and he positioned my head for a proper kiss. For long minutes, there was nothing but Todd and me and the fire that had started between us. One that was about to consume me. Todd broke the kiss. His hand pulled at the silk at his throat, the tie falling away at once.

I reached behind him and flicked at the hook holding together his cummerbund. We fought for the small studs against his chest, only undoing one or two before we were kissing again. Relief flooded me when he sought the tiny zipper at the back of my neck. It was going to be easier than I thought to forget about Jake.

Before Todd could close his broad fingers around the tiny zipper tab, there was a sound that came from neither of us.

"Bella."

Jake.

A millisecond after I heard him whisper my name, the overhead light snapped on, throwing the room into harsh light and shadows. Red paisley wallpaper pulsed.

I turned and looked over my shoulder.

"If you'll excuse us, Jake. Todd was telling me a bit about his time at Dartmouth." I wanted to get back to the kissing, and undressing, but the mood was irretrievably broken.

"Sheridan," Jake acknowledged.

Todd lifted me from him as if I were as light as a feather then stood and strode toward the window, his cummerbund and tie in hand.

"Wu Jian," Mrs. Li said, coming into the room. "You need to come out to the living room. There are some people your father wants you to meet." Her English was grudging. It wasn't to impress me, but probably Todd.

"I need to talk to Isabella."

Mrs. Li looked from me, shoeless, to Todd, his cummerbund still in his hand, to Jake.

"This is the last time I'm going to tell you to leave this girl alone. Let her trap another rich man."

Her insult was like a slap in the face. It hurt more than my mother's stinging palm against my cheek.

Neither Jake nor Todd jumped to my defense. Both men quickly followed Mrs. Li from the room. Just like that. Because the Wus owned everyone in Toms River. No one wanted to cross them. Everyone in town was waiting for the ever-promised plant to open and the good jobs to roll in.

I downed my drink, as well as the one Todd had brought in. The whisky or bourbon or whatever burned to my toes. Coughing, I shook it off. I shoved my feet back into the too pointy shoes and made my way back to the huge living room.

It was time for me to speak my mind. I couldn't continue to let the Wus treat Mama and me like second-class citizens.

Guests were talking and eating in nearly every nook and cranny of the room. Carefully, I took three steps up from the sunken area to a nook that held the piano Jake had practiced on more days than I could count. I lifted my hands high and banged both fists on the baby grand's keys filling the room with discordant sound.

The room grew quiet as half the guests turned toward me. I plucked a glass of white wine from a tray that had been abandoned on the shiny black wood.

"I have an announcement," I said. The next words from my mouth were going to include the phrase "sexually transmitted disease." The next unlucky victim of Mr. Wu deserved to know what she was getting into.

Before I could form the words on my slow-moving lips, a grip like a vise came around my arm.

"Come with me," Mr. Wu breathed into my ear.

I was frog-marched across the foyer to his office before I could squeak out a protest.

"What do you think you're doing?" he hissed. Gone was the indulgent papa side he'd been showing me for the last couple of years. But that charade had come to an end in the hospital.

"I was going to make a public service announcement. Clear up any misperceptions your wife may have had about your loyalty," I finally sputtered after he'd tossed me into a padded armchair and slammed the door shut.

"Don't be stupid, Isabella. You are a very smart girl who has had too much to drink."

"The price of my silence has just gone up." My demand would have been more effective if an unladylike burp hadn't come out right after.

"I don't know what you're talking about." He chose to ignore my words and my lack of manners.

"Don't be stupid, Mr. Wu. You're a very smart man who hasn't had enough to drink."

"What's your price?" He stood behind his desk and spread his arms wide, placing both hands flat on the shiny inlaid wood surface.

"Admission to Owen and tuition." It was the one thing I wanted that I couldn't get on my own.

He scoffed. "I have no control over the admissions committee. Perhaps you should have done better in school."

"I was planning to ace my SATs, but I was at the hospital the day they gave the last qualifying test."

Like I'd said, he was a smart man. It didn't take him more than a few seconds to connect the dots.

"If you go to Owen, you can't come back here."

"Get me into Owen and I'll never come back to Toms River again."

CHAPTER 17

TWELVE AND A HALF YEARS EARLIER

"ISABELLA, IS IT?"

I nodded, excitement speeding up my heartbeat. He'd taken the bait, and way earlier in the night than usual.

"Get your jacket and come out back with me."

I downed the remainder of my neat scotch letting the liquid warm me, help make me the reckless girl I wanted to be. I put on the jacket I'd hung on a brass hook and turned up the plaid designer collar. Through the sticky hall and past bathrooms I shuddered to think about, I pushed the heavy metal door.

A single bare bulb lit the dark alley. I looked right and left before I spotted the glow of a cigarette. I wrinkled my nose. Smoking wasn't my favorite, but another drink or two and I could get past it.

"Hi." I hated that my voice was breathless, but I was very close to not spending the next few hours alone with my thoughts. I'd have all of next week for that.

"You're a really beautiful girl."

I pulled the rubber band from my hair and let it fall across my collar. According to my roommate, Claire Harper, I looked softer, more approachable with my hair down. And since Claire always looked huggable, I took her advice.

"Thank you."

"What I'm about to say, I'm saying for your own good."

My mind wandered to a few hours ago. I was sure I'd brushed my teeth after leaving the dining hall. I'd showered, put on deodorant. I resisted the urge to sniff my pits. I braced for what was next, what was wrong with me. I could fix anything if I knew what needed fixing.

"Go ahead."

"You need to go home."

"Come again?" The only people sent home from bars were those too drunk to stand and troublemakers. I wasn't either.

"I've been working in Olde Haven for ten years, and I've seen a hundred girls like you come and go. Sex with me isn't going to fix what's broken. You need to find your father, or make up with your father, or forgive him."

He interrupted me when I started to protest.

"It's one of those three, or some variation. I'm not always on the money about what the dad did, but I could spot daddy issues the minute you walked in the door. The money you spend on drinks? Spend it on therapy."

"So—" I had no idea why or what I was trying to salvage.

"Go home. I'm cutting you off."

Louis Vuitton bags stood half-filled on my roommate's bed after I made the not-too-long trek from the bar to our room. At least I thought it was my room. I ducked my head back out of the door to check the number. Yep, this was the right room.

"Claire?"

My roommate popped her head out of the closet we shared. It was oddly shaped and as deep as the room, but hell to navigate without any real lighting.

"I'm here. What's up? You're back earlier than usual. How did your last class go?"

"Professor Muncy said I could turn in my paper after the October break." A cute blond bartender from a dive in Shelton had kept me way too busy to write a paper on comparisons between German heroic legend and Norse mythology.

"Maybe you should cut back on the partying."

"Maybe I should..." I hoped my wink was as broad as I tried to make it. That it hid the tears I was trying to swallow. The bartender had aimed his words right at the thing I didn't want to think about.

I needed *more* men in my life, not less. That's where he'd been wrong.

"But you're not, right?"

"Not now. What's the point? There's boys. There's beer. There are no parents. Totes winning combo. Enough about me. Where'd you get the glam bags?"

"You noticed?"

"I thought we agreed freshman year. I bring the bling, you bring the brains to this operation."

Claire folded and dropped two silk camisoles into a bag. I'd known this girl for a year. She did not own silk. Or at least hadn't brought any from Maryland's eastern shore. Our clothes sharing had only gone one way.

"What's going on, hon? Silk? Louis Vuitton. This does not compute," I said, doing my best robot voice.

She pushed the bags aside and sat on her bed with a sigh.

"I should probably tell you. You have to promise to keep it a secret, though."

I mimed locking up my lips with a twist and throwing away a key. "I'm a vault. You know that."

I'd shared little of my past with anyone here. But the one thing I'd gotten from living with the Wus was how to compartmentalize and how to keep a dammed secret. Whatever Claire was going to say couldn't compete with illicit affairs and secret abortions.

"I'm a Julie."

I searched my mind, but came up empty. "Is that some campus group?" There were about a billion different ones on campus for every damned hobby, not to mention ones for any geographical, racial, and religious affiliation you could imagine. "Wait, is that the new a cappella group? You'd said something about trying out."

"Those are the Jems."

"With a 'J.' Right, I remember. So what's a Julie?"

"Just Us Lying in Ecstasy. It's an acronym."

"What does it really mean?"

I could have driven a Mack truck through her pause. But I waited. After Jake and Toms River, I knew I would hear the grudging truth if I waited long enough.

"It's an escort service, Izzie. The girls who work there, we're called Julies."

My ass hit the bed next to hers before I realized I'd lost control of my knees.

"You once rescued a cat from a tree." It was one of the first stories she'd told me. It had cemented my belief that she was nearly perfect—the exact opposite of me. We'd been angel and devil last Halloween. Ethereal white robes had suited her like the spiked trident had me.

"It was my neighbor's crawl space and I was eight."

It wasn't only the cat story. It was that every single thing I'd learned about Claire Harper pointed to the fact that she was a good girl. I started to lay out the evidence I'd collected in the one and a half semesters we'd known each other.

"You go to bed at a reasonable hour. You eat vegetables in the dining hall. You don't drink alcohol because it's illegal. You turn in your papers on time."

"You're one of the rich kids, Isabella. It's hard here at Owen for the rest of us."

I was a little nauseous as a pang of guilt hit me in the solar plexus. Gone was the Mafia princess persona, and in her place was the rich dilettante from the Jersey Shore. Clarifying that my mother was a housekeeper, but that I had an unlimited credit card and no financial aid wasn't something I cared to explain—to anyone.

"That doesn't mean I'm an asshole, Claire. Do you need help? I'm sure I could charge food and clothes for you and no one would be the wiser." I'd tested the boundaries, and the sky was the limit with my platinum Amex.

"It's not the work, Isabella. The idea of work, I don't mind. Actual work, I don't mind. I worked all through high school at a bookstore.

"What I hate about the so-called student contribution is what class system it creates. You guys not on aid get to eat when you want, buy coffee when you want, study when you want. We, on the other hand, work to serve all of you."

I lifted my hand to cut her off, protest what she was saying, but she waved me off. There was a lot of that going on tonight.

"It's true and you know it. How much fun do you think it was, working in the dining room serving food and spraying down trays while the rest of you lounged around and ate the cook's chocolate chip cookies fresh from the oven after dinner? Or how embarrassing it is to dress up in a white shirt and black pants and serve wine and hors d'oeuvres to the same faculty that are teaching us during the day? All that service and I'm still going to graduate twenty thousand in debt."

She was right. I'd thought it weird at first that some students served others, then as quickly as the thought had come into my mind, I'd let it go. Dwelling on class disparities hewed too closely to my mother and Jake and Mr. Wu.

"So the bags?" I was not going to let that escort comment get buried in Claire's quest for social justice.

"My guy, the one I'm seeing, is nice. He's not some slobbering sicko who wants to keep me in a dungeon forever. He wants to go to Maine to watch the leaves change, drink apple cider, sit by a cozy fire. It's every woman's fantasy and I get to live it, all expenses paid."

"Don't you have to have sex with him, though, in between looking at maple trees?"

"He's not paying to discuss comparative religion, Izzie.

Although we have talked about the role of the Pope in the modern world."

"You don't want to serve other students and your faculty, but you serve men." If that wasn't putting lipstick on a pig, I didn't know what was.

"Pays a whole lot better. I'm not on the street giving twenty-dollar blow jobs for a hit of the crack pipe. I give him the girlfriend experience."

"Is it... Well, I think I'm trying to as...are you okay?"

"Isabella. You're infamous in our class for closing bars in Olde Haven by dancing on them and going home with the bartender. At the end of the day, what I'm doing is no different—except I get paid."

She had me there. By the gonads. Except what she didn't know was that it was my mother who did the dirty deeds for the money I got. I wanted to get up and hide in the ten-foot-deep closet Claire had gone back into.

I'd wanted to take myself and Owen seriously, but the situation in Toms River had wrecked my sense of what was important. Instead, I was in line to slide through with the school's easiest major and see how many guys I could do, all in the space of four years. We weren't different, Claire and I.

"Be safe, okay?" was all I said before I got out my nearly identical bags and started packing for the week.

"I will."

"And if you need a break, you can join me at the Mandarin Oriental in Boston. I've got a suite for a week. Going to do the weeklong spa retreat, maybe catch some local theater. I'd love the company."

"You have the life, Izzie. I'll hand you that," Claire said as she zipped her bags and plopped them by the door.

Sure, the life.

I had no family who'd miss me. Nowhere to go while school was out for the week. If I were Claire, I'd spray the trays and hand out drinks with a smile if it meant I could spend the week with Mama and Daddy and Arturo one more time, like it used to be.

CHAPTER 18

I TOOK a deep sniff as I unwound my scarf, hanging it and my coat on a hook by the front door.

"It's a bar, Isabella, not the cosmetics section of a department store," Claire said.

"But I love the smell of beer and old wood."

"Don't get too plastered. We're going to head out first thing in the morning and we agreed to split the driving."

"You can do the first leg," I said. "Or maybe you can have a drink."

"I'm underage," she said. Like that was an excuse.

"You know they don't give a rat's ass here about age. I'd have thought you'd have put all that legal versus illegal stuff behind you."

"Shhhh."

Ignoring the duplicity of the former kitten-saving saint, I found us a table that gave me a direct view of Mike the bartender's chest wrapped in a super-tight, long-sleeved shirt.

There were two things I loved about the Quotidian. First,

the bar was in a beautiful old building that had a long and distinguished history I never bothered to learn, but the plate with "George Washington and Abraham Lincoln slept here" was impressive. It reminded me of some of Owen's most historic rooms, but without the pressure of classes and grades.

Also, this bartender was on my conquest list. He was all huge biceps with tattoos that wound their way up his arms. I'd fantasized what it would be like to be under him with that ink stretching along his straining muscles.

It was Wednesday night before Thanksgiving. I figured it would be slow, and I'd get a chance to shimmy on up to him without distractions. I couldn't wait to take him to one of the hotel rooms upstairs. It all but promised to be a good time.

"Negroni, please."

Rather than automatically pull bottles from the carved wooden shelf behind him, Mike gave me a look.

"That's bitter, not sweet."

"Not everything in life has to be sweet. I like my drinks like my men, with a little bit of a bite."

In spite of probably having been fed lines his entire career, Mike huffed out a laugh. It was a very good start to the night. Turning, he pulled the blood-red Campari bottle from a shelf, then started preparing my drink.

"You're a bold one," he said, handing me the bright concoction. "Your friend over there want a drink, too?"

"She's the one driving for Turkey day. A Diet Coke with lime for her. There's no reason not to be bold, right? I like the way you look, Mike."

Too soon he was handing me the second drink and

moving away to serve another thirsty patron. But his "Back at you," was encouraging.

"Mike might be a candidate," I said as I passed the cola to Claire.

"We have to get an early start. The drive to the eastern shore is a solid four hours."

"I'll be good, I promise." I held up my hands like a Boy Scout.

Claire's phone rang. Her *other* phone. I knew what that meant. I got up and sauntered over to the bar.

"What does a girl have to do to get some music around here?"

Mike swirled his white terrycloth toward me. "What do you have in mind?"

"Gwen Stefani?" I couldn't quite move like the blonde in her videos, but I did a fair imitation.

"Hollaback Girl" blasted from the sound system and I did a simulation of the music video as best I could in the clear space in front of the bar.

When the song ended, Claire was waving me over to the table frantically. Giving Mike my best be-right-back smile, I sauntered over to our table.

"What's up? I was reeling the bartender in. He was all but caught."

"I can't go tomorrow."

"What do you mean?" We'd gone to her house last year. I was all set to pretend for a few days that all was normal. That I was the run-of-the-mill college student hanging out with friends over the holidays, not persona non grata with unlimited credit but no mom or dad.

"I need to be a Julie. He needs me for the holiday weekend."

"What are you going to tell your mom and dad?" From the care packages and stuff that came to the mailroom, Claire's parents seemed to think about her all the time. They may not have been able to afford Owen, but they kept us in blondies and snickerdoodles. Unlike me, she would be missed over Thanksgiving.

"That a last-minute project came up and I need to stay here to keep up my 'B' average so I don't lose my scholarship money."

"That's a lot of lies," I said. I'd been in the middle of way too many of those. I was starting to believe they always blew up in your face. I'd only met her parents a couple of times, but I didn't want her family to suffer like mine had.

"What are *you* going to do, Izzie?"

Fuck. I'd been so busy worrying about her, that I hadn't realized she'd left me stranded.

"Shit. The dorms are closing," I said absentmindedly. Only a few international students stayed over the holidays, and they had to get special permission way ahead of time.

"Tomorrow at noon."

"I'll go home. My mom will always be glad to see me," I said with false cheer. Like Claire, I was lying. I'd call around and see if some hotel could squeeze me in last minute. Maybe I'd spend the next five or six days actually catching up on my work before I flunked out of the school I'd tried so hard to get into.

"I've got to go pack. You coming?"

I left half of my Negroni on the table. Mike the bartender

would have to wait for another day. I was going to have to be good and sober to figure out where I'd be going fifteen hours from now.

After Claire left, I got on the phone. Turned out lots of people didn't stay with their families at Thanksgiving. I didn't want to risk my Amex with some thousand-dollar-a-night suite on the Sound, nor did I want to fight off local bedbugs in a by-the-hour motel room.

"Mama?" I asked tentatively, when I'd exhausted all my other options and had finally gotten up the nerve to call New Jersey.

Her "Yes, *cara mia*," didn't miss a beat. It was as if we'd talked yesterday, and not months ago when I gave her my summer address in New York, where I was interning for a fashion magazine.

"My Thanksgiving plans fell through and I was wondering if I could come. I'll stay out of everyone's way. I promise." It all spilled out in a rush, hoping there wasn't a "no" on the other end.

"Please come. I need you here," was all she said.

I threw my bags in the SUV and pointed the car north.

All the way up the Garden State Parkway, I tried to convince myself that turning up in Jersey was a good idea. My mother sounded like she missed me, even more than a little. She hadn't shown it with cookies and hand-knit socks like the Harpers, but in her own way, I knew she loved me. That she hadn't *really* picked Mr. Wu over me.

Two and a half hours later, I wasn't so sure.

"Mama, you're scaring me." I scooted closer to her on the couch and grabbed her hands, stopped their wringing.

She was scaring the *hell* out of me. Five seconds after I'd parked the car and turned off the engine, I'd heard what sounded like someone dying. I'd walked into our house and found Mama on the couch, crying her eyes out.

"Is it Daddy? Arturo. Is he okay?" I tried to think of the last time my brother and I had emailed. Maybe a couple weeks or even months had passed since our last messages. Between the time difference and me screwing my way through Olde Haven's bartenders, I hadn't really kept in touch. I knew he called Mama a few times a year, on the sly.

Guilt crushed me. He'd once been one of the most important people in my life, and now he was maybe dead or lying in the hospital after crashing into the side of some twisting, turning Italian mountain road. Everyone said Italy had the world's most dangerous drivers.

"Did he wrap his Vespa around a tree?" When he'd attached a picture of him on the tiny green scooter to an email, I was suddenly glad I was driving a brand-new SUV, the third generation of the one I'd had in high school.

"Noo," Mama wailed. I let go of her hands and got up and retrieved a box of tissues from the bathroom. She was like a leaky faucet.

It wasn't Arturo then. What else could it be? Then, with a sinking sensation, as I walked back to the living room couch, I knew.

Mr. Wu. What in the hell had he done now?

"Do you have HIV? AIDS?" I asked, skipping the polite preliminaries I'd have used with anyone else. But I was going to kill that rat bastard if gonorrhea was only the tip of the STD iceberg.

"No, *cara mia*," Mama said, her sniffling temporarily under control with a wad of tissues jammed under her nose. "Why would you say that?"

Um, because he gave you a fucking disease that landed you in the hospital on the verge of death. But I didn't say that. We didn't talk about *that*. Unlike the dust at the Wu house, which my mother carefully vacuumed away, the relationship dirt was all swept under the rug. We, all of us, stepped over it, pretended it didn't exist.

"Are you dying of cancer?" I scooted beside her and wrapped my arms around her. She smelled the same as always, a mixture of lemongrass and citronella from her Italian soap.

"No. Stop it." My mother shook free from my embrace. "I'm fine." My mother dried her eyes and smoothed back her hair. She gathered up the mountain of tissues and took them to the kitchen. I heard the garbage can lid lift, then fall. I waited a few minutes, but she didn't come back.

There was no smell in the kitchen. It was the day before Thanksgiving and there was no smell in the kitchen. I wasn't expecting a ten-course feast, but my mother always made something when she knew I was going to be home. Arturo may be alive and well, but there was something else going on. I wasn't sure I wanted to know.

"Mama. Are you making dinner? I mean, it's no big deal if you aren't. We can get Chinese..."

The moment I said that last, I regretted it. So many kids at Owen joked that when their families didn't cook, they had Thanksgiving and even Christmas dinner at Chinese restaurants. My mother, in the last several years, had become quite adept at making southern Chinese specialties. But of course she wouldn't want Chinese.

For the thousandth time, I wished we were a normal American family, not one tied to these other people for our very survival.

"Why were you crying?" Now that she was standing and not looking like someone had killed both her children in the town square, I hoped to get an honest answer from her.

"No reason. Just missing you and your brother. Olde Haven is too far away. Come sit with me and tell me what it's like at your fancy college."

"Mama. I'm tired. I drove a long way. Tell me what's wrong. On the phone, you said you needed me. I'm here, and not to tell you stories about Owen."

Her face crumpled.

I pulled a paper towel from the dispenser and handed it to her. It was a few minutes of bawling and hiccoughs before she was able to stand without her hand braced on the counter.

"It's Mr. Wu."

No shit, Sherlock.

"I'm sorry, Mama."

"He went back on his promise."

"What's that?" I tried to think of what he could have promised Mama—a pension, more vacation time, a new car. Though just like mine, he replaced the one she drove every two years.

Her face threatened to fold in on itself again, but she took a deep breath and looked me in the eye.

"He was supposed to leave Mrs. Li. He was supposed to

have told her last week. You and me, we were going to move into the big house. All of us, including Jake, we were going to be a family."

Hysterical laughter bubbled up in my throat. It took everything in me to keep it down.

I turned away and walked back to the living room. I sank into a wingback chair no one ever used in the corner. It was a paisley castoff from Mrs. Li.

For the first time ever, I wondered if I knew my mother. I'd always thought her a smart and savvy lady, but this...this took the cake. When she wandered in, I took a deep breath and spoke to her like English was her fourth language.

"Mama. The guy never leaves his wife, ever. You had to know that. It's been on *Oprah* more times than I can count."

"They have to leave sometimes, *cara mia*."

My heart, my ass. I wasn't her heart or her dear. Mr. Wu was.

"If they do leave, Mama, then they cheat on the new woman or divorce her. There's no way this works out."

I wasn't an expert, but how many times had I read about just this thing in every other women's magazine that came in our monthly mail?

"Mrs. Li's family has been paid back ten times over with interest. Their marriage was only about the money," my mother wailed plaintively. Because of course he'd shoveled some shit excuse about his marriage to Mrs. Li being one of convenience or a merger of families or whatever he thought Mama would believe. And she'd lapped it up like it was the best gelato.

"Why can't he leave?" I asked, though I was ninety-nine

percent sure whatever she said wasn't going to be the least bit believable.

"He's finalized a partnership and Dyno's cars will finally be available in the United States. It's the one thing he's been working toward all these years. He's made plans to build a factory here in Toms River, on that land that I've always told you about."

Ah yes, the fabled land that in Mama's mind made him richer than Croesus and somehow above the rules of the rest of us mere mortals.

"What does all that have to do with Mrs. Li?"

"Her family somehow secretly invested in this new partnership and are threatening to pull out if he leaves her."

I wanted to call bullshit so loud that our closest neighbors could hear me. With nearly seven acres, that would have been pretty far.

"Mama, I don't know if I'm the one you should be talking to about this." I wanted to back out of the room, run to my car, and stay in the Olde Haven motel next to the interstate. We were mother and daughter. Adults, sure, but this was the kind of divide that should have never been crossed. I'd wanted to know what was wrong, not be taken into her confidence about her immorality. Although I guess those were one and the same.

"You're twenty now, you understand the ways of the world. You love this family as much as I do."

I'd loved Jake once, I thought grudgingly. Mr. Wu and Mrs. Li, never. And this conversation had killed dead any good feeling I may have ever had about the family next door.

"Mama, I'm not sure this is love. I think we're in a dysfunctional relationship with this family."

"So glib, now that you're at that fancy school."

"I'm sorry, Mama. I'm sorry that you're sad about how this turned out. Have you thought about getting another job?"

"Feng said that he loved me. I can't believe this is happening again. I was going to be so much smarter than the last time."

"The last time?"

"Your father was a man named Paolo Leoni."

My head nearly spun. She'd never talked about this. Refused so often that I'd stopped asking.

"My...my father...my real father?" I stuttered out the question.

"My own mama had warned me that there was no good reason to be friends with Paolo, but I was young."

"Then what happened?" I was hanging on every word. No telling if she'd ever be this candid again.

"I fell in love. I was married. He was married. But Francis worked all the time. He didn't want to go out to dinner or dancing or anything. All he wanted was for both of us to work all the time to save up for a house near his aunt and uncle, as if that were the American dream.

"It started with lunch. I tried to break it off so many times. When I got pregnant, I was determined to end it with Paolo, make it work with Francis."

"Why didn't it work with either one of them?"

"Paolo came back. When you were about eleven and Arturo thirteen, he came back from California. He'd been in

Los Angeles for ten years. He said he was divorced. He said he was ready for us to be a family."

"Then why aren't you with him?" I'd missed out on one father, another would have been nice.

"We made a pact. I was going to tell your father, and then he and I were going to take you and Arturo and move to California."

"I've never been to California," I said stupidly.

"I went to Paolo's apartment, but it was empty. He hadn't divorced his wife. They'd had a bad fight, over him having an affair, then they got back together."

"And Daddy left."

"Francis Aconi took my only son and moved to Italy."

"I have a dad out there..." My mind whirled with possibilities, potential reunions, finding a man who looked like me, loved me unconditionally.

"Paolo isn't worth anything. Don't you waste any time on that man. Mr. Wu has been more father to you than Francis *or* Paolo. If that bitch Mrs. Li hadn't snuck her fingers into this new business, we'd be a *real* family."

My body felt hollow. I was hungry. Suddenly very, very hungry. Dining halls had been closed this morning, so I'd pulled over and had a coffee and muffin for the ride down. I figured I'd need to save space for dinner anyway. I couldn't think with all the blood rushing to churn my stomach.

"I'll make us something," I offered. "What do you want for dinner?"

"I made dinner."

I bent down to check, but the oven window was empty. There was no pie on the counter. No lasagna cooling on a rack. More blood rushed to my belly, filling with dread. It was the quickest cure for hunger I'd ever experienced.

"What have you done, Mama?"

"We're having dinner at the main house."

"Why would you do this? You have Thanksgiving off."

"He said that he'd never really had a traditional dinner. Dover Country Club does a passable job, but he should finally get to have a real meal."

"When, Mama?"

"Half hour. Can I borrow that face ice pack you used to use? I need to look my best."

While Mama iced her face, I plunked a cube of ice in a tall glass and added a few fingers of Amaro Averna. The bittersweet taste hit the back of my throat, but I held down a cough and finished what was probably the equivalent of three shots. I replaced the bottle in Mama's Italian drinks cabinet and went to change my clothes.

Truth telling shouldn't be done in jeans and my blue and white Owen sweatshirt.

♥

"Isabella, you're the last person I expected to see today," Mr. Wu said. We both knew I'd violated his one rule. After I'd left for Owen, I'd not set foot in Toms River when Mr. Wu was within fifty miles. Until today. Until I realized that I truly wasn't a part of this drama any longer. No matter what happened, they were all going to spin out the end of their little drama.

"Mama was quite sad, needed a little cheering up." I let the implication of my words linger like a bad smell.

"Do you like Owen?"

"I'm going to be a Humanities major. I'm learning a lot about human interaction."

"Why don't you have a seat right here." He gestured to the seat to his left. He was at the head, of course. Mrs. Li was on his right. The rest of the table was filled with DynoAutomotive people, mostly Chinese nationals who probably didn't know what to do with themselves over the long American holiday weekend.

And Mama.

And Me.

"Isabella, is it?" one of Wu's DynoAutomotive guests asked.

"Isabella Aconi, yes, and you?"

"Zhi Wei Jiang. I work in the logistics division. As one of the Americans here, I wanted to ask you about your Thanksgiving traditions."

"Which part? The part where the indigenous people here helped the pilgrims not starve, and celebrated their first harvest together before the pilgrims killed them with war, and famine, and disease? Or the part where Americans get together to give thanks for what they have?"

"Yes..." Jiang nodded tentatively.

"We have a big meal—turkey, cranberries, pumpkin and apple pies. But before we eat, we all go around the table announcing what we're thankful for.

"Why don't I start? I'm thankful for Mr. Wu's support in helping me attend one of the premier schools in this country,

Owen College in Connecticut. I'm thankful that my mom and I have been able to live on this lovely property for the last eight years.

"I'm grateful that their son, Jake, took my virginity then tossed me out like so much garbage. I'm grateful that father is just like the son, taking advantage of my mother for nearly as long and blaming it on his lovely wife. I'm grateful for Mrs. Li, and her complicity in all of this behavior from her husband and son. Oh, and I'm thankful I finally learned the true identity of my real father today. Yep, that's it from my list. Mr. Wu, maybe you should go next."

There was a long moment of quiet. My mother had her eyes cast down like she was praying the rosary. Mrs. Li's lips were pursed and her face twisted with the same disdain that she always visited upon me. I turned when Mr. Wu sucked in an audible breath.

"I warned you, Isabella. You leave this house now. You are never welcome back."

"Don't worry. I never want to come back."

I stood and strode from that man's damned house. When I got home, I picked up the bags I hadn't bothered to unpack and loaded them into the car. Ten minutes morphed into an hour as I waited for Mama. She had to come out of there. Come home so we could figure out our future.

At ninety minutes, I slammed into the red truck.

Mama hadn't chosen me. Jake hadn't chosen me. I chose me. Chose to take myself back to Olde Haven.

CHAPTER 19

"ISABELLA ACONI." I leaned across the desk as if there were answers in the pile of papers there. "I got a note about coming to this office."

The receptionist ticked my name on a long printout of names before her.

"Have a seat."

All the orange plastic bucket seats were free. I picked one closest to the door. The waiting room was as plain as the building. On a campus of beautiful architecture, this five-story brick building stood out, not for its beauty, but its abject plainness. If I hadn't known I was in the Ivy League, I could have been sitting in the county administration building across the street.

"Ms. Aconi," a woman called. She was standing in a door at the back of the waiting area. I stood wordlessly and followed the woman through the yellow metal door, its narrow window crosshatched with wire, then through a maze of cubicles to an office in the corner.

"I'm not sure why I'm here," I said as the woman lifted a cardigan from the seat, draped it across the back of the brown leather, then sat down heavily. "I know I have a few parking tickets, but I brought my credit card to clear that up."

"This is not about parking tickets, Ms. Aconi. This is about tuition."

I sat on the seat across from her and dropped my shoulders in relief. I thought for sure they were going to nab me for those tickets. I didn't like my designated parking spot in the back of beyond, and maybe parked in someone's reserved spot a time or twenty.

"My mother's employer handles tuition. Feng Wu, Dyno-Automotive," I informed her.

"Yes. I've had a look through your records, and indeed this Mr. Wu, is it?" I nodded and she continued. "He paid for the first three semesters. This semester, however, hasn't been paid."

"There must be a mistake," I said, dreading the truth I'd tried not to consider from the moment I drove away from Thanksgiving dinner.

"There's no mistake that there's no payment on record. Our calls to the number he gave previously haven't been returned."

I bit my lip to keep myself from crying in front of this woman with her blue sweater and long beaded necklaces stacked on her bosom.

That motherfucker. I mean, I hadn't heard from Mama since I drove away, but I figured she was stewing. Christmas at Claire's house had been fun. Winter on the eastern shore had been nothing like I'd ever done before. Rain, sure, but no snow, or ice, or sleet. We ate crabs and sang songs and I pretended her family was mine.

I'd been thinking maybe I'd go somewhere like that, on a quiet shore, when I was done here. But it looked like maybe I was done here already.

"I had a falling out with my family over the holidays," I explained in my most reasonable tone. "I never thought they'd pull tuition. Do you have financial aid I can apply for?"

Half the students at Owen were on some kind of scholarship. Supposedly the endowment was billions of dollars. I only needed a teeny-tiny fraction of that.

"Unfortunately, our aid has been allotted for the year."

"So there's nothing for people like me who have emergencies?"

"You're welcome to discuss this with financial aid, but unless you have some outstanding academic or athletic contribution, we don't make exceptions."

I almost stood up to tell her I used to be a hell of a gymnast...almost. But that dream, among others, had died somewhere between Philadelphia and Toms River.

"How much do I owe?"

"Eighteen thousand, five hundred. With the parking tickets, eighteen thousand, eight hundred sixty-two."

When you didn't have it, eighteen thousand may as well have been two million.

"How long do I have to pay?"

"Tuition was due November of last year, but we can give you until the end of add/drop." She consulted her desk calendar. "That's in ten days."

"Do you have a payment plan?" Maybe I could put Owen on layaway, like people did with expensive Christmas gifts at the mall."

"We normally require plans be set up at the beginning of the year. In your case, we could probably make an exception. Let's see."

Tension fled, I could do a plan.

She punched mightily into the adding machine on her desk. All she needed was a Kelly-green desk lamp and those sleeve protectors from British dramas to complete the look.

"Thirty-one sixty-four for the next six months. The first payment would be due by add/drop, though. We gotta know if you're committed. If you can't make that payment, you'll need to make arrangements to move out of your dorm and we will formally separate you from the college."

Formal separation. Sounded more final than Mama's divorce.

"I'll get the money," I promised.

"Good luck to you, young lady."

I took that as a dismissal.

I zipped up my coat, wound my blue and white scarf around my neck and made the lonely trek back to my dorm. Three thousand dollars. Three thousand one hundred sixty-four, to be exact. I could come up with that in a week, no problem. Sell some of the stuff Mr. Wu's credit card had paid for. I could do that.

But that left February and all the months after.

I shouldn't have had that drink or three. I thought that showing Mr. Wu's true colors would be the dynamite that crazy situation needed. The wake-up call Mama needed to get the hell out of Toms River.

Instead, I was the odd one out and they were all still there, enmeshed in total and utter craziness.

God dammit.

God dammit.

I'd been such a fool. *Was* such a fool. It was time for that foolish girl to grow the hell up.

When I got back to our room, Claire was squeaking an electric-blue highlighter through what could have been the Bible or Talmud or Koran. I closed the door behind me hard, getting her attention like I'd wanted.

"What's up, Isabella?"

"How can I become a Julie?"

CHAPTER 20

TWELVE YEARS EARLIER

THE MOMENT I handed my truck keys over to the valet, I knew I was no match for Greenwich. I walked to the heavy wood door thinking about turning back, but knowing that I wouldn't. Finishing this night would be the difference between dropping out and making my February payment to the bursar's office.

Choice made, I took a deep breath of the bracingly cold New England air, then stepped through the door.

"I'm here to meet Daniel van Dijk," I said to the maître d', coat already in hand, heeding my first lesson from Henrietta DeSimone's Julie training: look like you belong.

With a single dismissive glance, he looked me up and down, taking in the color-block crochet dress and mahogany stilettos with rhinestone ankle ties. Two hours ago, I'd put on these clothes I'd bought with money I could scarcely afford, and thought I'd be the belle of the ball.

The curl of his lip toward his too-long nose told me that I

looked like what I was—a hooker, and not even a high-class one. He didn't offer to relieve me of my coat.

"Let me take you to our private lounge." He turned on his heel so fast, it squeaked. It took me a few seconds to realize that I was supposed to follow him, which I did with a bit of hobble in my step. I'd barely mastered stilettos even after lessons from Claire, but running was well outside my skill set.

When he led me to a tiny room with a fireplace and four high-backed chairs, I was grateful I'd have a minute to compose myself with no prying eyes.

"Mister van Dijk." He stressed the last name, pronouncing it like Deek. "He will be with you shortly."

Of course, I'd pronounced the unfamiliar name like "dick," as in the kind I'd probably have to suck in a few hours.

I was alternating between self-flagellation for not looking up the proper way to say the name, and swatting away something tickling the back of my neck, when I turned around.

Was that a mane?

Motherfucker. Was the fur seat I'd been sitting on skin from a damned horse? I stood and jumped away from the chair. It *was* a mane. And not a horse's mane, either. It was a motherfucking zebra. The three chairs were upholstered in zebra fur, fringey mane and all.

Men thought everything that wasn't nailed down was theirs to possess. Land, property, women, animals.

Disgusted at the chair, at myself for what I was about to do, I was eyeing the window seat when the door opened. So much for artfully draping myself like a buffet. I'd failed at Henri's number two lesson: presentation is everything.

"Daniel," an older man said as he strode toward me with more confidence in his gait than I had in my little finger.

"Hi...hello." I was flustered at being caught standing. This was not the way a Julie was supposed to act.

Daniel extended his hand and I shook it. His grip was warm and sure. I looked up at him. He was tall, thin, and, well...old. Not grandpa old, or assisted-living old, but north of fifty. His dark-blond hair was thick and artfully combed. His coat was camel, his scarf Burberry, and not in a super-obvious plaid way.

Coming back to myself, and remembering my Julie training, I walked behind him.

"Let me take your coat." I found a sturdy wood hanger and deposited the coat and scarf on them carefully taking in the scent of expensive cologne that wafted out.

He went to the hearth and warmed his fingers before the roaring fire.

"I love this inn. The restaurant is great, but I hate these chairs. It's like someone went on safari and didn't understand that you can't kill everything in Africa."

In spite of myself, I laughed. "Oh God, I was just thinking the same thing. It's like sitting on a lion or tiger or bear. Oh my!"

Daniel's eyes met mine as he laughed spontaneously. His smile reached his eyes, and I took comfort in dodging a psychopath tonight.

"Very clever. I do like a clever girl. You didn't tell me your name."

"Bella."

"Bella..."

I let the long pause hang there for a moment.

"Bella Ruse."

"Not your real name, but still clever. We'll find out more about you later. How about we have some dinner? I hope you're a girl who eats."

"My mama's Italian. Of course I eat."

"Excellent."

I wasn't sure if he'd pressed some hidden bell, but the moment I came to stand next to him, the door opened and the maître d' was standing there, menus in hand. Gone was his attitude. Daniel rated a warm smile.

"Mr. van Dijk, your table is ready."

"Very good."

The table was small and round, and rather than placing the chairs across, they were situated next to each other. Had he called ahead for this particular setup? It seemed like it would be a little too intimate for a business meeting.

I sank into the chair the maître d' had pulled out, grateful only the top half of my dress was showing. Every other woman here was dressed in navy or cream and dripping in pearls, no matter her age.

Daniel spoke and I turned back to him. Julie lessons were harder to put into practice than I'd thought. Listen to them as if they are the most fascinating person in the world, Henri had said. There's nothing sexier than a woman who hears her man.

"You like Italian food then?"

And Chinese, I almost blurted, then stopped myself. Sitting up taller, I said, "I enjoy almost anything that's well prepared. What do you recommend from the menu?"

Daniel eyed me, his blue eyes sharp, then he slipped reading glasses from a slim leather case and surveyed the choices.

"It's a seasonal menu. I haven't been in the States for a few months."

I watched him scanning the menu, proud I'd been able to follow one Julie rule at least. Men—I'd been schooled—liked to be in charge, make all the choices. They said they liked an independent woman, one who knew her own mind, but there was a wide gap between what they said and what they truly believed, I'd learned.

Nine times out of ten, Henri had told me, men, when given the choice, would happily make all the decisions.

A waiter in an impeccable black suit materialized at Daniel's elbow.

"Mr. van Dijk."

"My date, Bella, and I will have Chef prepare a tasting menu."

A second waiter appeared, scooped the menus from the table and filled goblets with sparkling water. A curl of lime zest twirled along the bottom like a mini cyclone.

"Where are you in school?" Daniel asked.

A moment later, the waiter materialized again.

"Morel with crispy pancetta and quail egg in puff pastry," he announced before I could answer. I was grateful for the moment to think. Henri's first and most important rule for Julies—safety. We were allowed to share as much or as little as we wanted. Though the way Henri had said it, I took away that less was more.

"I'm at Owen," I revealed. Twelve thousand students should be enough of a shield.

"Graduates some civic-minded people."

"What do you do? Henri mentioned something about staffing. Is that like human resources?"

"That's one way of putting it."

"Then how would *you* put it?"

"Have you heard of Dyken Staffing?"

"Sure. Don't you have a little office in town? There are men standing in line outside in the morning sometimes."

"Probably a temporary staffing location."

"You have more than one?"

"About four thousand."

"Of those offices. Amazing. Just temp work, like stepping in for sick people or women on maternity leave?"

"That, and finding people jobs at all levels, from sectary to headhunting for C suites."

"C suites?"

"Corporate levels. CEO, CFO, COO."

"How'd you start in this industry?"

"It was my dad's company."

"Dijk. Dyken. Of course, right." Julies were supposed to be high end, cream of the crop, intelligent and worldly. I sounded like a bumpkin from the back country.

"Bella, don't beat yourself up. You're young. You don't know what you don't know until you know it. That's the way it works for everyone. You learn. You add it to what you know. You grow up."

"I'm so bad at this. You should call Henri back. I'm sure

you want to be with someone more mature. With...God, a real woman. I'm so stupid to have thought—"

"Trio of Hudson Valley duck foie gras, terrine, truffled mousse, seared foie gras with an artichoke heart salad," the waiter interrupted.

The artfully sparse plates appeared before us.

I leaned forward. "I don't even know what half this stuff is."

Daniel's hand flew up. "Sazerac for the lady."

A cut-crystal glass appeared in minutes, a long peel of lemon curled through the amber liquid and over the side of the glass.

"What's this?"

"Drink it."

I gulped it down in two big swallows. Bittersweet warmth slipped down my throat and hit my belly. Calm followed.

"Feel better?"

"A lot. Actually. Thanks."

"C'mon. Stay. I can't wait to get to know you better. I think we're going to get along just fine."

Another Sazerac in and I stopped being self-conscious. I learned all about Russian Osetra caviar, and crab-filled cannelloni that would probably have given Mama a heart attack for its twist on an Italian favorite. The Maine lobster was great, the sweetbreads were better than expected. Following Henri's instructions, I took a taste of everything, but didn't indulge like I may have if Daniel wasn't with me. No man wanted a woman too full of dinner to enjoy what may come later.

"Shall we retire to my suite?" Daniel said. "They're happy to bring us a dessert sampler."

This was the moment of truth. We were not obligated to continue any "date" past dinner or coffee or whatever constituted the public portion of the evening. The pay, however, was commiserate with performance.

"If you'll excuse me for a moment," I said. Trying to muster the grace I'd learned from the mandatory ballet classes all those years ago, I stood and made sure to keep my footing as I wound my way to the powder room.

I nodded to the attendant, then locked myself in the first open stall. I put the toilet lid down, sat, and hung my head between my knees so I didn't hyperventilate.

I could do this. Men were all the same, right? It wasn't like I was a virgin. That ship had sailed years ago.

The gnawing feeling in my stomach was there reminding me of the past. I pushed it away. Even if some small part of me still yearned for Jake, it wasn't meant to be. The whole Wu clan was toxic, and I was far better off away from them, even if it meant I was going to be broke for the rest of my life, having to do things like this to put food on my table and an education in my head.

My heart calmed and I lifted my head. I was strong. I could do anything.

As if I were in pearls and silk, I strode back through the dining room. I scanned the tables, not spotting ours.

"Ms. Ruse? Bella Ruse?" a waiter said, pronouncing my name like the country.

"Yes."

"Mr. van Dijk wanted you to have this." He handed me a

creamy white envelope. Finally finding our table, I sat. Cleared, save for my purse, I took a moment to gather my wits. With my fingernail, I slit the paper along the top fold.

Dear Bella, it began, *You were a most enjoyable dinner companion. Where the night goes after this is up to you. I'd like you to join me for dessert in my room, 218. If you choose to return to school tonight, I understand.*

I peered inside the envelope and found thirty crisp one-hundred-dollar bills. He'd paid me the agreed-upon amount. The full amount. I could take the money, pay my February tuition bill and go home. No strings attached.

I tucked the envelope in my purse, stood and gathered my coat.

Five minutes later, I rapped on the door numbered 218 before I lost my nerve.

Gone was the expensive suit. Instead, Daniel had on a navy velour robe and what were probably pajamas peeking from underneath, the kind men wore on Nick at Night shows.

"Bella, I'd hoped to see you. This is a nice turn of events." He opened the door wide, an invitation to step in.

I took it. Heard, rather than saw him close it behind me. "My name is Isabella. Isabella Aconi. I'm a sophomore at Owen," I blurted as I walked a few steps into the sumptuous suite.

While he used two hands to lift my coat from my shoulders and hang it in a small closet, he rolled my name across his tongue almost silently, his slight accent adding gravel to the Italian words. I stood unmoving. My heart pounded hard in my ears, blocking out almost all sound, so I was surprised to see Daniel step around me to open the door.

A bellman appeared, hands pushing a large linen-covered cart. With a flourish, a dessert tray was slipped on the dining room table. Then we were alone again. Still, I waited for Daniel to say something. He walked to the mahogany table, flanked by no less than eight chairs, and lifted a silver lid from a tray filled with at least a half dozen different sweet treats. Finally, he spoke.

"Do you like ice cream?"

"Sometimes. Why?"

"Half the desserts on the menu are ice cream. It has always perplexed me. But if you want Bing cherry, chocolate, vanilla bean ice cream, or this trio of sorbet, then you should pick now."

"What are the other options?"

"I like a girl who wants to know all the options. Speaks of emotional maturity sometimes lacking in your generation. Chocolate soufflé, lemon custard tart, and a napoleon in puff pastry."

"What's your choice, Daniel?"

"Ladies first. It's my philosophy in more than dessert."

I glanced from the food tray and saw a telltale twinkle in his eye. Grateful that I wasn't one to blush easily, I swallowed and turned back to the food.

"Lemon," I said.

"Good choice." He handed me a plate, and using the heavy sterling silver cake server, slipped the delectable-looking dessert onto the heavy china. "I love chocolate." He helped himself to the soufflé and a scoop of vanilla ice cream.

"Do you mind?" I pointed to my shoes.

"Please get comfortable."

I took off the shoes, relieving my numb toes, then tucked my legs under me on of the plush leather dining room chairs.

The lemon was heavenly, tart and silky smooth. Reminded me a bit of the tarts Mr. Wu liked. That he'd tasted in Hong Kong but wanted in Toms River. Mama'd worked for months to get those just right.

"Where'd you go, Bella?"

"Nowhere, Daniel. I'm here in Greenwich. Where did you grow up?"

"Gronsveld. It's near Maastricht on the Belgian border."

"Is it nice?"

"Most beautiful place on earth."

"Do you live there now?"

"No, my business is headquartered in Utrecht. My parents are still rattling around the place, though I think they're going to try southern Portugal soon."

Just when I thought I'd won the fight to keep my face neutral, my dessert fork clattered to the table.

"I'm not *that* old, Bella," he said, as if he could read my mind. "My parents had me just after my dad came back from the war. The greatest generation, you call them here."

"Cool. Where did you go to college?"

"One day, dear Bella, I'll tell you all about my life and you'll tell me all about yours. Tonight, though, is not about that. I want us to get to know each other better...in a more carnal sense."

At the word carnal, a shiver ran through my body. The previous few hours had only been prologue.

Daniel lifted my hand, gripping it in his. I let him lead me from heaps of melted ice cream to the bedroom door. He opened it. The room was wallpapered in deep blue. A mahogany sleigh bed dominated the room.

"Why don't you freshen up in there." He pointed to a bathroom door.

I grabbed at the opportunity with both hands and fled to the white-and-blue-tiled room. A robe that complemented his, gold where his was blue, hung on a towel bar. Careful not to snag or tear the only clothes I had to wear home, I lifted the dress over my head. The full-length mirror reflected back to me, my flesh-toned lacy push-up bra and thong-back bikini panties. I'd keep those on. Older men grew up on porn that came in magazines, not videos that left nothing to the imagination.

I added a layer of mascara and slicked colored gloss on my lips. Breathing deep, I opened the door again. It was now or never. Now, I needed money so I could finish Owen. So I'd never have to rely on anyone ever again.

"Sit." I followed Daniel's outstretched hand and took the invitation to lower myself to the long bench that sat just beyond the footboard. He came around and knelt before me. He took my naked foot in his hand and massaged the arch. I closed my eyes and leaned against the curved wood of the footboard.

"I love the way those shoes make your legs look, but they'll kill you in the long run."

His hands were merciless. He finished with my left foot and picked up my right, kneading foot, ankle, and calf. He stood and the room was quiet. In a few seconds, I heard wood crackle and come to life under flames. Warmth from the fireplace quickly took the chill from the room.

Daniel came back to me and took my hands in his. He pulled gently and I stood. Even with my height, he dwarfed me, something that was unusual for me. I could look most men in the eye. For a second, I looked up. His eyes caught mine. They were full of lust, possession, and something else I couldn't identify.

Hastily, I looked away.

He let go of me and placed both hands on the ties of my bathrobe's belt. One tug and the robe fell open.

"You're amazingly beautiful, Bella."

"Isabella, please."

"Bella means beautiful in Latin, dear girl. There is no more appropriate word for you."

I closed my eyes as if in modesty. Behind my lids, I was trying to let his use of Jake's name for me be okay. I only wanted one person to call me Bella.

God, my obsession with Jake was stupid. If I were being honest with myself, something I didn't try to do too often, I knew I still yearned for Jake. Knew that it took everything in me not to drive up to Cambridge, drop on my knees, and beg him to be with me.

"Bella?" Daniel's inquisitive tone shook me from thoughts of Jake. I wouldn't let that happen a third time. Planting myself firmly in the present, I met his gaze.

"Daniel. Let me," I said. I reached for his belt and undid the knot at his waist. I pushed the heavy garment from his shoulders. His pajamas looked and felt like silk.

He pulled me into an embrace. I wouldn't have put it past

him to have popped a little blue pill, because his rock-hard cock pressed against my belly, heat traveling through silk, impaling my skin. Despite the warmth, I shivered.

Daniel pulled me tighter, one hand on the back of my head, the other holding my mostly naked bottom. His nose was buried in my hair and he took a deep breath.

"You smell amazing, dear girl. Now come lie down so I can make good on my promise."

"What was your promise?" I made my voice husky to mask the momentary panic bubbling up as I tried to remember what in the hell he'd promised me. It hadn't been a million dollars. I'd have remembered that. Or that he wanted to tie me up. I'd have remembered that, too.

"Ladies first."

"You don't—" I swallowed the too big dinner and too much dessert that threatened to come up. This...with Daniel...was too intimate. If it weren't for the cash, I'd trade this guy for any of the bartenders who didn't give a shit about anything more than using me as a human Fleshlight. My heart thudded so hard I was sure the bed was shaking under me. My shoulders inched up to my ears.

"I like nothing better than giving a woman pleasure," Daniel was saying. He'd said some other things I was sure, but I couldn't hear any of it through the blood rushing in my ears.

Breathe, I said to myself as I forced air from my lungs.

Tensing up was only going to make this worse. I emptied my head and forced myself to relax and let my head sink into the down pillow. This was the best scenario Henri had laid out, where the girl was the only thing on the menu.

I wished for a long moment that I'd asked for another drink or five back at dinner, or while I was forking down dessert. 'Cause I desperately needed courage, and the lowered inhibitions that come with a tray full of drinks.

He lowered himself to the bed, the swish of the silk pajamas the only sound in the too quiet room.

"Do you have music?" I asked.

"Yes, I forgot all about that. Of course." He rolled to the edge of the bed and fiddled with one of the four black plastic remote controllers that littered the bedside table. The haunting notes of a flute from Ravel's "Bolero" filled the room. The rhythmic beat of sticks on the skin of the drum calmed me, gave me something to focus on when Daniel, done fiddling with the room's electronics, rolled back over and kissed me.

Henri's last bit of advice floated through my mind. Fake it until you make it—or fake it until you fake it.

I wound my arms around his neck and kissed him back. After the first few awkward moments where we bumped noses, it worked. Daniel kissing me. He was a good kisser. Rather than awkward, I felt the first stirrings in my belly. The topsy-turvy, twisty feeling I always got when the sex was going to be better than average.

I lifted my leg and cradled Daniel's erection. For a moment, he pulled away and sucked in air sharply. It was old fashioned how turned-on he was without the posturing that young men thought was on the menu thanks to ubiquitous porn on the web.

"Bella..."

With unerring precision, he opened the clasp of my bra.

One moment he was looking at me reverently, and the next he'd wrapped a large hand around my right breast and had sucked my nipple into his warm, waiting mouth.

Electricity shot from my tit to my clit. The sensation was so unexpected, my body nearly shot right off the bed, coming back down with a soft thump on the duvet.

"That's it, Bella. You're a responsive one."

I didn't want to be a responsive one. I wanted to be the best actress ever. Academy-award worthy, even. There was no time for a faked response when Daniel's hand spanned my belly, making it quiver. I couldn't let out the fake moan I'd practiced when a real one tore from my throat as his hands pushed aside my panties and his fingers slipped between my folds.

"Oh God," slipped out.

"Tell me, beautiful Bella...tell me what I can do to make you feel good."

"I don't know."

"Every woman should know."

"I...it's never come up." That was the sad truth.

"Oh, dear girl. This should always come up."

"What do *you* like, Daniel? I'm here to please you." I pushed him so that he was flat on his back. One button at a time, I released him from the gold-piped navy pajama top.

I was about to grab the waist of the pants, but he grabbed my hand. Not hard, but enough that I knew he wasn't quite ready to go there. I didn't know what to make of it. Every other man I'd been with would have been happy with them and their cock being center stage, having a solo, and a big finale.

"What I like, Bella, is a woman who knows her own body. Tonight will be a lesson in Bella Ruse."

I got all shivery at that, my nipples pulling tight, goose-flesh prickling my skin, liquid pooling between my thighs.

In the seconds before Daniel leaned toward me again, I chastised myself for not honoring Henri's rule about staying in complete control. Daniel's mouth and hands were everywhere. Shivers turned to sighs, then screams I couldn't hold back.

Next time, I promised myself. *Next time, I'll keep control.*

Control was long gone by the time I'd come not once but twice, first from Daniel's tireless hands, second from his magical mouth. Control was an illusion when Daniel finally shed his bottoms and came to rest over me and fitted himself at my opening. I couldn't have exercised any control when he pounded into me in a way I wouldn't have known I liked, but loved from the first thrust to the last.

"You're an 'A' student, Bella," Daniel said, the moment he caught his breath.

"Excuse me," I replied, sliding from the bed and running to the adjoining bathroom.

I'd barely shut the door before I lost dinner and dessert in the very white toilet bowl.

I stood and looked at myself in the mirror. Smeared makeup and twisted underwear reflected back. My stomach went topsy-turvy again and I lifted the toilet seat just in time. This time I didn't bother standing after I'd flushed. Instead, I snatched off the offending lingerie and tossed it in a corner.

I was normally cold when I was naked, but I was warm now. Flushed with mortification.

I was a prostitute, a hooker, a lady of the evening. Mary Magdalene had nothing on me. I didn't know which was worse—what I'd done for money or that I'd enjoyed it.

Daniel was a skilled lover. Made the men who came before him seem like bumbling fools. All except for Jake, who I forgave because it had been our first time.

At the thought of my first love, I was back over the toilet bowl. This time it was only dry heaves, nothing more.

Daniel had done something Jake hadn't been able to do— give me pleasure during sex.

I flushed and stood. Ignoring my naked body—rubbed red where Daniel had kissed and sucked—I pulled the remaining robe from the hanger on the back of the door. I shut off the light to hide me from myself, then washed my face and brushed my teeth to the light of the moon.

CHAPTER 21

ELEVEN YEARS EARLIER

THE BUBBLE of good feelings I'd wrapped myself in popped when the waitress came around, lighter in hand, touching flame to wick on every table. Startled to look up and see that the sunlight that had poured through the windows when I'd come in was long gone, I stole a quick glance at the Tissot watch Daniel had bought me during a weekend in Geneva without once looking at the price.

It was almost nine in the evening. The lengthening day had tricked me into thinking it was much earlier in the afternoon. There weren't many rules Daniel had while I was staying with him here in Holland, but there was one—that I was home by eight.

My heart sped up, nearly stealing my breath.

It was late.

I was late.

I was *never* late. It was an unspoken rule. And I'd broken it.

Now what? The question pinged through my brain until the voice of my coffee date intruded.

"Don't tell me, lovely Isabella, you have to go?" Mathijs asked, his voice a rough purr.

The way he asked made me want to throw caution to the wind and stay. He was smart, and funny, and liked me—the me I'd let him see. His accent soft like the Flemish in this part of Holland. Like Daniel and so many men here, he was blond with blue eyes. But where Daniel was stoic, Germanic, Mathijs was different, kinder looking. I liked the softness that creased the corners of his eyes when he smiled. In the last couple of months, he'd been smiling at me a lot. I was sure I'd smiled when he'd finally asked me out.

"I'm late," I said, though I made no move to get up, get my coat, or the keys to my bike lock.

Going to class then going home to Daniel had been good enough. It's what I'd done through the warm late summer, the cold wet winter. With spring, life in the eight-bedroom, ten-bathroom manor had begun to feel claustrophobic. I hadn't yet decided if I was living in a castle where all my dreams could come true or just a really beautiful prison.

"Late for what? You're a student. There are no more classes until Tuesday. Monday is Koninginnedag."

Screw it. I was already going to have to face the music when I got back. Might as well stay. I scooted next to Mathijs and looked into his warm blue eyes, more the color of the Caribbean and less like Daniel's stormy blue gray.

"Koninginnedag," I repeated. The word was a mouthful, like all of Dutch. "The Queen's Day?" I was pretty sure of my translation, but still.

"You Americans aren't fans of royalty. Right?"

"It's not that." I took in the disbelieving set of his mouth. "Okay, it's that. It seems after a few wars, Europeans would have happily given up royalty. I mean, what's democratic or even mildly socialist about people having a birthright to wealth?"

"Are you against wealth? That watch on your wrist says you enjoy having money. You're a rich American abroad." He said it in a way that made me think he didn't admire wealth.

"Everyone thinks we're rich. I mean, some kids are. This watch was a Christmas gift from a friend while we were in Switzerland. Trust me. I'm not one of them. My mom is a housekeeper." Something about Mathijs brought out the honesty in me. I liked who I was with him. I wanted him to like the real me, not the rich dilettante I pretended to be ninety percent of the time.

"Really?" He seemed genuinely surprised. High school had been a great training ground. Maybe I was too good.

"The thing about America is that we believe everyone should get a chance, no matter how humble their beginnings. Mine were the humblest of all, but a school like Owen, it gives people like me a chance in life."

The speech was a little rehearsed, but I'd practiced it in my head for days to try to redeem some of the shitty behavior I'd displayed over the last few months. I'd swanned about like the Mafia princess of old, except in the class we shared. There, with Mathijs, I was me—more me—because I knew he wouldn't date that image I'd created.

Mathijs waved his hand and a waitress brought a round

of Belgian beers. "Got you the kriek. You seem to like it. I saw you order one a couple of weeks ago."

"Well we may have meritocracy instead of royalty in America, but you all beat us with beers," I joked.

I was all calm on the outside. Inside, I was squirming with happiness. He'd noticed little things about me in the same way I'd noticed that he liked a bit of honey in his coffee, and that he dipped the tip of his tongue in the foam of his beer when he thought no one was looking.

"Have you done the Heineken Experience?" he asked.

Finally.

We'd been playing around, circling each other for the last weeks. But like I'd been advised during orientation, I'd followed the rules of the culture. One that seemed progressive on the outside, but was really traditional at heart, and let him lead the chase, all the while making it so I could be caught.

"No. I skipped it during the first week." That bit was a lie. But a small white one. I was willing to see a brewery and taste beer again if it meant getting to know Mathijs better. "Is it worth it?" I asked, riding the line between cool girl and giddy teenager.

"I'm happy to take you tomorrow if you're interested."

"I think that would be a lot of fun. I'd love to." It was the truest thing I'd said in a long time. I nearly patted myself on the back. Here I was, sitting in a café, glimpsing at a normal future. I liked the look of it, the potential to end up somewhere different than I'd started. The true promise of Owen, realized.

"I can meet you," he offered. "Where are you staying? Host family, right?"

The house that was really a castle with just me and Daniel. I'd probably stretched the host family lie a little thin. Until I could find a way to explain Daniel, and God knows there was no way to really *explain* Daniel, I needed to skate over that one.

"You know what? I'm staying at someone's house a bit out of the way. Why don't I meet you at the Utrecht station? We can take a train in."

"Great. Maybe I can convince you to go to a Koninginnedag parade after the tour."

"Does the queen come out and wave to her subjects?" I lifted my eyebrow so that he knew I was being playful.

"She's one of the oldest monarchs in Europe. There will be that, of course. Even better though, there's food and beer."

"Cheese? Fries? Pancakes?" I was working my way up to liking the food here. My classmates seemed to like it. I missed Mama's cooking.

Banishing my mother from my mind, I put my elbow on the scarred wood and bumped shoulders with Mathijs. He smelled like the yummy European blocks of soap I saw in lots of stores. Like goat milk and olive and earthy essential oils.

"All the Dutch culture in fried foods?" His smile was self-effacing. "Sure. I even promise to get you fresh stroopwafels."

"Ooh, those sugary waffle things? Warm and gooey, they're the best."

"Nothing but the best for you. It'll be a grand day tomorrow."

I know it was crazy girl behavior, but I wondered if we'd

hold hands on the train, maybe share a sugary kiss over waffles.

I was about to slide my hand over into his lap when the café door opened, letting in streetlight and a cool breeze. I looked up. Froze.

Then snatched my hand back as if it had touched fire.

"Bella!"

With that one word, the fantasy of me and Mathijs evaporated like Dutch colonialism. It was Daniel, his face thunderous.

"Geez, is that your dad, or the dad of the family where you're staying?" Mathijs muttered. "Protective?"

"He's the head of my host family," I said. I omitted that it was a host family of one. "I've gotta go." I stood, jerking the table, sloshing beer.

"Tomorrow, then." Mathijs stood as well. The warmth from his jacket and heat from his body enveloped me as Daniel drew closer. Lust and desire and dread twisted into a ball of lead in my stomach, threatening eruption. Mathijs pulled back then offered his outstretched hand as he introduced himself.

"Mathijs Twilhaar."

Manners didn't allow Daniel to refuse.

"Daniel van Dijk." He took back his own hand sooner than I thought polite.

"I'm surprised to see you here," I said to Daniel, my tone conversational. I didn't know what in the hell else to say. All I wanted to do was diffuse the ticking time bomb that was Daniel.

"Figured you might have gotten sidetracked between

school and home. I came looking for you because you have to get up early tomorrow."

"Tomorrow? Mathijs invited me to the Heineken Experience. You always said I should go."

Too many times to count, Daniel had said I was young and that I should experience all the Netherlands had to offer a young college student.

For the first time, I was hearing the truth behind that message: choose me instead.

"You *should* go." Daniel's voice was equally as conversational. "I'm more than happy to take you. But tomorrow we're going on a private tour of the Keukenhof Gardens. The tickets and guide have already been booked."

I scrambled to integrate this new plan into my brain. Did Daniel really have plans? Up until this very moment, he'd always had his assistant share his travel itinerary and any planned excursions months in advance. Spontaneous was not an adjective I'd have used to describe him.

"The tulips are great this time of year," Mathijs said, helpfully. "I went with my family when I was a kid." Mathijs was bobbing his head good-naturedly. I wanted to pat the crown of his blond hair at his naiveté. He'd been bested by a corporate mogul who ate men like him for breakfast.

"They only bloom for a short time, so we have to go now." Daniel's tone had gone from strident to friendly, now that he had Mathijs' tacit acceptance of our so-called urgent plans.

"Sorry, Mathijs. Another time," I said. What I didn't say is that there would never be another time. I'd confused what Daniel had said for the truth. That he'd bought and paid for me and he didn't share.

"Another time, beautiful Isabella." He leaned in and kissed me softly on the lips. I tried to keep my body still, but I was sure the little vibrations of arousal rippling through me were as plain as the nose on my face.

"Excuse us," Daniel said. At least I hoped that's what he'd said, because he'd spoken in Dutch and the words hadn't seemed all that nice.

"You didn't mention anything about tulips," I said on the short walk through the dark café and onto the cobbled street. I could barely keep up with Daniel as he strode ahead of me, his steps brisk. Through the bustle in the busy square, I could see the waiting limo. Daniel's driver, who I thought must have had some kind of psychic powers, was already up and out of his seat. He stood at the ready, his fingers grasping the back-door handle.

"My bike—"

"In the trunk."

Objections thwarted, I had no choice but to slide onto the plush leather back seat.

What would have been a pleasant twenty-minute bike ride home was scarcely ten minutes in the hulking car.

"We have to talk." Daniel had barely gotten through the front door before he made the pronouncement.

"In the hall?" I was being bratty, but so be it. If he was going to treat me like a child who couldn't make her own decisions, I was going to act like one.

"Not here, Isabella. How about my study?"

"Here" was a huge entrance hall where our voices echoed off the black and white floor tiles that were probably older than all of the United States of America. "Here" was Daniel's childhood home, which was more castle or manor than the suburban ranch house I'd imagined. "Here" was where the servants could hear, though they probably knew everything there was to know anyway. Daniel paid them well for their discretion.

"I'm thirsty. I think the kitchen would be better." Without looking behind me, I stalked toward Cook's domain, where the balance of power would be, if not even, a little bit tilted in my direction.

Daniel's study is where we discussed things like money and negotiated the ins and outs of our bedroom encounters. I didn't want to contaminate my feelings for Mathijs with all that. The kitchen was by far my favorite room in the house anyway.

When the cook was off, like today, I'd light the fire in the hearth. Lay out my books on the farmhouse table and relax. The room held no expectation. Not like Daniel's study or his bedroom, where I had to answer or perform on command.

The room was L-shaped, with the same black and white tile floors as the entry, just on the other side of the wall. Taking my time, prolonging whatever was coming, I lit the fire, then stood in front of it as it took the chill from the room.

I'd never understand the Dutch. They had radiators everywhere, but seemed to loathe to turn them on, instead bundling up in sweaters and gloves like they were living in Camden with no money for natural gas.

I went to the huge modern fridge and got myself one of the tall blackberry sodas I'd come to love. I drank it down in a few gulps, knowing it was going to land on top of coffee and beer and would probably make me feel like crap, but not caring anymore.

The slap of leather on tile let me know I wasn't alone.

"Do you want something?" I finally turned and looked at Daniel. He was casual today, in a crisp navy-and-white-checked button-down shirt and dark slacks.

"Tonic water."

I found another tall glass and poured him the bitter drink. Tonic was an acquired taste, which I hadn't yet learned to appreciate.

"Are you enjoying your time here, Bella?" Daniel asked after a few sips and a long pause, during which he agitated his glass, looking at the liquid swirl around as he moved his hand in small circles.

"What do you mean? Of course I'm enjoying my time. It's my junior year abroad. The classes are great, and it's beautiful in the Netherlands." All that was true, even though we probably both knew I wasn't really answering the question.

"Why then were you going to go out with that boy?"

"Mathijs?"

Daniel nodded, his eyes squinty, as if I'd mentioned the local neo-Nazi instead of a college kid. I was quiet a long minute as I tried to think of how to frame it.

"I thought it would be fun to hang out with someone who shared the same interests as me. We're in Comparative Analysis of Global News Coverage together."

"We talk, right? Just last week, I was telling you about the difficulties of entering the markets in former Communist countries."

"That was interesting—"

"Don't humor me, Bella."

"I'm not humoring you, Daniel. It was interesting, what we talked about. And the class is interesting. Mathijs is a nice guy. That's all there is to it."

"What is this between you and me, Bella? What are we doing?"

"What do you mean? You pay Henri some ridiculous amount. She pays me a percentage of that. And I live here with you. Available according to the agreement we set out last summer. God knows where you got a lawyer to draw that one up." The fact that some anonymous attorney somewhere knew I had sex for money shamed me more than the agreement itself.

"So that's all this is? A boss-employee relationship?" Daniel banged his glass on the long farmhouse table. Liquid sloshed on its highly polished surface.

I retrieved a towel hanging on the oven door and blotted the liquid before it made one of those ghosting stains. Tossing the towel, I sat heavily at the far end of the table. In my heart, I'd known this was coming. Except for those moments in his study where we discussed business, Daniel acted like we were man and wife, or at least partners. I'd gone along because it had been the path of least resistance...until now.

My sigh was deep and long.

"What this *is*, Daniel, is The Girlfriend Experience. Some call it compensated dating. Sugar Daddy, Sugar Baby. High-end escort. World's oldest profession. There are probably a thousand more euphemisms, Daniel, but we both know what's going on here."

Wearily, as if feeling every one of his sixty-plus years, Daniel took a seat in a padded leather armchair at the head of the table that was probably older than him and me combined.

"This is more than that, Bella. A lot more. I love you, dear girl. I'm wildly, passionately in love with you."

Of all the things in the world I'd expected to come out of Daniel's mouth, "I love you" wasn't one of them.

It was clear though that it was true. One hundred percent crystal clear. If I had been paying attention, I'd have seen it in the way he tried to give me whatever I wanted, in how he had Cook make all my favorite meals, stocked the house with my favorite foods, bought me gifts, pleasured me in bed.

I closed my eyes for a long moment.

I didn't love him back.

I wasn't sure I ever *could* love him back. I'd used up all my love with Jake. Even with all the years between us now, I hadn't gotten it back, the ability to fall, to love with abandon.

"That's against the rules," I whispered instead of confessing.

"What rules? Whose rule?"

"The rules for this kind of thing. What we're doing. It's not *Pretty Woman*. I have no expectation that you're going to climb up my trellis or fire escape or whatever and hand me some ten-carat ring and ask me to marry you, or that we're going to live happily ever after. Fairy tales are for other people. We're both more practical than that. Right?"

He was a CEO. That had to be the very definition of unsentimental.

"Wrong, Bella. You're young and naïve and plain wrong. Love comes along once, maybe twice in a lifetime."

Silently, I agreed with him. It had come once for me, and was long gone.

"We're not lovers, Daniel. You know what kind of relationship we have. Why are you trying to make it something it's not?" I pushed back because I didn't want his love, didn't deserve it.

"It's different for me, Bella. Where are we not compatible? We laugh at those TV shows you like. We can talk about almost anything, from economics to politics to all those social issues you're so passionate about. We're good in bed together."

It was all true and not true at the same time. I worked hard to keep up with current events. When he was traveling, I read the *Economist*, *Wall Street Journal*, and even the pink-hued *Financial Times*. I was as real in bed as I could be. He was a skillful lover who worked tirelessly to pleasure me each and every time we were together. I *was* probably naïve and stupid to believe that there was more, that sex would be transcendent with someone I loved.

But I did believe it, held out hope that something like that could be in my future.

Anger ripped through me. He was the one breaking the rules now. Feelings, having them and sharing them, had been as much off-limits as my dating.

"Seriously?" I lashed back. "I can't believe this. You were the one with all the signed agreements and lists and duties and boundaries. Now you're the one crossing the line."

"Then I'll take the money out of it."

Daniel's calm infuriated me. I had to stop myself from shaking before I could answer.

"What do you mean now?"

Was this it? The end? Would I have to suck it up and sleep with a dozen different men to get my last year paid? The thought made my skin crawl. I'd been able to stay with Daniel because our relationship had an expiration date: my graduation from Owen.

Daniel rose and retrieved a bottle from the stash the cook kept on the back of the black granite counters. To his tonic, he added a substantial amount of Dutch gin. The faint smell of pine wafted my way.

After a long sip, he asked, "Why are you doing this? Living with me? Doing this job?" He said the word job as if it were the most distasteful in the world. Shame at the truth of it washed over me. Most days I could compartmentalize, but he was ripping down the walls.

"You know why. I need to pay for Owen. This is the only way I can pay for Owen."

Daniel stalked from the room, returning moments later with his sleek laptop, the color of the cobalt tiles below our feet.

"Do you have a bank account?"

"At Olde Haven Community Bank." I didn't mention the bank account probably had less than a thousand US dollars in it. Everything Henri paid to me, I turned right over to the bursar the moment it hit my account. It wasn't even in the bank long enough to earn any interest.

"Do you have a...damn, what do you Americans call it...a checkbook?"

Robotically, I retrieved it from the leather book bag he'd bought, his first gift to me, and handed it to him.

Daniel looked at it for a moment, then typed, the hundreds of keystrokes the only sound in the kitchen other than the crackling of the fire in the hearth.

"There. It's done." He slid the slim leather case back toward me, slammed the laptop shut and pushing it across the table.

"What's done?"

"I've transferred forty-five thousand US dollars to your account. That should cover tuition, books, fees, whatever you need."

"Why—"

"You're free. I don't want you to be with me if it's only about money. I want you to be here because you *want* to be."

"Why, Daniel? Why are you doing this. Everything was fine between us."

"I was pretending. It wasn't fine. It *isn't* fine. It hasn't been fine for months. Being with you is like living with a closed door. Tells you you're welcome to come in, while still shutting you out."

My brain hurt. Even though that was probably a bad translation of some Dutch saying, the message was loud and clear.

"Shutting you out? I live with you. You have access to my time, my body..."

"That is not enough. I want access to your heart, too."

My head was spinning. I couldn't make heads nor tails of what had happened here. One minute I was laughing with Mathijs—acting my age—and the next minute I was getting declarations of love and devotion and money from Daniel. All sixty-two years of Daniel.

If he wanted love, did that mean marriage, kids? He was practically at retirement or death or both.

He rose, ending the discussion.

"I'm going to bed, Bella. You can stay or you can go. But don't do it for the money. Do it because there's a chance for you and me."

"Daniel..."

I don't know why I called him back. Why I didn't let him go.

When he turned, I reached out, touching first his shoulder, then sliding my hand down his arm, finally capturing his hand in mine. I slipped my fingers between his. The contact, his warm palm against mine, was oddly reassuring that nothing was wrong. That things could go on just as they had been.

It was so wrong, but I leaned in close, kissing him along his jaw in a way I knew he liked. The sigh that escaped him preceded the relief I could feel when his jaw went slack and the tension left his shoulders and hands.

He relaxed into me, his large body bumping mine back against the table. We stood like that for five, maybe ten seconds before I gave in. Before I kissed him, slanting my mouth across his until he gasped, his arousal nearly instantaneous.

"It's not Sunday, Bella," Daniel managed.

Normally a statement like that would lead to a protracted mediation about substitute days.

"It doesn't matter today. For once, can we not make this a lesson in negotiation?"

"Such sweet words, my beauty."

I placed my fingers to his lips. Talking wasn't going to make anything better. I pulled at his tie and he came forward, tipping us so that I was lying on the table. He didn't hesitate to push the painted silk dress above my hips. Navy lace underwear slipped off, leaving me bare. Daniel slipped his tie through his collar. It probably joined my panties somewhere on the kitchen floor. He spread my legs so they straddled the table. I'd never been so exposed.

"You look beautiful in firelight. I have to..."

Then he did. Put his head between my thighs and used his lips, tongue, and fingers so expertly that it wasn't more than a few minutes before I was moaning his name into the cavernous room, not giving a care about which servants may have heard me.

My bones were jelly, but I lifted up to my elbows anyway. I made quick work of Daniel's belt and zipper. The slacks fell to the floor in a whisper. I lifted the dress up and over, unclipped my own bra. In seconds, Daniel fell upon me like a starving man. His hands and mouth were everywhere, my face, my breasts, my belly, before he impaled me.

The coil of arousal twisted tighter. I scraped my nails along his back, seeking relief. He pulled my legs up and over his shoulders, bringing me to the edge of the table. One minute my mind was whirling with the consequences of what I was doing, the next it was soaked in pleasure and unable to form a coherent thought.

Without any more words, Daniel came, then pulled out. He retreated to somewhere in the house, his study or his room. I don't know. I wouldn't venture close to either door.

Instead, I put myself back together as best I could and for

a long time, nursed some of the Dutch gin Daniel hadn't finished. Eventually, I went up to my own room in my wing of Daniel's small castle.

I opened the wardrobe and looked at the brown designer bags on the top shelf. I didn't pack a single item. I wasn't going anywhere.

CHAPTER 22

SEVEN YEARS EARLIER

JULIUS, the doorman, rushed from his post and sheltered me with his oversized black umbrella.

"You okay, Ms. Aconi?"

"No one ever died from a little sleet, Julius. I'm good."

I looked down at my once-black suede boots. People didn't die from precipitation, but these shoes had. What in the hell had I been thinking? The leather was white from salt stains around the toes. I looked up at the Philadelphia sky and cursed the God who had rained down on my head.

The weather forecaster who worked across the hall at WCBT had promised me it was going to be a clear, sunny day. All those satellites and Doppler and maps hadn't worked worth a damn. I'd trudged home the remaining few blocks after the stinging rain had started. Maybe I should have just taken the Broad Street Line, or worn different boots, or maybe started the day differently.

Julius' "Going up?" shook me from my thoughts—thank goodness. I'd been second-guessing myself and my choices for the last few months. What happened with the Wus or my mother's family all those years ago wasn't my fault. The relationship with Daniel, though, that was all me.

"Let me get my mail and then I'm going up. Have to come back down in a few for the party in the bar."

"Right. You're having a special Ivy League thing. Good for you, Ms. Aconi."

"Also, Daniel will be in tonight or tomorrow morning. Please be sure to bring his bags up for him."

"He likes to do it himself."

"He's almost sixty-six. I just don't want him to hurt himself. If you can think of an excuse..."

"Gotcha, Ms. Aconi. My father's getting on up near that age. Don't want to retire from city sanitation. Nobody can tell him anything. My momma worries every day that he's going to break his back. Don't worry, I'll get him."

"Thanks for keeping an eye out," I said, mentally shaking off the comparison. Daniel was nothing like a father.

That indescribable feeling was in my body again. I wished I could dislodge it. That mix of hope, dread, expectation or some fourth thing I couldn't name was filling me up because Daniel was coming into town tonight. I'd gotten the message this morning in a succinct email from his assistant.

Of course, Daniel didn't take commercial jets, so I didn't have a time to pinpoint, get ready for. His pilot flew when Daniel was ready. Like everyone else who worked for him, I had to be ready when he was.

I hadn't canceled my plans for tonight though. It was a networking session of the Philadelphia Ivy League association. When the email had gone around about venues, I'd volunteered the huge bar in my building. I'd charged the private meeting fee to Daniel. The upside to my extended-stay apartment were the amenities, like the doorman Julius and the bar and restaurant on the premises. Until I found a job of my own and could pay for things like that myself, I planned to take advantage of every single one.

None of the women I'd met since Owen had a man like Daniel in their life. They all had a million roommates and were struggling with dating and relationships.

Daniel and I had a new agreement, one that excluded Henri. One that made me a Bella and not a Julie anymore. But one that came with all the strings for the apartment, the clothes, the job at WCBT.

"Oh, before I forget," Julius huffed. "There was something that came for you. Didn't fit in your mailbox."

While he fiddled around under the reception desk, I went to the bank of mailboxes. They were at maximum three-inch-by-three-inch brass with antique dials and decorative features. Probably as old as the beaux arts building itself. Cute, but nothing much fit in them. I pulled out some rolled-up neighborhood flyers, but there wasn't much else. All the bills went to Daniel.

Julius pressed number twelve once the elevator opened and handed me the large square envelope. My name in over-large script jumped out at me from the stark white stock.

"That there looks like a nice wedding invitation for you. When you come back down, use the private entrance to the bar with your keycard. No need to put your coat back on then."

"I'll do that, thanks."

Julius stepped back and the elevator door slid shut.

I looked at the return address on the envelope. Maryland. Holy crap. I wondered if it was what I thought it was. Too quickly, the elevator pinged and the door whispered open. I walked the few steps to my apartment and slipped my keycard against the door. Green lights flashed and I pushed my way in.

It was as quiet as a tomb and nearly as dark. I released my breath, grateful I'd have some time before Daniel came, that he wasn't here already. I needed time to shift gears from single girl to sugar baby. It was sometimes a rough transition. I didn't get to have migraines or bad period days. Ready, willing, and flawless is what Daniel expected...paid for.

Shaking off more water, I dropped everything on the floor, picking up and putting away items one at a time, making sure the apartment was as neat as a furniture showroom.

The event downstairs was scheduled to begin in ten minutes, but they could start without me. The anticipation of the mail was too much to save for later. I curled up on the couch, the heated room drying my dress quickly. I pulled the thick white envelope towards me and slipped my finger under a space in the flap.

My presence was requested at the wedding of Claire Harper.

Wow. My heart sped up in excitement and a bit of envy. Claire was getting married. Twenty-five seemed too young, but like me, Claire knew her own mind. Knew what she wanted in life. For her, that was a husband and a few kids in some Maryland suburb. For me, it was career success and independence I didn't yet have.

I stared at the calligraphy in disbelief. My college roommate was getting married. In my mind, I already saw the picture the two of us would take and submit to the alumni magazine. If the invitation was coming today, then she was having a spring wedding. I scanned the card to see where it was: indoors at some country club on the shore. Good.

I hopped up and scrounged the BlackBerry from my purse. I scrolled. There weren't any new messages from Daniel or his assistant. I closed messages and opened the calendar, not that my weekends were too full, but I couldn't go if it interfered with one of Daniel's visits, because bringing him with me was out of the question. I did not want to explain him to our former dorm mates.

Sitting on the armchair this time, I pulled the invitation across the coffee table, searching through all the elaborate writing, looking for the date.

"January fifteenth," it read.

Wait, that couldn't be right. I checked the BlackBerry.

Today was Friday the fourteenth. I was sure of it because I'd typed in the date for the teleprompter myself a few hours ago.

My heart sank.

I shook the stiff white envelope. An RSVP card fell out. No additional matching envelope. I turned it over, in case it was a postcard.

Instead of an address and postage stamp, Claire had scrawled a note on the back.

My fiancé, Leland Phelps, is from a very prominent family.

They know nothing about Julie or what happened while we were at Owen. I'll always love you, but have to cut ties with my past. Wish you luck with your life and career. Love, Claire. P.S. One piece of advice. You have to break away from Daniel. It was only after I quit Julie and Henri that I met Leland. I know that he'll be able to give me all that I need.

I dropped the card as if it were on fire.

I was her sordid past. One she didn't want to soil her life with. It was the same message I'd received from my mother's family when I came back to Philly.

Didn't Claire think that I wanted to be done with Daniel? Maybe if I'd had parents like hers, it would have been easier. But I didn't have anyone or anything to fall back on.

Resolved to be the architect of my future, I got up and went into the bathroom. I did the best I could with gel, slicking my damp hair back into a low ponytail. Claire's note had sapped my energy to repair the weather's damage and make myself perfect again. The houndstooth mini dress I'd worn to work would have to do.

I trudged to the bedroom and replaced my scarred boots with tights and ballet flats. Daniel liked me in fuck-me pumps at least three inches high, but I wanted to be comfortable for once. After I tucked the invitation back in the envelope and cleaned up any stray water, I shoved some business cards in my pocket and headed down to the bar.

I didn't get five feet through the back door before the activities chair, Priscilla Holland, accosted me.

"Call me Prissy," she started, before I could utter a single word. After air-kissing me, she said, "Isabella, so great to see you. Fab location you picked. The bartender even made a signature drink for the night. The Ivy, it's called. It's dark green. Isn't that fabulous?" She secured a green drink from a tray and handed it to me.

Fabulous, I thought, but kept my mocking tone to myself.

"What's in it?" I didn't need to be drunk while trying to network.

"Doesn't matter. It's good. Drink up."

I downed it in two gulps. Probably not what I was supposed to do with something that wasn't in a shot glass, but the sweet, tart drink was just what the doctor ordered.

"This *is* good."

I put down the empty glass and helped myself to another. Suddenly Claire's non-invitation didn't hurt so bad.

"You're from Toms River, right?"

That bit of Jersey history harshed my mellow quickly. I wished I'd never mentioned the place, but I'd been caught unaware by some stupid icebreaker during my first time joining one of the Ivy gatherings. When I was on my game, I told everyone I was from here, blotting out everything between then and now, minus Owen.

"By way of Philly," I said, hoping she'd forget about the Jersey Shore.

"You're from Philly? I never knew that. I thought it was all New Jersey for sure."

"I was born here. Lived on Pemberton Street until I was eleven."

"Wow. You have family here?"

My mind scrambled as I tried to think of a way to answer that question honestly. I'd been naïve about so many things, one being that my mother's family would welcome me with open arms now that I was back. But my attempted reunification with my grandmother and aunts had been anything but welcoming. I was the bastard child of a sinner. A single visit to that neighborhood had wiped away every single childhood fantasy of a joyful reunion, the kind that made my mom cry when she saw them on TV.

"No, not anymore." It was all but true. Family in name only wasn't family.

"Admit it, then. You're really a Jersey girl. You went to high school there and everything, right?" My new friend Prissy was like a dog with a bone. Since it was so important to her, I went full Jersey.

"Yup, I went to high school in Toms River, spent my summers getting my tan on at Ortley Beach. Why, you from there too?"

"Oh, no, I'm Pittsburgh all the way. There's a guy here I want you to meet. He's a few years ahead of you. Went to Harvard. He's getting an MBA at Wharton. I think you guys would hit it off."

Sighing out my relief that this wasn't going to be some awkward reunion where my past and present collided, I dropped my empty glass on the nearest tray. This was how it was done, networking. You met someone you had something in common with, and maybe the next time they had a job available or you were looking, maybe they'd think of you. The taste of freedom from a world influenced by Daniel propelled me forward.

"Lead the way," I urged.

In a moment, we were facing the backs of two men in

well-cut blazers. Daniel had schooled me on clothes, and I recognized expensive but not flashy when I saw it now, most of the time. I was still working hard on being on the sophisticated side of that line, but it was a daily challenge not to bring the bling. These two guys had probably never had that problem.

"Cole," Prissy snapped.

Cole turned around. His carefully crafted smile slipped a centimeter or two when recognition crossed his face.

The expensive clothes and haircut belonged to none other than Coleton Lehman, the cause of the most humiliating moment in my life.

Fuck. I should have known this wasn't going to work out. Me. Out here on my own, trying to make my way in the world. I wanted nothing more than to run upstairs and hide in the cocoon Daniel and I created whenever he was here. A world where no one existed except us.

"Isabella Aconi. She's an Owen grad. You guys know each other, by any chance?"

"He was in the class ahead of me—"

"For a hot minute. Went to Woodward Tillman." He turned around. "Hey, man, guess who's here? POTP."

The second dark suit and expensive haircut was none other than Jake Wu.

Immediately I regretted not blowing out my hair, freshening my makeup, and changing into the pencil skirt and white blouse I'd chosen this morning. I looked like the kind of girl her ex would be happy to be well rid of. I wasn't dressed to inspire regret.

"POTP?" Prissy questioned. "You're Jake," she asked,

squinting and bending her knees to read the name tag under the dim lights. Thrusting out her hand, she shook both of theirs. "Wellesley. Just a seven-sister school, but with the rule change, here I am! You both went to Harvard. Wow. Where are you from, Jake? Isabella and Cole are from Toms River."

"As a matter of fact, Jake was my next-door neighbor. POTP is 'pussy on the premises.' It's Cole's nickname for me, though maybe it should have been Jake's. Now if you'll excuse me..."

I turned on my heel and walked toward the back of the bar. I had my hand on the resident's exit when someone grabbed at my upper arm. I turned back. Prissy.

"I'm sorry about that! I hate it when they get all frat guy on us. It's why I went to a women's college. I got into Dartmouth and Princeton, but picked Wellesley instead so I could avoid guys like that. Anyway, I know you're looking to possibly transition into a new position. Give me your card and I'll keep an ear to the ground for you."

I fished out one of the cards I'd stuffed into my pocket, back when I was hopeful and determined, and handed it to her.

"Thanks. I'm going to go up, nonetheless." I never thought myself fragile, but the one-two punch of Claire and Jake had broken my spirit.

"I understand. I'll have no problem holding down the fort. Thanks for the venue."

"Anytime."

I made it from the back door to the elevator unmolested. After my keycard lit the green light, I pushed into my apartment. Unlike the last time, it wasn't empty.

"I wondered where you'd disappeared to, Bella."

Daniel turned from where he'd been staring at Rittenhouse Square through my panoramic living room window.

"I can't do this anymore." I let out my breath and kicked off my shoes. They fell haphazardly near the coffee table. Despite the tiniest frown that creased his brows, I didn't rush to get my flats and tuck them neatly in the closet.

"Do what, my beautiful Bella?"

"Us."

For the smallest second, Daniel's carefully crafted façade slipped. I'd only seen it happen once before, when he'd told me he loved me in the Gronsveld castle's kitchen. I was sure I'd never see it a third time.

"What has changed?"

"Nothing. Everything. I'm twenty-five and I don't have anything approaching a normal life."

"I saw that invitation on the table. You can't let what that naïve girl says get to you."

"It's not Claire." Though in a way, it *was* Claire. My roommate had been the final straw. I couldn't avoid reality much longer.

"That girl will learn that secrets always come out. I met Leland Phelps, Junior many years ago, when... It doesn't matter when. That man either already knows about Claire, or it's only a matter of time before he finds out, and tells his son Leland the Third, her fiancé. Then the whole thing will come unglued."

"You don't have to try to make me feel better." Although I'm not sure if that made me feel better that Claire couldn't hide, or worse because her life would be ruined because of narrow-minded men.

"I'm not." He must have seen my not-too-subtle change of expression, because his face softened. "I am. But I'm telling the truth about Phelps."

"The women I work with...they have roommates. They go to crappy restaurants and drink cheap wine."

"You Americans believe everything has to be hard, Bella. It doesn't though. There's no nobility in poverty. Nice people are rich *and* poor."

"Maybe there is something to achieving without a leg up." Daniel's castle popped into mind. "No offense." I lifted my hands in apology. Daniel worked hard, but the business had been inherited.

"None taken. That's the phrase, right?"

"Daniel. You do not need help with English or colloquialisms." Although he sometimes pretended he did to get a smile out of me.

A heavy knock sounded at the door. I checked my watch. It was nearly nine o'clock.

"You got the restaurant to send up something?" It was unusual, because the private jet was stocked with his favorites. But he was getting a sweet tooth as he got older, and only the cannoli I'd introduced him to from the Termini Brothers hit the spot after he'd landed from a long transatlantic flight.

Daniel was shaking his head as he stepped away from the windows. Without looking through the peephole or asking who it might be, I twisted the handle and pulled the heavy steel door open. They were one of the unoriginal elements in the historic building, but fire and burglar safe, Julius had assured me.

"Bella..." It was Jake Wu, the only other person in the world to call me by that name.

That awful moment—when all that was wrong with my world collided—was now.

I stepped back from the door. Jake stepped in, then took a half step back when he noticed I wasn't alone.

"I'm sorry, I didn't know—"

"Jake. Meet Daniel van Dijk," I said. "Daniel. This is Jake Wu."

In the most awkward slow motion ever, the two men who had mattered more to me than any others, except my father, shook hands.

"Jake Wu? The one from Toms River? The one your mom worked for?" Daniel asked me, his eyebrows creeping up his forehead.

I'd long ago abandoned Henri's rule of secrecy. With Daniel, confidences had come easily. I had never feared he'd turn into a stalker or use anything against me.

Except for his blind spot concerning the nature of our relationship, I didn't think he wished me anything but the best. He didn't think the Wu family was the least bit noble, and that kind of thing, treating people nicely, was fairly well ingrained in Daniel's DNA.

"Yes, Daniel. That Jake Wu. He was just downstairs at the bar. I left when his friend referred to me as 'pussy on the premises.'"

Daniel's face did something I'd never seen, turned nearly puce with anger. "And you have the audacity—"

"I'm here to apologize." Jake cut Daniel off. "I can't believe Cole said that. It's out of character—"

"Oh, for fuck's sake, that's the biggest lie you've probably ever told," I said.

"What are you talking about?" Jake tried to arrange his face into a mask of innocence. But without the long bangs covering his eyes, it was impossible for him to hide.

"Cole called me that during that spring at Woodward Tillman. I very distinctly remember all your friends laughing —and you not doing a single thing to defend my honor."

"You heard that?" His voice broke like it had when his voice had changed.

I wanted to believe that he was shocked, surprised, but after so much duplicity from everyone in Toms River, I wasn't sure any of them would know the truth if it smacked them in the face.

"I was in the bathroom. I'm not hard of hearing, though. I would have probably heard it from your room."

"I think an apology is in order." That last was from Daniel, who'd come closer and stood not two feet from us. Like when we were kids, I'd forgotten he was in the room. Jake had always had that effect on me. He and I were our own little universe.

"I *am* sorry, Bella. He's an ass. Always has been," Jake said.

"So were you for saying what you said. Then why are you hanging out with him?" Cole had gone from bully to friend. I didn't understand it one bit. Jake looked like he wanted to say more, maybe give a reason for what he'd said, but he was silent a long beat.

Finally he said, "We're working on a marketing project."

"That's why you're at a bar drinking and socializing? Because you're working on a project?"

"His dad's company designs and manufactures auto-safety systems. Dad thinks having him as a friend would be advantageous," Jake admitted.

"Advantageous. That's why he's still married to your mom, right? Because access to her family's money is advantageous. You Wus love to take *advantage*..."

"It's not—"

"Yes, it is exactly. I heard your apology, so if you'll excuse me..." If I had to excuse myself one more time, I was going to scream.

Jake lifted the messenger bag he'd dropped by the door and turned his back. His hand lingered on the handle before he turned back around and looked at Daniel and me more closely.

"Aren't you leaving too?" he asked Daniel.

"I am not."

A look of pure confusion screwed up his handsome features. How had he only gotten better looking in the last few years?

"Who are you again?"

"Daniel van Dijk."

"Bella?" Jake was looking for an explanation this time.

I wanted to tell him he was the last person I owed anything. I found myself stuttering out an answer for my former confidant anyway.

"Daniel is...Daniel is..." I'd never had to explain Daniel before. Claire knew. Hotel receptionists and restaurant hosts got it. Jake Wu lived in a completely different universe, where expensive homes, education, and clothes came easily. "My sugar daddy."

"Bella!" Daniel's reproof was sharp.

"Why sugarcoat it?" I locked eyes with Daniel. "You pay for my companionship. We may be friends, but that's the bottom line."

"Why?" Jake asked, his face still a mask of confusion and possibly hurt, though that was probably my own projection.

"Because," I said plainly. "Your father refused to pay for Owen. He said he would, then cut me off when I wouldn't do exactly as he said."

"My dad isn't like that," Jake protested.

"Feng Wu is *exactly* like that. The car, the phone, the clothes. All of it was extortion. He paid. I kept silent about, well...you know what about. When he broke his promise to leave your mother for mine, I broke my silence. I was young and stupid, I'll admit. But he hit back hard. Pulled the tuition blanket right out from under me. Just days past the financial aid deadline. I couldn't go home, so I did what I had to do."

"Prostitution." Jake spit out the word like I was a murderer instead of someone engaged in a victimless crime.

"Call it whatever you want, Jake. Your father made me the woman I am today."

"If you...I can't..."

"Pick your jaw up off the floor and go home, Jake."

"What does your mother think?" he retorted, not ready to end the argument. As if Maria Sofia Aconi held sway over me anymore.

"My very devout Catholic mother chose to stay with a

man who's married. She chose a man who won't let me back on his property. She doesn't get a say anymore. Maria Sofia Aconi made her choice, and I made mine."

Shaking his head in disgust, Jake opened my door and walked out. I slammed it behind him, happily shutting the door on my past once and for all.

I thought my feet would go out from under me, the exhaustion hit me so quickly. They did the minute the back of my knees hit the couch. Leaning my head back against the cushions, I closed my eyes.

I was wondering how much Jake would share with his dad, and in turn my mother, when I felt the cushions next to me sink down. The smell of Daniel's top-shelf cologne tickled my nose. I opened my eyes when Daniel took my cold hands in his.

"I've done this all wrong, Bella. Forgive me."

"There's nothing to—"

"There is. I...am a cad."

"A cad?" I sifted through my mind, landing on words I hadn't seen since my first-year literature classes at Owen. "You're not dastardly. You haven't treated me badly. Everything about us has been honest and above board." At this moment, I was eternally grateful that Daniel didn't pretend.

"Marry me, Bella."

CHAPTER 23

NOW

SQUID-INK PASTA APPEARED in front of me, and a seafood risotto was eased onto the other side of the table in front of Daniel. I'd tried hard to talk myself out of coming, but I'd failed this time like I had all of the others.

I looked around at the dozens of other diners in the cavernous space. How many of them were starting out, on the verge of breaking up, or somewhere in between? How many thought I was out with my father?

"Looks good." I complimented the food presentation, training myself to get back into the Daniel zone.

Years of practice made my smile look genuine and me at ease, though I was anything but. I'd promised myself while I was using a wire hanger to zip up the Dior dress I knew he'd love, and smoothing on his favorite shade of red lipstick, that tonight would be our last together. For real this time.

It had to be. My mind couldn't hold space for him anymore. It may have been selfish, but I needed to figure out what I wanted my life to look like going forward. Catering to the needs of a rich, elderly Dutch man didn't figure into it. I didn't know much, but that I was sure of.

At least, I'd been sure when I'd checked to make certain I had my keys and had closed the penthouse door behind me.

"Damn, Bella. It's loud in here. All this post-industrial design is just another way of saying that they don't have any sound control," he yelled from across the small reclaimed-wood table.

I did have to lean forward to hear anything more from Daniel. He was unhappy. It was my job to fix it.

When I'd suggested the Italian restaurant in a former factory space, I didn't ever think I'd be here with him. Like the rest of the people who worked for Daniel, I knew he liked perfection, or as near to it as any flawed human could get. In the past, I would have come here a week before our date, scoped it out, and made sure all accommodations were made for Daniel to feel comfortable.

"Excuse me a moment," I said and stood not waiting for his permission. I found the restaurant manager and pulled him aside. My—or rather, Daniel's—black American Express got us instant access to a private dining room.

I sat in one of four leather armchairs and waited. In minutes, the manager was escorting Daniel to the room. New plates of food and a pristine bottle of Vigneti Massa Timorasso appeared in the sommelier's hand. He uncorked it, we sipped, and he poured. The whole fix took under fifteen minutes.

It had been a hard-fought skill, working for Daniel. Hopefully I could use it to keep my job at CBT, or at least dazzle some hiring executive at another network.

"You were always a smart girl," Daniel said, happily ensconced in a leather armchair, a twin of mine, the room funeral-parlor silent.

"Your risotto?" I enquired after he'd had a bite or two.

"As perfect as you are beautiful."

The seemingly offhand compliment, given only to soften me, firmed my resolve instead. I lifted the flap of the new Christian Dior bag. It and my dress were the last gifts to myself on Daniel's dime.

I opened the leather, still heavy with new-product smell, and extracted the BlackBerry. I palmed it, rubbing my fingers over the smooth glass and plastic one last time. It was as familiar as an old shoe. Before I could second- or third-guess myself, I laid it face up on the scarred wood.

"I need to give this to you," I said, pushing the phone across the table.

Daniel looked up, a bit startled. "Is it time for a new one? Did Hendrika not get the dates right?"

I pushed my pasta aside. It looked beautiful, the squid ink turning the once yellow pasta a shade of midnight blue, plump peach shrimp in sharp contrast. I'd lost my appetite, though, when I realized what I'd have to do, what I'd needed to do years ago.

"Hendrika is not at fault here," I was quick to say. No way did I want Daniel's assistant to get into trouble. This woman and the last had worked for him tirelessly. What I was about to do was no fault of theirs.

"Why the phone, then?" Daniel's face was a mass of confusion among the slight wrinkles. He'd been just past middle age when I'd met him. Now he was firmly in the realm of the aged.

"We need to..." I faltered, just as I'd promised myself I wouldn't. I tried again. "I can't see you anymore."

"Oh, Bella. Every few years you do this. I know you're not going to marry me. I've settled on that, but there's no reason we can't remain friends."

"Daniel." When he put down his fork, I took his hands in mine. They were warm and strong, and surprisingly young looking. I still thought there was some magic serum the rich kept to themselves. Maybe if I'd walked down the aisle with Daniel, he'd have let me in on it. Now, I'd never know.

"Daniel, I need to be on my own now. I love that we've had the last twelve years together, but...I can't do this anymore. Live this double life. Two phones, two credit cards. Two separate lives. This month I turned thirty-three—"

"Is this because I didn't call on the first of April? We used to celebrate our birthdays together."

Daniel and I had been born forty years and one day apart. This had been the first year in a dozen we hadn't celebrated together. I'd assumed that he'd finally respected my boundaries.

"No, it's fine," I replied, vindication waning.

"I was in Vladivostok trying to hammer out a deal. I knew I'd see you here."

"Daniel. It's fine. It's better than fine, in fact. I think we're growing apart naturally." That last wasn't exactly true. But I sensed that he needed to be let down very gently.

"What are you saying?" He pushed his plate aside. A

waiter, concern pinching his model-perfect face, materialized and asked if everything was okay.

"Please bag everything and bring us a second bottle of wine," I said.

"Dessert?"

"Just a doggy bag and the wine, please. We have something important to discuss."

He brought and uncorked another bottle of wine. "You won't be disturbed," he promised.

I nodded my thanks. The tall glass door glided shut with a muted thud. Like it had been that first night in Connecticut, it was just the two of us. Except I was in Dior, not mall-rat chic. I had changed in more ways than one.

"Look at me, Daniel. You've done a wonderful job. I'm VP. I don't dress like a hooker anymore. I know how to make my way in the world. You raised me well. It's time I fly out on my own. I have to close the door on my past. Not to forget, but because I can't move forward if I let you do everything for me. I need to find out what I can do on my own."

"You Americans—"

"I know. We Americans like to do everything the hard way. Climb uphill both ways in a blinding snowstorm and all that. Maybe that's true for a lot of people. But this isn't about my culture, it's about me growing up."

For a long time, Daniel was silent. His hands lay on the roughhewn table. Diamond cuff links winked, reflecting the old-fashioned bulbs that were popular everywhere now. The death of incandescent bulbs having given rise to a certain nostalgia for dim yellow light everyone had hated until some government official had decided we couldn't have it anymore.

"I have a birthday present for you."

"I can't accept any more gifts, Daniel." In the last nights, when sleep was nowhere to be found, I'd catalogued all that he'd given me, or that I'd worked for, depending on perspective. The list was long. I'd gotten out of bed the last few mornings realizing I'd have none of it—the custom luxury car, the designer clothes, or the jewelry—without Daniel.

But without it, without that armor, I didn't know who in the hell I was.

"Let me give you this one final gift. It's my way of making sure you don't do the American thing too hard. To ensure you can do whatever you want, and not remain beholden to me or the Wu family."

The way he said it, as if he were some benevolent grandfather, set me to wondering if he'd known all along this day was going to come, that this day would be today.

"The Wu family. I left them years ago." I shook my head. The Wus—Jake Wu, specifically—had been the main thing chasing sleep away.

"I don't live in a hole in the ground, Bella. Just the opposite, in fact. I know that Woo Dyno-whatever-in-the-hell they call themselves now, bought CBT. Management at your building let me know too late for me to veto it that Jake Wu is renting the apartment next door, or across the hall or something. Your mother refuses to leave. I know how much that fact hurts you. I don't want the same for you."

Daniel reached down and lifted his briefcase onto another chair. He lifted the flap of the worn brown leather and extracted a thick Kraft paper file folder. The kind my Owen professors used to carry around.

"What's in the file?"

"It's my Bella file," he announced matter-of-factly, as if every john had a file for his escort. He extracted several pages with care. "Hendrika tells me this is the title to your vehicle. Your name and address are there as owner. This second is your bank account statement."

I took first the car title. I'd never seen one before, but if Daniel and Hendrika said the car was mine, I believed it was. My BMW was listed there, along with an impossibly long string of characters, the vehicle identification number. The rest of the embossed paper allowed me to transfer ownership to anyone else I wanted.

With trembling fingers, I slid the red-and-gold-colored bank papers over so I could read them. Before I could peruse them though, Daniel spoke again.

"I thought about giving you a check. But I've watched enough American television to know you could have ripped that up. So this is your latest statement."

I took a closer look. At the bottom of the fourth page of words and numbers was a balance that nearly had me falling out of my chair. I was grateful that sturdy leather-clad arms held me secure.

Daniel had added seven zeroes to my bank balance, or my new brokerage account balance. Turns out my bank has private banking and brokerage options I'd never been invited to partake in.

"What happened to flowers?" I teased.

"I was going to do that thing your mom's favorite talk show host did, give you a million. Then I had Hendrika print me a list of house prices in Los Angeles and New York and

London. You can't buy a garage for under four. There's enough for a house, and for you to live on while you decide what you really want to do."

"I can't accept this."

"You can ignore it. You can take it all out and burn it in the street. But you can't give it back."

"The services rendered were not this good."

"I regret that our relationship started out the way it did. But I don't regret meeting you one bit. You're a wonderful, smart, and beautiful woman. I'm glad to have known you."

"Are you dying?" I was only half-joking.

Daniel's smile turned to a chuckle, then full guffaw. "Yes, Bella, I'm dying."

"Oh my God! Are you okay? Is it cancer?" I wanted to run around the table and clutch at the man I'd wanted gone all of ten minutes before.

"No, I'm not dying of cancer. I'm dying of old age. If you're lucky, you will live another fifty or sixty years. That's not true for me. I have maybe twenty good years left, probably fewer. You always said I had enough money to spend in ten lifetimes." He pushed the bank documents a little closer. "Here's one lifetime for you."

"Jesus, Mary, and Joseph. That's the first joke you've ever told. Scared the hell out of me."

"You always said humor is all in the timing. How was mine?"

"Impeccable."

"Happy birthday, Bella."

CHAPTER 24

NOW

WHEN I WAS nineteen and sitting at Henri's knee, taking in her advice and warnings, if someone had asked me what I needed most, the answer would have been a million dollars. It had been so clear then. Tuition was due, I needed money to pay it. I had to graduate, get a job and live on my own. Simple problem, easy solution.

Now I had ten. The problems weren't so simple anymore or easily solved, though. It was more than Blue or Revival or CBT. It was more than home ownership or the title to my car. It was the fact that I hadn't made a single choice about my life in twenty years.

Or possibly, it was that I'd made a series of very shitty choices over the last twenty years. I looked over at the clock on my beside table. Twelve hours I'd been in bed, waiting for an epiphany, and I had nothing.

I'd never been one of those people with clear goals— become a doctor, become a lawyer, write a novel. I'd ping- ponged from avoiding one man, to running to others, then

Daniel stepped in and took over. If I wanted this life I had, or if I wanted another, I could not say. Either way, I had no idea where to start.

I got up and ran down the short flight of stairs to the living room. I needed to get out of my own head for a moment. How in the hell people did that meditation crap, I'll never know. Maybe meditation was for people with simple minds, that they could clear of thoughts. I needed pulse-pounding, loud music to obliterate them from mine.

I dialed up Stone Temple Pilots and "Plush" on the iPod. Plugged it in and turned it up to ten. In an hour—in an hour when the iPod had shuffled its way through *Core* and the album had run its course—then I'd get to the figuring-out-life part, but not before that.

It was a long ten minutes before the pounding fully registered. Damn. Was there another new tenant? Maybe Daniel had something. Maybe I should buy a house here in the City of Angels. All four walls would be mine. I wouldn't share them with anyone. If I blasted my stereo, no one would give a shit.

Finally turning the music down halfway, I undid the locks and pulled open the door.

Jake.

I'd nearly put the fact that he'd moved here out of my mind. Nearly.

"Yeah, yeah," I started, stepping away from the door. "I'll turn it down. Thinking about moving anyway. Don't think this place is my jam anymore."

"It's not the music."

"Then why are you here at...I don't know?" I looked

around wildly until I found the slim black hands and Roman numerals that made up the time. "Noon on a Sunday."

"I knew you were home. The music."

"Your office not working out?" I asked. I'd silenced complaints about the office shuffle by pointing out our department had direct access to the man who could save their jobs. Maybe, I'd pondered at our last meeting, Woo DynoMedia would be less likely to fire people whose faces they knew personally. The complaining stopped and Jake had moved in.

I personally hadn't seen much of him. I think he was probably using it as a base to spy on other departments more vulnerable than my own. Or I'd invited the fox to the henhouse and we were all going to be eaten in a matter of weeks. Either way, I'd let go of what I couldn't control.

"The office is fine, Bella," Jake said, bringing me back to the present.

"Isabella," I corrected him.

"You haven't said anything about us. Not since I—"

"There is no us," I retorted, my words automatic. I turned away for a long second, trying not to let his use of the word "us" make me yearn for something that could never be.

"There used to be," he insisted.

"In two thousand one." Seventeen years had passed. That was no small period of time.

"So—"

"Jake. You have to, I don't know, go. Home. Across the hall or New Jersey or even China. China would be good." China was on the other side of the earth. My heart could be safe if he was there.

"I'm not going back to China."

"Ever? Woo everything is there."

"I'm not going back today or tomorrow or until whatever this is between us is resolved."

Resolution. It was a strong word. Better than closure or forgiveness—the former I'd never get, and the latter I wasn't ready to give to myself, much less anyone else.

I decided right then I'd start with what I'd always wanted.

Jake.

It had always been him.

I reached around behind him and pushed the door closed. Without a word, I took his hand in mine. It was so familiar, and yet new at the same time. I led him up the short staircase and to the single door at the top of the landing. Pushed it open and propelled us to the biggest piece of furniture in the room, the mussed king-size bed.

"Bella?"

Without answering, I gently pushed him to sit. I remained standing. I kicked off my sneakers, pushing them under the bed with my toes. My pajama bottoms were next, the soft cotton pooled at my feet.

"What are you doing?" Jake made no move to leave, but his eyes were clouded with confusion.

"I've missed you. For seventeen years, I've missed you. I'm done with that. Missing you, that is. You're here. I'm here. Let's be on the same page for once."

I pulled off my tank. The air was cool against my naked breasts. I took a deep breath. Normally I'd feel exposed, or even unsure of how my body would be received. But not now. There wasn't anything to hide.

My panties were the last to go. I pushed the clothes into a corner of the room then came to the bed. Stood before him.

"This is me."

"I thought we'd have lunch or something. I wasn't asking for this, Bella," he stuttered out.

"We've eaten a thousand meals together, Jake. Chinese. Italian. You taught me how to use chopsticks. I don't want all the pretense of forks, knives, and cloth napkins. I only want us."

I could see him there in his gray button-down shirt and black slacks and his brain trying to wrap itself around nude me in my apartment. It was probably the last thing he'd expected when he pounded on my door.

I could practically see in the softening of his back when he relented. He bent, easing off one leather shoe, then the other. Black-and-blue-striped socks followed.

Touching his shoulder, I said, "Let me."

I knelt before him, me on the floor, him on the bed. I smoothed my fingers against his hair, across the sharp black sweep of his eyebrows, over the softness of his lids.

He closed his eyes, but I didn't stop my exploration. Touching him the way that I never could when all our meetings were clandestine stolen moments.

I resisted the urge to touch the rest of him. I'd save that for later. Instead I moved to the strong column of his throat and eased open the first button, then the next. The remaining five followed in quick succession. I spread the starched cotton, laying my hands against the black ribbed shirt underneath.

Jake shrugged his shoulders and I followed his cue, taking

off the shirt fully and laying it on the duvet folded at the foot of the bed. When my hands got close to the silver buckle at his waist, his breathing quickened.

Relief flooded through me. I wasn't alone. All the yearning and longing. It wasn't just me. For once, it didn't feel one-sided, me and him.

Leather unhooked from prong, slid through the metal with a soft chink. The snap, then zipper followed.

"You're going to have to stand."

I stood slowly, myself, then held out my hand. Without hesitation he grasped it, and with my other, I shoved the black wool from his slim hips. Next, I made short work of the undershirt and dropped it to the floor, no longer worried about keeping anything neat. It was all cotton and could be washed easily.

I didn't dare glance down. I wasn't as ready as I thought for that next. Instead, I looped my arms around his neck. Reflexively, or hopefully more deliberately, his arms came around my waist. Skin to skin for the first time in nearly twenty years. It was at once new and exciting and like a homecoming.

Air seeped from my lungs as I laid my head against his shoulder. I could have stayed like this, me against him, us swaying only slightly.

But the comfort of being in his arms slowly gave way to an awareness of another kind. His erection pressed against my belly, throbbing with a slow, steady pulse.

Heat shot through me. One moment gooseflesh had raised on my arm and now in the next, sweat prickled my skin.

Despite my experience with men, my hands shook with nerves as I unbraided my fingers and bracketed them on the sides of his face.

"Bella..." Jake whispered before he lowered his head, his lips meeting mine.

I thought I would go up in flames from that first contact. It was like the bus or the shed all over again, but without the worry of discovery. We were adults now, free to take pleasure where we could find it. I wanted that, the pleasure without the guilt, without the recriminations, without the second-guessing.

I could have lived in that kiss forever. His lips were soft but sure, his tongue a tool of both exploration and pleasure. Slowly, never coming apart, we sank down into the fluffy down of my comforter. Reluctantly, I pulled away. I wanted to see him in the light of day.

My God. I sucked in then hissed out my breath. He was as beautiful as I remembered, probably even more so. I traced a hand along his neck, shoulder, and arm. He was as lean as a swimmer, his biceps hard, not bulging, his skin golden against the snowy-white cotton.

I was surprised to see a tattoo on his arm.

"Trust me, Father doesn't know."

"What is it?" I asked, tracing the Chinese character with the tip of my finger.

"Just something I needed to remember."

I wanted to ask more, know more, but when his hand moved from my own shoulder down to the crown of my breast, I lost my train of thought. His fingers circled one nipple as it strained toward his touch, then the other. Before I could get used to it, his mouth kissed a path from a freckle on the slope of my breast before zeroing in on the center. His hot mouth and exploring tongue heated me up like a furnace.

From one breast to another, his mouth traveled while his fingers skimmed from my quivering belly to the delicate flesh between my thighs. His fingers parted me, and he played me like he'd played the piano all those years ago. My mind flashed to watching his long fingers move up and down the black and white keys during lessons back in New Jersey.

Finally having what I couldn't all those years ago made longing surge through my body.

I wanted to hold out, to make it last, but he played me like a symphony, my body winding up, my moans the crescendo.

I wanted to pay more attention, sear this moment of pleasure into my memory forever, but it wasn't to be. One minute I was pulling a condom from my bedside drawer and in another, he'd stripped his underwear, sheathed himself, then pushed inside me.

It was the same as that first time, but different as well. What was different was that this time, he was there in the room with me. What had happened last time had been him going through the motions.

"Look at me, Bella," he commanded softly.

I opened my eyes and met his above me.

"I never stopped loving you," he blew into my ear when he bent his elbows and covered me with his body, his chest rhythmically moving over mine, making the most delicious friction.

Blinking furiously, I looked away then, at the generic painted trio of wood tiles that had come with the apartment.

At the heap of clothes we'd made on the floor, at the diagonal crack in the accent wall from a minor earthquake. Anywhere but at Jake.

I'd wanted this. Minutes ago, this had been the most important thing. And now, before it was over, I was regretting it.

I took a deep breath willing my mind to go blank. In two minutes or ten, Jake's rhythm stuttered and he was grunting his release.

"That was...that was everything. I love you, Bella."

My heart lurched. It was the one thing I'd always wanted to hear. It was about seventeen years too late, though. I'd needed all that—the love, the tenderness, the declarations—when it would have made a difference. Not now. It was too little, too late.

When Jake rolled off the bed to go to the adjoining bathroom and take care of the condom, I stood and lifted my robe from where I'd carelessly thrown it on a chair the night before. Belting it securely around my waist, I took a moment to breathe, then spoke up when he'd made himself comfortable against the pillows and padded headboard.

"I think you should go," I said, meeting his eyes, lazy with that fog of sleep men got after sex.

"Now?"

"Yeah, now. I need time..."

"To think about us?"

Twenty years ago, or even two months ago, I would have nodded, been agreeable to get him out of my apartment. But lying and deception had gotten me nowhere. I spoke up and told my truth.

"There is no 'us,' Jake."

His eyes went wide. Drowsiness cleared from his features.

"What just happened here?" he demanded.

"We had sex. The sex I wished we'd had back in Meriden. But this has kind of healed that old wound, you know?"

"Are you saying there's no future for us?"

"I'm saying that I'm going to take a shower. Then do some laundry. Then I think I'm going to look at my calendar and put in for some vacation days. The controversy around Blue has died down a bit. The FCC will do whatever they do, but will take their time in doing it. Maybe I'll go to Paris. It's supposed to be beautiful in spring. Or maybe Italy."

The moment I said it out loud, I knew I'd be on a plane to Europe next week. I wanted to see Arturo, maybe talk to the man who'd been my dad for the first dozen years of my life. I needed to understand, resolve my past before I could even think about a future.

CHAPTER 25

NOW

JAKE'S FACE took on a look I hadn't seen in years—panic. It was the face he'd had when his mother announced she was flying in, and he was days behind on Mandarin and had skimped on piano practice. His mouth twitched like it had when Mr. Wu was shuffling down the hall in his ugly rubber slippers.

"Can we talk? Not here. Brunch. Where's good?" He was off the bed and pulling on his clothes much quicker than I'd taken them off.

"You know what? Brunch is a great idea. Meet me at the man door in thirty minutes," I said. It would give me enough time to perfect my brush-off, solidify my fortitude.

"Man door?" Jake had the look when an Englishism went over his head.

"The gate." There were only a few entrances to our complex by car and two for walking. Daniel had thought I'd needed all this protection and safety. It hadn't kept me safe enough.

Jake walked out of my apartment looking apprehensive.

"Thirty minutes," I promised as I gently closed the door.

Not having to worry about how I looked was a relief. I showered and put on leggings and a T-shirt. I wasn't trying to impress Jake. I certainly didn't have to tart up for Daniel. No TV executives to wow either. Maybe what money gave me wasn't happiness, but relief.

"Ms. Aconi, you know Mr. Wu?" Gerard asked, his hand hovering over the button, but not quite unlocking the gate.

"We grew up together. Next-door neighbors. New Jersey."

"Imagine meeting up here! You're in the same building, right?"

"Neighbors. We're on the same floor."

"What a coincidence. That's fate." His smile was practically beatific. Fate was a fucker, I wanted to say, but couldn't. Instead, I smiled like I did for my boss or Daniel.

"Right, Gerard. We're off to brunch to get reacquainted." Finally, the elderly guard hit the buzzer.

"Good eating."

"Gerard?" Jake asked. "You know his name?"

I wanted to point out that Jake knew my name and my mother's, and the Perezes'. But rich people didn't like to be reminded about how much they had or that we all served at their sufferance. I knew Gerard like I knew Julius like I knew all the rest of them. I might have looked like one of the privileged, but I hadn't ever forgotten where I'd come from.

"He's been here since the dawn of time."

"The building is only fifteen years old or something like that."

"There's an older complex in the back. Nearly everyone who's come to L.A. has lived there in Park La Brea. I think he dates back to that era."

"I like that about you."

"Like what?"

"That you get to know stuff about people. You knew all this stuff about the Perez family. Remember them?"

"Are they still at Casa Wu?"

"No, they retired a few years back. Moved back to some town close by."

"Brick."

"It's that kind of thing." We stopped to cross Beverly Boulevard. "Where are we going?"

"Farm to Table. They have a hangover special."

"You hung over?"

"Went to dinner last night in the Arts District. Probably had an entire bottle of white wine. Italian, so not too alcoholic, but still a whole bottle."

"Celebrating?"

"In a manner of speaking. This is the place."

We didn't talk while the host seated us and offered bottomless mimosas.

"Water for me, thanks," I said. I'd already had that bottle last night while Daniel had changed my life. Plus, I needed to be stone-cold sober for whatever Jake was going to throw my way. I'd never let my guard down with the Wus.

"So, how do you like the building? Good management?" he asked innocently, playing with his fork like we were two normal people out at a meal.

"Are you asking about the apartment?"

"Sure. I've only been there a few weeks, maybe two months by now."

"Jake. This is a one-time-only thing, this meal we're having, so maybe you want to get to what you want to say. I'm happy to talk about Gerard and the nuances of the building complex, but it's probably not the best use of your time."

I didn't know if I was grateful that our server came or annoyed that we couldn't get this awkward reunion over and done with. Maybe he would do his spiel, I would do mine, and I could take my hangover special to go.

I tried not to tap my sneaker-covered foot while the waiter went over the specials and all the variations this place had made to simple breakfast foods that had been fine until L.A. had gotten its hands on them, spicing up their eggs with organic jalapenos, jazzing up their pancakes with maple foam and candied nuts.

"Hangover special," I said when the waiter finally took a breath.

"Steak and eggs," Jake ordered.

"Didn't go bold," I teased as the waiter retreated.

"Never got used to sweet American breakfasts."

"You act like you haven't been here for the last twenty years."

"I've been in Shanghai for the last six years."

"Building cars?"

"Learning how to market cars, then working to start DynoMedia."

"Mm," I said noncommittal.

"Have you thought about me? I thought about you all the time."

I had to hand it to L.A. Brunch service was fast. Restaurants had to turn over those tables and keep the lines moving outside. I was never more grateful to see a plate of food in my life. What in the hell was I supposed to say to that?

The truth—that I'd thought about him practically every day for the last twenty years? How good it had been when it was good, but there was only, what...a year or two before it had all gone bad, which had been all the rest? All the times I'd gone over my stupid trip to Woodward Tillman, or the time we'd met up in Philadelphia? All the times my mother had mentioned him and my stomach had alternately flipped with excitement then plummeted with dread?

"What did you think...about me?" I couldn't imagine it had at all been the same for him. He'd been the one with the money and the secured future, whose life didn't change on the whim of one rich man or another.

"I wondered how you were."

"How...I...was..." Did he want to hear the truth? Did I want to tell him? "I graduated from school, had a series of jobs, ended up at CBT." I left out all the bartenders, and worries about being poor again, and Mr. Wu's betrayal, and my mother's. And Daniel. Instead, I finished with, "I was fine."

"Are you dating someone?"

"Now, you ask. Not before your big declaration of intention, but now?"

"*Are* you free?"

It hit me then. He wasn't asking about boyfriends or whether I was swiping right on Tinder or had mutual likes on OkCupid.

"You're asking about Daniel. About whether I'm still sleeping with men for money?"

"I wasn't going to put it exactly like that."

"Why skirt it? No, Daniel and I broke up once and for all."

"When?"

"Last night."

"Oh. So there's hope for us. I was thinking..."

I didn't hear anything else he said. Because I wanted to say yes. Desperately, hopelessly wanted to go back and grab the past with both hands.

Instead, I pointed my internal compass toward the future.

I leaned down and eased the thick ivory linen envelope from my purse and put it on the table.

"What's this?" He took the envelope I'd shoved in his direction, flipping it to and fro.

"Maybe you should open it."

"Why do I feel like I shouldn't."

"I'm handing this to you as Vice President of Program Practices at CBT. I've already sent this same letter to HR and my direct boss via email."

He slipped his finger into the envelope, removed the single sheet I'd only printed minutes ago.

"I hereby tender my resignation from my position as Vice President of Program Practices for CBT, effective immediately..." he read, then dropped the page on the table. Looking up at me and meeting my eyes, he said, "Not even two weeks?"

"When I started here, I jumped the line. Connor Quinlan can step into this job tomorrow and probably be much better at it than I." If making amends was going to save my eternal soul, I might as well start with Connor. There were so many more to come.

"So this is it?"

"I'm sure CBT will be fine without me."

"And us?"

"This isn't our time."

"Are you serious?"

"Deadly. It's not that your offer isn't appealing. But I can't be bought."

"I'm not trying—"

"CBT. FCC fines. You're probably a billion-plus into the hole on this one."

"Good investment strategy—"

"Dictates that you want a return. I hope you get one. Keep CBT pushing the envelope and you'll be golden. As for me...I think I need closure, and I can't get it here."

"Is there hope for us?"

I wanted to say yes. I wanted to say no. Pulling my trench close around my body, I gave Jake my best Mona Lisa smile and left to get home. I needed to pack.

CHAPTER 26

TWO WEEKS LATER...

BEFORE I PICKED up my brand-new iPhone, I looked to make sure the leather-padded club chairs on either side of me were empty. Sure I wouldn't disturb anyone in the rarified air of the airline's first-class lounge, I tapped on Maria Sofia Aconi's photo. She answered on the first ring.

Without preamble, I said, "Mama, I'm going to Italy."

"Oh, honey, when are you going? I wanted to be the one to take you, your first time."

"Do you have vacation?" I tamped down the hope bubbling in my chest and braced myself for her reply.

"I...I can't take it right now," she said, as I'd expected. "Mr. Wu needs me."

"So when can you take me?" My question was perfunctory. I'd given her one last chance. One last test and she'd failed...again.

"Well, I can't this year. I'd have to check Mr. Wu's schedule..."

"So...never, Mama?" I probed. I wanted to pull the mask

off. No longer was I going to let her get away with excuses and promises.

"Never say never," she answered vaguely.

"I'm going to Italy alone, then. I've bought tickets."

"Then why did you ask me? Was this a trap? It's always something with you, Isabella."

"To give you one last chance, Mama."

"One last chance at what? Why are you judging me? Not everyone has a sugar daddy. Not everyone can travel at the drop of a hat."

From where I was sitting in the nearly empty lounge, it looked like my mother was the only one with a sugar daddy. One she couldn't leave. One she'd chosen over me time and again.

I lifted my head and sent up silent thanks to Daniel and the universe for forever freeing me.

Today, I was going to choose myself.

"Don't think Francis Aconi is going to welcome you with open arms."

"I'm not holding out any hopes."

And I wasn't. I was going to take it as it came. I may not have Jake, and I may not have Daniel, and I may not have Mama, but I did have a single person I could count on.

I had me.

Thank you for reading WHAT WAS PERFECT. I loved this book so much. Isabella is my heart.

WHAT WAS LOST is next in the series. It's their story, this time from Jake's point of view. It may not surprise you to find out he saw things a little differently. It certainly surprised me, though.

What Was Lost

We were never in love at the same time.
I have to fix that.
I have to fix us.
Because I broke us.
I was young, stupid, impulsive.

Now that I've grown up, I know what I want.
It's not money or status.
It's just Isabella.
My Bella.
I have to get back what was lost.

Order **WHAT WAS LOST** now so you don't miss out on Jake's story. **WHAT WAS TRUE** the last of the trilogy is out now.

If you love crazy, beautiful, love stories, then you'll want one-click TAMING THE BAD BOY now!

Sometimes good girls do bad things... Can Ivy League Daisy tame bad boy comedian Raphael? Or is Ivy League out of his league?

"Read it. Loved it. The depth of characterization is beautiful. The story feels rich and real. Two flawed individuals that fall in love and must overcome their own personal challenges and resistance to love."

—*USA TODAY* BESTSELLING AUTHOR
MAGGIE MARR

ABOUT THE AUTHOR

I write crazy, beautiful love stories because I believe story-telling is magic. I love complicated heroines with secrets, strong heroes who fall hard, and a long winding road to happily ever after. When I'm not writing, I love to travel to witness the diverse tapestry of humanity, photograph the beauty of the world, visit museums, and watch live theater. I live in West Hollywood, California ten miles from the nearest airport.

xo Jolie Moore

I haven't found my own happily ever after, but I'm not done trying. This year I'm going to go on fifty first dates. Join me as I try to find my Mr. Right or maybe Mr. Right Now. #50first-dates #joliemoore #crazybeautifullove

Sign up here to get weekly date updates as well as new release notifications.

joliemoore.com/50firstdates

facebook.com/xojoliemoore

twitter.com/xojoliemoore

instagram.com/xojoliemoore

pinterest.com/xojoliemoore

amazon.com/author/xojoliemoore

goodreads.com/xojoliemoore